Estate of the Heart

by

Janet Franks Little

TELEMACHUS PRESS

This book is a work of fiction. Names, characters, places and incidents are either the product of the author's imagination or are used fictitiously. Any resemblance to actual persons, living or dead, or to actual events or locales is entirely coincidental.

ESTATE OF THE HEART

Copyright © 2017 Janet M. Little. All rights reserved, including the right to reproduce this book, or portions thereof, in any form. No part of this text may be reproduced, transmitted, downloaded, de-compiled, reverse engineered, or stored in or introduced into any information storage and retrieval system, in any form or by any means, whether electronic or mechanical without the express written permission of the author. The scanning, uploading, and distribution of this book via the Internet or via any other means without the permission of the publisher is illegal and punishable by law. Please purchase only authorized electronic editions and do not participate in or encourage electronic piracy of copyrighted materials.

The publisher does not have any control over and does not assume any responsibility for author or third-party websites or their content.

Cover designed by Telemachus Press, LLC

Cover art:
Copyright © dreamstime_1_6263835_Lucy Clark.jpeg
Copyright © dreamstime_1_84636220_©Syda Productions.jpg

Published by Telemachus Press, LLC
http://www.telemachuspress.com

Visit the author website:
http://www.janetfrankslittle.com

Library of Congress Control Number: 2017944962

ISBN: 978-1-945330-63-6 (eBook)
ISBN: 978-1-945330-64-3 (Paperback)

Telemachus Press, LLC
7652 Sawmill Road, Suite 304
Dublin OH 43016

10 9 8 7 6 5 4 3 2 1

Version 2018.11.14

Table of Content

Chapter 1	1
Chapter 2	8
Chapter 3	15
Chapter 4	22
Chapter 5	29
Chapter 6	36
Chapter 7	43
Chapter 8	51
Chapter 9	59
Chapter 10	65
Chapter 11	71
Chapter 12	79
Chapter 13	86
Chapter 14	95
Chapter 15	103
Chapter 16	110
Chapter 17	117
Chapter 18	126
Chapter 19	133
Chapter 20	141
Chapter 21	149
Chapter 22	155
Chapter 23	162
Chapter 24	169
Chapter 25	176
Chapter 26	185
Chapter 27	193
Chapter 28	200
Chapter 29	208
Chapter 30	213
Chapter 31	220
Chapter 32	227

To Steve, my fellow rehabber who has lived in the estate of my heart for more than forty years.

Estate of the Heart

Chapter 1

"'SCUSE ME, I'M looking for Cam-er-on Coleman."

Cam cocked her head. The speaker sounded like one of the Hemsworth brothers. *Could Liam or Chris be here?* She stopped sweeping cut wisteria off the flat roof.

Anthony Antonnuci, C.C. Restorations' only full-time employee and her right-hand man, was on the ground stuffing the vines which had grown like werewolf hair into trash bags. "Boss, someone's here to see you."

Cam laid down her rake and glanced over the edge. A tawny-haired stranger in pressed jeans and a white dress shirt with rolled cuffs stood on the walkway which meandered to the patio from the side yard. Cam crossed the roof to where the ladder was propped and put her foot on the top step. She had descended several rungs when the rear screen door squeaked open. Nate Adkins came out. His insulation company was working inside the house.

The newcomer moved toward him with an extended hand. "G'day. I'm Jack Reynolds."

Nate shook the man's hand. "What can I do for you?"

"I'd like to talk to you 'bout the property."

The contractor looked toward Cam who was now on the ground behind the stranger's back. She shook her head and pointed with a you-talk-to-him gesture.

Nate shoved his hands in his pockets. "Uh, I can talk for a minute. But we're pretty busy here."

Cam moved closer but stood off to the side. She brushed leaves and debris from her clothes, arms, legs and cocked her ear toward Jack's Australian-accented voice.

"I saw the sign out front for C.C. Restorations," he said.

"That's right."

"So, the new owner hired you to work on the place?"

"Yeah. You need an estimate done?"

Cam took a half-step closer. The movement caused Jack to jerk his head in her direction. Cartoon-like, his eyes widened when he saw her.

He dragged his gaze back to Nate. "No, uh, I wanted to help with the restoration for free."

Whoa.

"Free?" Nate uttered the word like it had never come out of his mouth before.

"You see, last month I graduated from uni with a degree in architecture. I'm looking for experience in historic restoration before I return to Sydney. My mum's family owns a construction firm here in Akron, but I'm more interested in preservation. Since C. C. Restorations is rehabbing The Harte Estate, I was hoping to apprentice with you, Mr. Coleman."

Nate's eyes pleaded with Cam. She moved to stand next to the two men. "He's not Cameron Coleman. I am."

"You?" His eyes raked from her face, down the sweat-stained gray tank top, past the denim cutoffs to her scuffed brown work boots.

"I'm always happy to meet someone offering free labor." Cam pulled off the worn suede glove and held out her hand to him. The instant their palms touched a current raced up her arm and made her heart beat faster.

Most people, especially men, did not expect Cameron Coleman, the owner of C.C. Restorations, to be a woman with a killer grip. This wannabe apprentice was no exception. She took a moment to study him. He was a head taller than her. His dark blonde hair had a loose, natural curl which gave him a boyish appearance. She was enthralled by his bright, sapphire-blue eyes.

Nate cleared his throat. "Cam, we need to talk about the attic above the second-floor sunroom. I think we've come up with a solution to our access problem."

Cam pulled her hand free. "I need to deal with this first, Jack." She motioned to her employee. "Anthony, why don't you take lunch out front? Jack can sit with you until I get back."

Cam followed Nate inside.

As they climbed the wide, main staircase, the contractor pulled off his cap and scratched his head. "What do you make of him?"

"Don't know. He looks too neat and clean for manual labor."

Cam surveyed the attic and gave the okay for an unobtrusive rooftop vent to access the space. Before heading back downstairs, she detoured to the only upstairs bathroom with running water and stared into the mirror over the sink. "Shit, I look like hell."

She pulled off the grimy Cleveland Indians baseball cap. Her blonde hair was darkened with sweat. Loose pieces of wisteria were trapped in her ponytail. She sniffed her armpit and gacked. There wasn't enough time for a shower, and she had only one set of clean clothes stashed in a closet here. Besides, there was more messy work to do this afternoon. Cam washed her face then wiped the worst of the perspiration and dirt from her arms and legs with a threadbare washcloth.

She left the bathroom and shut the door behind her. The house was quiet. She descended the main staircase, walked the length of the thirty-foot foyer, and exited the front door. Cam turned in a circle to view her latest renovation project and grimaced. The amount of work needing done at The Harte Estate was staggering. With the toe of her boot, she brushed at a thin layer of gravel that barely covered the quarter-mile-long drive.

Paving is out of the question unless I win the lottery.

The condition of the main house and gatehouse as well as the six acres of land surrounding them cried out with decades of neglect. Cam had created a list of long overdue repairs and maintenance issues but more were added on a daily basis.

Her reverie was broken by the startup growl of a wood chipper. It was deep in the trees on the south side where what was left of a clay tennis court was buried under a foot of leaves and dirt. The brum-brums of chainsaws followed. She had hired a local arborist to remove dozens of diseased or dead trees, including the one which fell on the carriage house roof. The several acres of lawn consisted of grassy patches and weeds. Most of the overgrown property looked like the Ohio version of Jurassic Park without the dinosaurs.

The once cream-colored, stucco walls of the eight-thousand-square-foot main house were veined with discoloration from the dead ivy Anthony had pulled off. She shook her head at the biggest travesty—mismatched aluminum storm windows. They were as appropriate on a historic home as a spoiler on a Model T.

The low rumble of men's laughter drew her attention. She headed toward the voices. Anthony, Jack, and three of Nate's workers lounged on the kitchen porch. Several pizza boxes lay on the wooden floor next to a cheap Styrofoam cooler filled with ice and cans of Coke.

"Hey, Boss." Anthony pointed the end of a pizza slice at her. "We saved you some pie."

Cam crossed from the driveway through the weeds to where the men were gathered. "Who ordered this?"

"Jack brought it with him."

The Aussie shrugged. "I figured lunch was the best time to stop by, so I brought pizzer and soft drinks."

Smart. Bribe the help.

She bit into a slice and viewed the would-be apprentice with narrowed eyes. He smiled back at her. Neither of them spoke while Anthony and Nate's workmen discussed Cleveland's baseball season. After the empty boxes and the cooler were tossed into the dumpster, the men returned to work.

Cam slid her hands into the back pockets of her shorts and straightened her spine. "So, Jack Reynolds, why do you want to work here?"

"I'll show you. It's in my ute."

Ute?

He walked over to a showroom-new, white Ford pickup parked with the other banged-up trucks and vans, opened the door, and bent forward to retrieve something. Cam's breath caught in her throat when his muscular thighs pulled his jeans taut. She lowered her head and studied the toes of her boots.

"Here you go." He handed her an inch-thick sheaf of paper in a two-hole binder. "That is a project I did at the University of Queensland. It's a restoration plan for this property."

Cam leafed through the report. There were floor plans of the gatehouse and main house. Several pages showed old photos of rooms in both buildings. A site drawing indicated the boundaries and each structure on the six acres. There were numerous pages of text. Jack had researched how to update both houses to make them more energy efficient and functional while preserving their architectural integrity.

She glanced up from the open binder. "How did you know about this house?"

"My mum lives next door to Susan Gardiner in San Diego."

Mrs. Gardiner had inherited The Harte Estate from her great aunt, Lavinia, and sold it to C. C. Restorations.

Cam closed the binder. "Can I have a day or two to read through this?"

"Keep it. I have another copy." There was an awkward silence, then Jack flashed a devilish smile. "Are you going to give me a chance to work under you?"

An image of this man lying on rumpled sheets wearing the same infectious grin made her hesitate. She leafed through the pages of the binder to collect herself. "I'll need information from you to check out. Write me on the C.C. Restorations website so I can email you an application form."

After he left, Cam returned to the patio to help Anthony finish taming the wisteria and set up scaffolding for their next project. Later in the evening, with a meatloaf takeout dinner from Boston Market, Cam read Jack's report. It was titled: *Energy Efficient Solutions for the Preservation of a Century Home*. He was very thorough in his research and options for a full restoration. She had evaluated the same issues before making her offer to purchase the property.

Maybe he will be a good apprentice if his background and references check out.

#

On Friday, Cam received an email from a jtreynolds1287. It read:

Ms. Coleman,

I am most interested in working with you on your restoration project. Please send any paperwork I will need to complete.

Regards,
Jackson Reynolds

Cam scanned an employment application and attached it to her return email.

Dear Jack,

I read your research project for The Harte Estate. It was impressive. You and I have a similar vision for the property. If your background information checks out, I would welcome your unpaid assistance. How long of an apprenticeship do you need?

Cameron Coleman

The next day she received his return message with an attachment.

Dear Ms. Coleman,

I have completed the application. You are welcome to contact any reference listed. I am ready to work as soon as you say. I would appreciate an apprenticeship for six months before my return to Australia. I know I can learn a great deal from you.

With regard,
Jackson Reynolds

She studied his application. Jack had been born the same year as her, but she was ten months older. Cam had estimated he was much younger than her twenty-seven years. He displayed the eager, boyish charm of a recent college graduate. Unlike her, he was not yet hardened with the reality of a daily job and the struggle for financial security.

The most important lesson you'll need to learn, Jack, is that restoration is all about the bottom line.

Cam leafed through his project again. The cost analysis was on the last few pages. His figures didn't allow additional funds for unforeseen problems. She had never rehabbed anything without encountering an expense not budgeted in the initial estimate. For Cam, a twenty percent contingency was a requirement.

The next lesson, Jack, is you need to expect the unexpected.

Chapter 2

ON SATURDAY AFTERNOON Cam pulled into the parking lot of A to Z Salvage. The twenty-thousand-square-foot warehouse was jam-packed with every kind of antique or vintage architectural element imaginable. The inventory was varied and ever-changing, but Zane Coleman, Cam's father, had a military affinity for order. Voices echoed from the area where doors of various functions, sizes, and woods were stored. When she stepped into the sales office, a middle-aged woman with graying blonde hair was sitting behind a banged-up wood counter. The vintage counter had been in a downtown hardware store until 1950.

"Hi, Mom."

"Hi, honey. Your dad's with customers in the warehouse. A young couple wants some vintage doors for the house they're building."

"Are they going to use them as intended or bastardize them into something else?"

"Now, Cam, at least they'll be resurplused."

"You mean repurposed?"

"Isn't that what I said?"

The door from the warehouse opened. "Abigail." A booming voice echoed through the room. "Write up an invoice for eleven hundred. What are you doing now, Cameron?"

"I'm going to pack my things and move to The Harte Estate."

"The packing can wait. Go get the forklift. I'll grab the ratchet ties. We need to load up some doors." He slapped the sales tag on the counter.

Cam followed her father, a spare man with a salt and pepper crew cut, out the door. "We need the forklift? How big are the doors?"

"Each one is twelve panels and weighs around three hundred pounds."

On the way to get the forklift, Cam spotted a large pile of maple floor boards. "I didn't see these here before. Where did you get them?"

"An old roller skating rink in Canton is going to be torn down. Adam and I spent the last two days removing four thousand linear feet before the wreckers got there. If you got time this weekend, there are still a few nails that need to be pulled from them."

More like a few thousand.

Cam climbed into the cab of the forklift and drove it between aisles of inventory. They loaded the old library pocket doors onto the forks and secured them to the vertical face. At the loading area, a fresh-faced young couple stood beside a newer Cadillac SUV. Cam stopped ten feet from the open bay.

She turned in the driver's seat and spoke over her shoulder. "Uh, Dad, we have a problem."

Zane strode up to the forklift. "Goddammit, why'd you stop?" Then the former jarhead spotted the customers and their vehicle. "What the fuck. Freeze."

The husband had just hooked a bungee cord to the luggage rack on the roof. He stiffened at Zane's command as if shot by a cannon loaded with Botox.

"Dad, let me handle this."

Zane muttered as he marched back into the warehouse.

Cam turned off the humming forklift and hopped down. "Hi. Don't mind my father."

The wife was a perky redhead with a headband sprouting a silk blossom. "Is there a problem?"

"You could say that. These doors are too heavy for your car. They'll crush the luggage rack. They need to be transported in the bed of a truck. And you'll need at least four people to off-load them. It's why we had to use a forklift to get them here."

The husband rocked back and forth, heel to toe. His wife glanced nervously at him. Underneath the salon-styled hair, spray tans, and expensive clothes, there was a barely disguised uncertainty.

The husband spoke. "Well, maybe we should—"

"Have your builder come pick them up. It's what you're paying good money for. Let him use his equipment and manpower to get them to your new house."

"That's a good idea." The wife beamed at her dour-faced spouse. "Denny should get the doors."

"I'll handle this, Brittany." The man assumed a wide-legged, blustery stance with his fists on his hips. "The price we agreed on with your father was eleven hundred out the door today. I'm not sure when the builder can get here. There better not be any storage fees."

"Don't worry, there won't be. I'll cover them for safekeeping. We can store them in the back. Why don't you leave the name and number of your builder so we can hassle him if he drags his feet?"

Brittany smiled. "Would you? He never seems to listen to us."

Her husband glowered at his wife. "If I call Denny, he'll take care of it. Sometimes these construction people need to be reminded who they work for."

You're right. But at least we know six hundred pounds can't be hauled on a luggage rack with bungee cords.

After the couple went to the front entrance to complete their purchase, Cam shut and locked the overhead door. She backed up the forklift and headed to the Waiting for Pickup area. Her father was there with a long roll of transparent shrink wrap on a handle and a stack of flattened cardboard. Without a word, they got to work securing the doors then headed to the sales office.

The customers were gone.

Cam's mother was perched on a stool behind the counter. She looked up from the computer monitor. "Is everything okay?"

Her husband grunted, went into his office, and shut the door.

Abigail rolled her eyes. "Thank goodness you showed up when you did."

"Where's Adam?"

"He and Sasha went crib shopping."

A stab of maternal envy hit Cam. "How's she doing?"

"Great. Both of them are so ready for this baby."

Cam's brother and his wife were expecting their first child in two weeks. Adam was the one who usually dealt with customers. He was warm and personable. Even Sasha with her limited English was better than gruff and abrasive Zane.

"I guess I'll go pack."

Her temporary living quarters was the loft room above the sales office.

"I got you some boxes from the grocery store. They're sitting on the steps. Before you go, tell me what you've done at the house this week."

Cam described the projects she and Anthony had completed as well as the various contractors who had been onsite.

A frown creased Abigail's forehead. "Are you sure this house is not going to turn into a money spit for you?"

Cam's friend and realtor, Jeanine, had assured her that she got the deal of the decade when Susan Gardiner accepted her three hundred and fifty thousand dollar offer.

"It won't be a money pit, Mom. Besides, I may now have someone who'll be working for free."

"Who would volunteer to work without pay? Can you trust him?"

Cam explained about the recent college graduate who wanted an apprenticeship. "He's familiar with the property because his mother is friends with the woman I bought it from."

"I don't know, Cam. Sounds fishy to me."

"Don't worry. I'll check him out before taking him on."

#

All the references on Jack's application, except one, were in Australia. Cam emailed a professor at The University of Queensland. She also sent a request to Brady Connors of Village Builders in Sydney. The only reference in the U.S. was Susan Gardiner. Cam called her.

"Hi, Mrs. Gardiner, this is Cameron Coleman from C.C. Restorations. Am I calling at a good time?" She had taken into account the three-hour time difference between Akron and San Diego.

"It's perfect. Are you calling about Jackson? Did he show you the project he did?"

Cam's eyes flitted to the binder on the table in front of her. "He gave me a copy. I'm impressed with his ideas and all the work he's done. Have you read it?"

"No. I just provided him with the history and photographs. How does it fit in with your plans?"

"They're very similar. It's why I'm considering his application for an apprenticeship."

"I'm so pleased." The woman hesitated. "You know, I accepted your offer, even though the price was *very low* because your company does restorations. The other buyers only wanted the land. I couldn't bear not to have, at least, the main house saved."

"My plan is to restore it and the gatehouse."

"Then I wish you all the best. Now, let me tell you about Jackson." Mrs. Gardiner paused. "Let's see. The one thing I've always noticed is he opens doors for women, unlike American men his age."

Okay. It's not a requirement on a job site unless someone is carrying a load of supplies.

"I've never heard him swear other than to say bloody hell."

Shit. He's going to hear a lot worse coming out of my mouth.

"He's very athletic. His mother, Brooke, has his soccer trophies on display in her den. Jackson was recruited for a professional team in Australia, you know."

Good. Then he can be coached and follow directions.

"He graduated at the top of his class in the school of architecture which is a very demanding program."

I hope he doesn't think he knows more than me. "Thank you. Those are all good things to know."

"Uh, Jackson told me you might call, of course. I have to admit I was surprised to learn you're a woman. I assumed Cameron Coleman was a man." Mrs. Gardiner cleared her throat. "He said you're very attractive."

How could he tell?

"Be careful, my dear. You don't want to fall in love with that charming Aussie."

"Don't worry about me, Mrs. Gardiner. My only love is old houses, not charming men." *I've learned my lesson there.*

#

The following day, Cam received an email from Dr. Dunwoody of the School of Architecture, Queensland, who sang the praises of his former student. An email also came from Brady Connors. Jack worked for him the past two summers. She waited until the end of the week before she called the cell number on Jack's application.

"'Allo."

The accented greeting made her heart flutter. "Hi, Jack. It's Cam Coleman."

"Thank you for calling, Ms. Coleman. Have you decided to take me on as your apprentice?"

"There's one condition before I can say yes."

"What?"

"You have to stop calling me Ms. Coleman."

He laughed. "What shall I call you? Boss, like Anthony does?"

"Or Cam is okay."

"Not Cam-er-on?"

"That's what my father calls me."

Jack's voice became soft and husky. "I certainly don't want you to confuse me with your father."

Before she could stop herself, she giggled. *Fuck. Where the hell did that come from?*

"Do I have the job, Cam?"

"You can start Monday morning at eight. You'll work until five with a thirty-minute lunch and two fifteen-minute breaks."

"What 'bout tools?"

"You just need work gloves. I'll provide whatever else is needed for the job. Bring a cooler or thermos with your own beverages. You'll be immediately terminated if you drink alcohol, including beer, on the job. Do you smoke?"

"I don't and my amber fluid is limited to after hours. I'll see you Monday morning."

Yes, you will my new apprentice.

Chapter 3

CAM SAT ON the concrete step which led from the rear foyer to the back patio. She sipped from a near empty cup of coffee and read the Akron Beacon Journal.

"G'day."

Her head popped up. Jack stood a few feet away. Cam closed the newspaper. "What are you doing here?"

His eyes darted back and forth. "Uh, I work here?"

"Not until eight o'clock." She checked her watch. "It's only seven-thirty."

Jack spread his arms wide. "I'm your early bird." His gesture stretched his snug tee-shirt with a soccer ball logo and the words Sydney FC across his toned pecs. His shirt and eyes were of a similar blue color. "You're here bloody early too."

"Because I live here."

"You do?"

"I always live in my projects. Saves money and provides onsite security." Cam stood and opened the warped screen door. "Before everyone gets here, let me explain what you'll be doing."

They entered the back foyer, walked through the dining room, butler's pantry, and into the kitchen. Cam placed her empty coffee cup in the sink. It was filled with other unwashed dishes in greasy water. She squirted in liquid soap, added some hot water, and turned to face Jack. She was startled when her elbow bumped against his firm abdomen. The running water had muted his approach. Cam took a quick step to the side.

She leaned her hip against the counter and affected a casual stance. "I read your report on this house. I liked your ideas for the kitchen remodel, but this'll be one of the last rooms we do. Let's head upstairs."

He eyed the sink. "Not going to wash those first?"

"They can soak. I'll get to them later."

Jack seemed unable to walk away from the dish-filled, soapy water. "It'll only take a few minutes but."

"But what?"

"Sorry. Ozzy way of saying it. *But* it'll only take a few minutes."

Geez. Between him and my mother, I'm going to need an interpreter. She shrugged. "Knock yourself out. I'll get things ready on the second floor." She pointed to the bottle of Dawn dishwashing detergent which sat on the apron of the sink. "Bring that with you when you're done."

Fifteen minutes later, his voice called up the stairs. "Cam? Where are you?"

"I'm in the room on the right."

His first job would be to remove wallpaper in the smaller bedroom of a Jack-and-Jill combination bath. This was where she slept on an air mattress. After the walls were bare, she would set up her bed. As she closed the closet door where her clothes and bedding were stored, he stepped into the room.

Cam turned to face him. "You're going to take down this wallpaper. Have you ever stripped before?"

He flashed a snarky grin. "No one's ever paid me to do it."

"Good, because you aren't going to be paid this time either."

Cam filled a pump sprayer with a gallon of hot water and a small amount of the dishwashing soap. They laid out canvas drop cloths.

Jack used the toe of his shoe to maneuver the covering into place. "Why do we need to put this on the floor?"

Cam looked around the room to ensure every square inch of hardwood was protected. "Stripping is a messy job. After you get it off, it's wet and sticky."

Jack barked a laugh then converted it into a cough. "Sorry 'bout that."

Cam showed him how to wet down a section, wait for the solution to work, and lift the paper off with a wide scraper blade. "Just don't dig at it. You'll gouge the plaster. Wet it again and wait."

He rubbed his hand where she had removed a vertical section and grimaced. "The wall is gummy." He grabbed her hand and laid it on the plaster under his. "Is it not to feel like this?"

His palm was warm and strong. He stood so close she was able to see where he had missed shaving a spot of dark gold whiskers along his jawline. Her eyes closed for a second with the desire to lean against him.

Instead she slid her hand down the wall to free it from under his and shifted away. "The wallpaper paste is still on the plaster. I'll bring you a bucket and sponge. You'll need to wipe down the walls with clean water. We can't paint unless all the adhesive is removed first."

Cam left him alone when she heard the other workmen arrive. At lunchtime, she climbed the rear staircase to view Jack's progress.

He should be ready to start in the next bedroom. In the doorway, she shook her head in disbelief. "What the—" She bit back the expletive before it crossed her lips.

Jack rose from the floor. "What's wrong?"

Cam strode into the room. "You've been in here for four hours and only two walls are stripped. This whole room should be finished."

"I did what you told me. Sprayed the paper and waited, then scraped, and rinsed."

She rubbed her face with her palms. "Jack, you don't do a strip at a time. You do the whole wall. While you wait, you spray the next one, then the next one."

"I'm sorry. I wanted to not do a bodgy job." He looked like a contrite schoolboy.

"No, it's my fault. I didn't realize how inexperienced you are." She heaved a sigh. "It's time for lunch. Take a break, then you can finish this."

When he went downstairs, Cam checked the walls Jack had completed. There wasn't a smidgen of paste left anywhere, even in the corners.

At least he's thorough. I just have to speed him up.

Cam ate a container of yogurt and a banana under a tree in the backyard. She had just finished when Jack sat down beside her.

His shoulder bumped against hers. "I'm not leaving today until that bloody room and the next are finished." His mouth was set in a tight line.

Cam needed to instruct him but didn't want to lose his free labor, so she chose her words with care. "When it comes to any restoration project, time is money. The sooner I can turn a property around and sell it, the faster I can move on to the next one. But the key is doing it right. You did a great job getting all the paste off the wall. It just needs to be done quicker."

"What's your timeline on this place?"

"I'd love to say it'll be ready to sell at the end of your six-month apprenticeship. Realistically, nine months to a year if there are no major setbacks."

Anthony's voice called out behind them. "Boss, I'm ready. You want me to get to work on the windows?"

"I'll be right there."

Cam stood up. She put out her hand to Jack. He wrapped his fingers around it but made no move to rise to his feet. A tingle went up her arm, and her breath caught in her throat.

She swallowed. "Um, time to get back to work."

He rose in one fluid motion, her hand still in his. As soon as he was upright, she pulled free and headed to the front of the house.

In the afternoon, she worked with Anthony to remove the last of seventy vinyl-clad storm windows covering the original wooden ones. To Cam, the windows of a house were its eyes and had the most visual impact. She was told the cheap white insulating panels were installed thirty years ago when natural gas prices skyrocketed.

Cam grew up in a household where the thermostat was locked on sixty-five degrees, no matter how cold it was outside. When she complained, her father handed her a package of sandpaper. "Go in the basement and sand those chairs I brought home. You'll warm up." After that, she kept quiet and layered on more clothes.

At the end of the work day, half the windows lay in piles on the grass. The rest filled the bed of Cam's pickup. She and Anthony had just secured them with ratchet ties when Jack emerged from the house. He pulled up the hem of his tee-shirt and bent his head to wipe his brow. Cam caught a glimpse of a ripped abdomen.

Jack pointed to the windows in her truck bed. "Whatcha doing with those?"

Cam stood on the tailgate. "I'm donating them to the Habitat for Humanity ReStore."

Jack stepped forward and put his hands on Cam's waist. "Let me help you down."

No workman had ever treated Cam like a damsel who needed assistance. She peeked at Anthony who watched with wide eyes.

He's probably waiting to see if I slug Jack.

She put her hands on her apprentice's broad shoulders and bent her knees. He swung her off the tailgate and set her on the ground.

To cover her fluster, she brushed her palms on her pants and spoke in measured tones. "Is Habitat for Humanity in Australia?"

"They've built houses in most of the states on the mainland. Don't know 'bout a ReStore but."

Anthony scratched his cheek. "But what, Jack?"

"Eh?"

Cam was now clued into the quirky speech pattern. "Jack puts *but* at the end of the sentence instead of the beginning. We say *but I don't know*. He says *I don't know but*."

Anthony nodded. "I get it." He touched the brim of his baseball cap with two fingers. "See you guys tomorrow." He whistled and headed to his vehicle.

Jack stared at the piles of windows still on the ground. "What's a ReStore? Is it like the Salvos?"

"It sells donated building materials. I've bought things there for a few of my projects. All the proceeds from donations go toward their home building program." Cam eyed Jack's shiny, not-a-scratch-or-dent pickup. "Tomorrow, let's load up the rest of the windows in your truck so we can take them in one trip."

Jack looked at his vehicle then her beat-up, five-year-old Chevy. He didn't say no to the hauling job but he didn't look happy.

Cam gave his bicep a playful punch. "Preservation Lesson Number Two. You can check out the store and see how to keep reusable materials from landfills."

#

Jack soon mastered wallpaper removal. By the end of his first week, he had all nine bedrooms in the house down to clean bare plaster and ready to paint.

Anthony found Cam in the kitchen. "Boss, you mind if I go home for lunch? My mom had a pretty rough night."

Mrs. Antonucci suffered from crippling arthritis. Anthony was not only the family breadwinner but his mother's caregiver. His teenage sister, Sophie, worked part-time and also helped with their disabled parent.

"Was it her arthritis?"

"The doctor switched her medication 'cause he's worried about her liver and kidneys. But this new one doesn't seem to work as well."

"You won't have much time to eat. Here." She handed him a peanut butter and jelly sandwich and a chilled bottle of Snapple. "Eat this on the way. I'll make myself another one."

"Thanks, Boss."

Cam joined Jack at a metal table and chairs she had set up under the covered patio. He unwrapped two thick slices of multi-grain bread, loaded with ham, cheese, and vegetables. He lifted half of his sandwich. "Want some of my cut lunch?"

"Thanks, but my *cut lunch* is fine."

They ate in silence for several minutes, then Jack cocked his head at her. "Howzit you started doing this work?"

"I come from a long line of junk collectors. Today, they're called pickers. When my dad was a kid, he and his father would go to flea markets or rummage through peoples' trash before the garbage truck got there. They would bring things home and fix them to sell. After Dad got out of the Marines, he and Mom opened a salvage store with everything my grandfather still had left. Their place is called A to Z Salvage. When I graduated from high school, I got my grandfather's old house ready for sale after he died and decided this was what I wanted to do. I saved my money, bought a fixer-upper, and C.C. Restorations was born."

Jack drained his can of soda. "Is it not easy being a woman in this field? Were you ever harassed?"

"Not really. Remember I'm not collecting a paycheck, I'm signing them."

Jack put the empty wrappers in his lunch box. "You ever do the work of the contractors here this week?"

"Some jobs are best left to the professionals because they're faster and better. I'll watch and ask questions while they're working. A lot of times, I'll help out so they can teach me. I'm paying them not only for their work but to share their expertise."

"The blokes don't mind?"

"People like to talk about what they're good at."

"I can only dream 'bout learning everything you're good at. Can't wait for what you'll show me next."

His words, accompanied an engaging grin, sent shivers of delight racing through her. She stuffed the remainder of her sandwich in her mouth as heat leapt into her cheeks.

Chapter 4

THE FOLLOWING WEEK, Nate's crew from *Energy Solutions* drilled holes into the brick mortar and the stucco exterior of the main house. Insulation was blown into the spaces between the inside and outside walls. The openings in the brick were plugged with matching mortar. Round disks were inserted into the stucco which would need to be covered with stucco patch.

When the insulation work was finished, Jack and Anthony repositioned the scaffolding to reach the second floor. Cam mixed the powdered patch and water in small buckets. Jack proved to be the most proficient with a rubber float. Cam praised his flush and well-blended repairs.

Anthony cuffed Jack's shoulder. "We got us a Stucco Stud, Boss."

A warm dampness gathered between Cam's thighs whenever Anthony teased his co-worker with the nickname.

Cool your hormones, girl. Don't forget he's your apprentice.

With the scaffolding still in place, they also prepped the windows for a fresh coat of paint. Cam instructed both men in how to replace cracked glass and re-glaze the pane dividers. They worked on the front walls and windows in the morning when the west face of the house was in shade and switched to the back in the afternoon.

Over the next few days, Jack's skin became golden-brown. His eyes appeared bluer, and the curled ends of his hair were streaked lighter. He hadn't shaved and his face sported a short gold moustache and beard.

When he showed up for work on Friday in cargo shorts and a tight, sleeveless tank, Cam peeked out the library window. He stood by his truck and slathered sunscreen on his exposed skin. She stared at his broad shoulders, veined arms, and muscled legs. He turned toward the house and looked straight at her. She pretended to examine the window latch.

In the afternoon, Anthony received an urgent phone call from his sister. Her clunker of a car wouldn't start and she needed to get to her part-time job. "I'll come back as soon as I drop Sophie at work, Boss."

"It's already three. Take the rest of the afternoon off—" She smiled as Anthony bit his lip. "With pay, of course. You deserve it for all your hard work."

After he left, Jack stopped scraping. "That was spiffy of you."

"I wish I could pay him more. Between my dad and me, we'll keep him employed until he finds a better job."

"Is it hard to find one 'round here?"

"Yeah, it's tough to get a good paying one if you have no degree or technical certification." *Like me.*

"Then he should go to school."

Why do I have the feeling Jack never worried about money before? "Anthony is the sole support for his family. His mother is disabled and his sister works while she's in high school. I'm hoping he can get hired with a good company and his employer will pay for his training. Some of my dad's contacts said they'll consider him when business picks up. He's a good guy who deserves a break."

She and Jack finished with the last stucco and window repair on the rear of the house. Only the windows and insulation holes of the first and second floor sunrooms were unfinished. Jack jumped down from the bottom step of the scaffold. "Shall I tear this down?"

"No. We'll move it on Monday. Let's get things cleaned up and put away."

"Uh, I have a favor to ask."

Cam released the hose nozzle and waited.

"I'm to meet some blokes at Portage Country Club. They have a reservation for five-thirty. If I go home and clean up, I'll be late."

The prestigious private golf, tennis, and swim club was less than a mile away. Cam checked her watch. "It's a quarter to five now. Would fifteen extra minutes help?"

"May I shower and change here?"

The only functional bath in the house was next to the small bedroom where Cam slept. It had been re-muddled about twenty years ago. The cast iron tub was removed and disappeared. In its place, the elderly homeowner, Lavinia Harte, had installed the cheapest, one piece acrylic shower unit ever made.

"You can use the shower next to the room with the bed. It's the only one with water running to it right now."

When he went upstairs with clothes on a hanger and a shaving kit, Cam walked around the property. When she entered the house from the back patio, there was no sound of running water upstairs. After taking off her boots, Cam padded in sock-covered feet across the foyer and unlatched the front screen door. Jack's truck wasn't in its usual spot on the driveway. She checked her watch. It was five-thirty. After locking the screen and front doors, she climbed the stairs, pulling off her clothes as she went. In the bedroom, she threw everything into a basket in the corner and entered the bathroom.

Cam stopped dead.

Jack rubbed his face with a towel then leaned forward over the pedestal sink to peer at his clean-shaven reflection in the mirror. She indulged herself with the view of his nude body in golden splendor. His darkened, wet curls were beaded with water. Crystal droplets hit his wide shoulders then ran down his muscled back. He leaned sideways to flip the towel over a rod mounted on the wall then turned. Jack's firm, hairless chest and flat abdomen tapered to narrow hips. He was well-hung beneath a mat of light brown curls. His legs were bunched with the sleek muscles of a soccer player. Cam's gaze rose to his face. His mouth lifted in a lopsided grin.

A rush of breath whooshed from between her lips. "Sorry. I thought you left. I didn't see your truck."

"I moved it to let Anthony out."

"Okay, I'll let you finish."

Jack's hand shot out and grasped her elbow. "Cam—"

They came together as though pushed from behind. Jack's mouth latched onto hers as their bodies adjusted to each other. Her arms closed around his neck. He varied the angle of their lips and plunged his tongue into her mouth. She wove her fingers through his damp waves and curls.

When his lips moved to her jaw, Cam rasped a hoarse whisper. "You taste golden."

He nibbled tiny love bites down her neck. "Your skin is so warm, sweet." His palms brushed against the sides of her breasts before they closed on them. "I've wanted you since the moment we met."

They continued their mutual exploration of each other's mouths and bodies. His taut buttocks tightened under her assessment. Her hand closed on his hot arousal. He inhaled a shuddering breath. Without a word, Jack drew her down to the floor. She reclined onto a fluffy rug on the cool marble.

His eyes drilled into hers like blue diamond bits. "Do you want this, Cam?"

Her whole body cried out in silent demand. "More than this house."

Jack's inquisitive hands and mouth traveled her body. He plumped her breast and nibbled the swollen peak. He trailed kisses down the flat valley between her ribcage. His tongue dipped into the dimple of her navel. He stopped at the pale hair. "So pretty."

Her thighs opened. She throbbed with desire. Her eyes fluttered closed.

His fingers parted her and probed. "Look at me, Cam." He lifted himself over her. His knees spread her legs wider. With their eyes locked, he rocked back and forth, inch by inch, until he was fully seated.

Cam relished the fullness of him. He eased back then slowly filled her again. She tilted her pelvis up to meet him. Her fingers wound through his silky locks. He moved in and out at an unhurried pace. She expected him to pick up speed. He didn't.

Oh, my God, he's as slow at this as he was at stripping wallpaper. "Faster, Jack. Please."

He gave her a look like he had just scored a game-winning goal then set a pounding rhythm. Cam's legs tensed. Her body quickened. Several powerful lunges later and she exploded into a million pieces around him.

Jack followed her into the abyss. Her one cry was echoed by his repeated shouts. "Oh, fuck. Oh, fuck. Oh, fuck."

Well, Susan Gardiner was wrong. He does say something other than bloody hell.

They lay without moving. Their breathing slowed. A phone rang on the bathroom floor. Jack pulled out, rose to his knees, and reached for his shorts lying in a heap.

He dug a cell phone from the pocket. "'Allo." He listened. "Sorry. I'm not going to make dinner. Something came up at work." He flashed a toothy grin. "Go ahead and eat. I'll meet you later for a pint."

The caller spoke more.

"Don't worry. I'll grab a bite." He leaned forward and nibbled at her breast as he made a nummy noise.

Cam pushed his head away and sat up.

Jack moved his mouth back to the phone's speaker. "I'll let you know. G'bye."

She stood and stepped past him to turn on the water taps. "I need to take a shower."

"Want company?"

"You better get dressed. Oh, and push the lock in on the kitchen door when you leave." Cam stepped inside the acrylic stall and pulled the curtain closed.

Oh my God. What the fuck have I done? Regret made her hang her head. She was physically attracted to Jack, but his free labor appealed to her more right now. *You just screwed yourself out of unpaid help, in more ways than one.*

While she air-dried her body and blow-dried her hair, she rehearsed what she would say to him on Monday, if he showed up. She stepped naked into the bedroom.

Jack sat on the edge of the mattress dressed in a blue shirt with the cuffs rolled up and gray pants. His eyes lit when he viewed her unclothed body. Embarrassment flooded her like she was the only nudist on a public beach. On unsteady legs, she walked to a laundry basket stacked with folded clothes. With her back to him, she bent forward to rifle through it. There was a sharp intake of breath from behind her. She pulled on a pair of gray jersey shorts and a tank top with a built-in bra before she turned around to face him. He leaned forward, his elbows on his knees.

"Why are you still here, Jack?"

He lifted his eyes. "We should talk."

Shit. She sat on the bed but left a two-foot gap between them.

He rubbed his palms together. "Do I still have my job?"

Glee filled her. *He's not quitting.* "I'd like you to finish your apprenticeship, if you want."

"Reckon that." He straightened with a wide smile.

She slapped the tops of her thighs. "All righty, then."

As she rose partway, Jack's hand on her forearm stopped her, and she sat on the mattress again.

He fixed his eyes on her as if she were a test he was determined to ace. "What 'bout us?"

"There is no *us*. There was just *this*." Her hands made a back and forth motion between them.

"Will there be any more of—" He mimicked her gesture. "*This?*"

Cam wet her lips. "I've never done *this* with, you know, someone who works for me. But I'd like it to continue. Do you?"

"Too right."

"Okay. Then we're good."

"Uh, there's one more thing." Jack stared straight ahead. "I didn't use a franger."

"A what?"

"A condom."

"Oh. Don't worry. I'm on the pill."

The relief in his expression was laughable. Being the lone woman on job sites, Cam learned to take precautions. She used birth control, once a month she took a refresher self-defense class, had a pistol, and carried Mace on her person if she was alone with a new contractor.

I have all these safety measures for physical attack, but how do I protect myself from a good-looking con man? She stood and headed for the door. "Well, I'm going to have my dinner. I'm starving."

"What do you have to eat?"

She stopped. "I wasn't offering to feed you."

"Fine, I'll feed *you*. Let me check out your fridge and pantry." He placed his hand on the small of her back and propelled her through the door into the hall.

"You can cook?"

He nodded.

Cam took him by the hand and led him to the back staircase. "Let's see what you can make." She chuckled at what he was *not* going to find in her kitchen.

Chapter 5

TEN MINUTES LATER, Jack viewed the paltry pile of food he scavenged from the refrigerator and one cupboard. "Do you not have salt?"

"Here." She opened a drawer and lifted out several paper packets saved from a McDonald's carryout order.

"Milk?"

Cam pulled on another drawer under the coffee maker and showed him tiny cups of non-dairy creamer. "Will this work?"

With his hands on his hips, he shook his head. "I moved to this country less than a month ago, and I have more staples in my kitchen than you."

"I have frozen dinners in the freezer."

Jack grimaced like she had just offered him yellow snow to eat. "Step aside. Let me work my bloody magic. Do you not have a fry pan?"

She pointed to the cupboard next to the old Aga stove. "Over there."

"A spatuler?"

She left the room and came back with the wide-bladed scraper he used to remove wallpaper.

Jack took it from her and sighed. "A bowl?" She handed him the one she had for instant oatmeal. "I need a bigger one."

Cam retrieved a plastic one gallon bucket. "Will this do? It hasn't been used yet."

He rolled his eyes and began to work. In a short time, he had a large, steaming omelet in the skillet. "Plates and utensils?"

She opened a drawer with extra plastic forks and spoons from Chinese takeout piled next to paper plates with balloons which read, *Happy Birthday*.

Jack divided the omelet in two with the scraper. They took their food, paper towel napkins, and cold bottles of beer to the metal table and chairs on the patio.

Cam leaned close to the omelet and gave a loud sniff before she cut into it. Her first bite made her moan with delight. "Mmm, mmm, mmm." When a thin strand of melted cheese dangled between her and the plate, she slurped it with gusto into her mouth. She swigged a long draught of cold beer. "Ahhh." A delicate, but audible burp passed her lips.

Jack shook his head. "You make more noise when you eat than when you come."

After they finished, Cam threw the empty beer bottles into a recycling bin. The paper plates went into the trash. Jack washed up the bucket, fry pan, wallpaper scraper, and plastic utensils. He left at seven o'clock after an awkward goodbye kiss at the door.

#

The next week's work schedule was set back by the Fourth of July on Thursday. Anthony was scheduled to be off on Friday, the day after the holiday. His extended Italian family had planned a reunion near Lake Erie that his mother and sister were eager to attend. It was Monday morning, and he left to check on his mother during his lunch break.

Cam and Jack ate on the patio. "I guess I won't see either you or Anthony after Wednesday."

"The fourth day of July isn't a holiday for me. My country's Independence Day, or as we call it, Foundation Day, is January twenty-sixth."

"Does that mean you'll paint windows with me on Thursday?"

"Is your family not celebrating the holiday?"

"My parents are going to my aunt's house in Columbus. My brother, his wife, and new baby are visiting her family in Chicago. I'm staying home to work."

"How 'bout going with me to the country club for dinner and the fireworks show?"

"No, thank you." *There is no way in hell I would ever go inside Portage Country Club again.* "It would be like we're on a date."

"It's just dinner. My mum will be in town and mentioned she'd like to meet you. She told me to ask you to the club if you didn't already have plans. We'll be there with my uncle and his daughter."

"Why would she want to meet me? You're just my six-month apprentice."

"Aren't I more now?"

An angry panic rose inside her. "We agreed to hookup now and then. But I'm not your girlfriend."

Color flooded Jack's face. His voice took on a steely quality. "During business hours, I'm your apprentice. After hours, we're lovers."

She kicked back her chair and jumped to her feet. "No, we're not. We fucked one time. That doesn't give you any kind of control over me."

He stood and placed his fisted hands on the table. "All I want to do is feed you and introduce you to my mum."

"At the damned country club."

"What the bloody hell is wrong with the country club?"

Anthony came around the corner of the house. "What's going on, Boss?"

Cam and Jack glared at each other like prize fighters in the center of a ring.

Jack spoke first. "It's a difference of opinion 'bout independence, mate. Nothing more."

The men worked together on the sunroom windows. Cam left them alone and tackled the front door. She scrubbed harder than usual at the three-inch-thick oak with stripper and steel wool to remove the old varnish. By the time she finished, she'd worn through two pairs of heavy duty rubber gloves.

#

On Tuesday morning, Cam checked her email and text messages for Jack's resignation, but his truck pulled into the drive and parked in his usual spot. They maintained an icy civility. By the end of the following day they had all the windows on both houses re-glazed, repaired, and ready to paint. In two weeks, a painting contractor was scheduled to do the stucco and wood batten exteriors.

"Why not have the painters do everything?" It was the first time in two days Jack said more than 'allo and g'bye to her.

"The windows alone would cost more than double what I was quoted for the walls."

"That much?"

"It's the man-hours, not the materials. The painters will have all the walls and trim done in five days. We'll be lucky if the three of us get the windows painted in two weeks."

His question and her answer signaled the thaw in their interactions. At five o'clock, Jack opened his truck door to leave. "What time shall I be here tommo?"

"Tommo?"

"To-mor-row."

"Same as usual but I think we'll quit at noon since it's a holiday."

Cam was tired. Her plan was to labor through the long July Fourth weekend but not for ten hours each day.

Jack studied her face. "Sounds like an ace ideer."

#

Early the next morning, Cam's phone rang. She reached for it on the pillow next to hers. It was Jack.

I knew it. He's bailing on me. "Yeah?"

"Cam? Where are you?"

"What do you mean? I'm here at the house."

"I'm outside. All the doors are locked."

The time was seven fifty-seven. "Oh, shit." She had overslept. "Hang on. I'll be right down."

Cam threw off the sheet, rushed into the bathroom, and splashed water on her face. She flung a tee-shirt over her sports bra and grabbed denim shorts out of the laundry basket. She pulled them up her legs as she duck-walked to the stairs and fastened them on the way down. She opened the kitchen door to find Jack on the porch. In each hand was a large cup of coffee. A white bag from a bagel shop was clenched between his teeth. She held the door open and grabbed the bag when he swung it toward her.

"You won't let me feed you dinner so I brought brekkie." He set the coffee cups on a nearby counter.

"Thank you."

When she walked past him, he reached out and pulled her into an embrace. After a comforting squeeze, he released her.

She frowned. "What was that for?"

His face crinkled into a smile. "It seemed like you needed a hug this morning."

#

As they set up to paint windows, the blare of a loudspeaker sounded. "Wake up, Delaware. It's parade time." The announcement was accompanied by *The Stars and Stripes Forever* music.

Jack stopped, his paintbrush held aloft, and cocked his head. "Who the bloody hell is Delaware, and why are they waking him up?"

Cam laughed. "Delaware is the street behind us. I was told every year there's a neighborhood parade for kids the morning of the Fourth."

"When we take a break, let's go. I'd like to see how you Yanks in Akron celebrate your independence."

Cam bit her lip and looked at the wall of windows in front of them. "Okay, but just for a little while."

#

At ten-thirty, as they walked down the block, the loudspeaker rang out. "This is entry number twenty-six. We have the O'Connor sisters on their bikes dressed as Lady Liberty. That's it, girls. Ride in a big circle for the judges to see."

The cross-street was blocked off with barricades. A group of more than a hundred people stood, sat in lawn chairs, or lounged on the grass. In the street was a large, white circle. A crowd of milling children on bikes, in wagons, or strollers were dressed up or carrying banners in various patriotic themes of red, white, and blue. The announcer sweated in a George Washington costume.

They watched the judging of some bike riders and several groups of children who sang songs while coached by a parent. It was definitely a family-oriented neighborhood celebration. Jack talked with the young father next to him who held a sleeping baby. They smiled at two adults trying to corral a preschooler riding a Big Wheel who didn't want to leave the judging circle.

Cam glanced down at her paint-spattered work boots. She was a temporary homeowner who would be gone as soon as The Harte Estate was sold. The other women present were wives and mothers who, if they had jobs, didn't do the kind of work she did. She wasn't in attendance with a family member or friend. Instead, her Australian apprentice and lover stood at her side. He was more comfortable with her neighbors than she was. She moved to the outside edge of spectators.

Jack caught up with her after she crossed the street and headed up the block. "You're leaving?"

"I've got too much work to stand around. Stay if you want." She picked at paint which dotted her arms.

Jack eyed her for a moment. "You're right. Those windows aren't going to paint themselves." He grasped her elbow, and they headed up the street.

#

Cam called a halt to painting at one in the afternoon. After Jack left, she took a shower, lay down on her bed and slept for three hours. Hunger drove her to the kitchen where she knew the only food available was French bread pizza or canned soup.

For the first time in a long time, she was lonely. During the last four years, she had closed herself off from getting close to anyone except her family. It was the only way she was able to dig out of the hole her former fiancé had created in her heart and bank account.

Now this damned Aussie has come and made me feel vulnerable again.

If her parents or brother were in town, she would have spent the evening with them. Maybe she would have had some barbecue, drunk a few beers under the stars, and watched a fireworks display with the people she loved most and who loved her. After eating frozen pizza for supper, Cam grabbed a mover's blanket and headed outside. She lay down in the front yard's grassy area. When it got dark, the whistles and concussive bangs of fireworks from the country club boomed. Above the treetops, the colorful explosions reached high in the sky.

A beam of headlights and the crunch of gravel signaled a vehicle had entered the property.

Chapter 6

JACK'S TRUCK CAME into view and parked. He ambled over to Cam and sat down next to her. The night was lit with brilliant hues of white and red.

He lifted his eyes to the sky. "I came to watch the fireworks."

"Why? The view is better at the country club."

"The company's better here. My uncle was fine until he got a gutful of piss."

Cam did a quick contextual interpretation of drunken behavior. "Too bad."

"And I had forgotten what a silly girl my cousin is."

"How old is she?"

"Twenty-two, I think."

"She's a woman, not a girl."

"Amelia may not be an ankle biter, but she's still a pain in the arse."

A loud whoosh was heard, then a bright flash illuminated the tree tops. They lay back on the blanket with their heads cradled in their hands. When the final, spectacular pyrotechnic display ended, they continued to recline side-by-side. Neither said anything while they gazed at the stars and listened to the sounds of night insects.

Finally, Jack rolled to his side and propped his head on his bent arm. "Tell me 'bout the man who hurt you and what happened at the country club."

Cam gave a startled twitch. "What are you talking about?"

Jack said nothing.

After a minute, she spoke while staring at the velvety sky. "The name he was using at the time was Oliver Armstrong. He was handsome, charming, and a thief. We were engaged and the wedding was to be at the Portage Country Club. I knew he wasn't going to show up when he was an hour late for the ceremony." *There's no more pathetic sight than a heartbroken woman in a wedding dress.*

"The bugger left you at the altar?"

"Yeah. My dad was out thousands of dollars for a wedding that never happened. Oliver was the one who wanted it at the club. He said his business associates and wealthy mother wouldn't want to attend a ceremony and reception in my parents' backyard. I later found out there was no mother, rich or not, and the so-called business associates were suckers just like me."

Jack placed his free hand on top of Cam's which rested on her abdomen. "Go on."

"I guess he did me a favor by not going through with the marriage. It would have cost me a lot more. The properties he and I *bought* together to renovate were actually owned by someone else. He dummied the paperwork."

"How much did you lose?"

"Fifty thousand. I worked hard for that money, and it was all I had in savings. I've been going nonstop for the last four years to pay back my parents and get myself financially secure again. Buying this place was the biggest risk I've taken so far." She rolled to her side and faced him.

"I'm sorry I pushed you 'bout going to the club. What happened to that mongrel?"

"Oliver was later caught in California pulling the same scam. The last I heard he was in prison, which is some consolation, but the money is gone for good."

Jack closed the distance between himself and Cam. Their lips touched, and their noses bumped. He lowered her to the blanket. His mouth opened over hers. The heat of it competed with the summer air on her skin. Their legs sandwiched together as they adjusted to get as much contact as possible.

When his tongue flicked in and out of her ear, she gasped. *Oh God, that's what it's going to feel like when this Down Under man goes down under.*

"You're so beautiful, Cam."

His lips found hers once again. He rolled over and pulled her on top of him. Jack raised his head to capture her mouth as his hands lifted her tee-shirt and caressed her back. His fingers worked their way down to her baggy shorts. The loose elastic waistband and her bikini panties were no barrier. He rolled her off and sat up to remove her clothes until she was naked from the waist down. He laid back, unfastened his pants, and lifted his hips off the ground. When he pushed his pants and boxers to his knees, Cam flexed her fingers around the girth of his erection.

He put his hands behind his head. "Do what you want. I'm all yours."

His face in the moonlight was luminous with amusement and desire. Cam leaned forward, her hair falling around her, and took him into her mouth. His hips juddered. She teased him with her tongue. The muscles in his thighs tightened when she pushed him to the back of her throat. He groaned. She cinched her lips around him, again and again.

When she sensed him teeter on the brink, she stopped. He blinked up at her. Cam swung her leg over his hips like mounting a horse, sat down, and nestled him between her thighs. She rocked back and forth in the saddle. Her damp warmth stroked him and created a friction which made her tremble with need.

Jack's face twisted, his teeth clenched. "Please, Cam. I need—"

She smiled with triumph and rose to her knees. He positioned himself beneath her. She eased onto him with exquisite slowness. Cam didn't move as she savored the sublime sensation. Jack flexed his hips. The motion radiated through her.

She groaned. "Do it again."

He obeyed. Cam bent forward and laid her palms on his chest. She lifted her pelvis and brought it back down. Ragged breaths matched their rising passion. She rode him up and down, back and forth. The oh-so familiar pulse tightened her belly.

She climaxed with a shout. "Yes. Yes. Yes."

Jack grabbed her hips, tipped his head back, and came with soft grunts. She lay down on his chest, overwhelmed. It was a place where she was both vulnerable and invincible at the same time.

#

Jack spent the night in Cam's bed. He left in the morning to put on work clothes and returned with hot coffee and a dozen doughnuts from Krispy Kreme. They painted until mid-afternoon when they cleaned up to go shopping. The first stop was Big Lots where Jack insisted she buy some inexpensive pots, pans, cooking utensils, dishes, and silverware.

He grabbed a shopping cart. "I refuse to cook with a bloody wallpaper scraper or bucket again."

She agreed to purchase all the kitchen supplies except for a hand mixer. "You want it, you buy it. I'll never use it." She paused to look at the picture on the box. "Then again, with just one beater, it might be good for mixing paint in a quart can."

He snatched it from her and put it back on the shelf. The trip to the grocery store took twice as long as usual for the same reason. Almost half the items Cam put in the cart Jack removed and returned to the shelf or freezer cabinets.

"You don't need chuna salad in a tin. You can make it better and cheaper." He put a small jar of mayonnaise and one of relish in the cart with several cans of tuna fish.

She spread her hands wide. "How can this be cheaper? Two cans of *chuna* salad with crackers are less than five dollars. All this other stuff is almost ten dollars, and that's without the crackers."

"The pre-made packs will feed you for two meals. The fresh-made will feed you for days."

"Who the hell wants to eat tuna fish for days?" When they exited the store, Cam eyed the shopping cart filled with bags of groceries. "Are you sure we have enough space in my refrigerator for all this? Remember, it's not full-sized."

Jack hugged her to his side. "Trust me."

They arrived home and put away most of the purchases. Jack assembled meat, vegetables, canned tomatoes, and spices next to the stove. Cam opened the refrigerator to put in a quart of milk.

Jack took the carton from her hand. "I need that."

"I thought you were making spaghetti sauce."

"Too right."

Cam's mouth twisted in distaste. "With milk?"

"It's my Dad's recipe for spag bol."

"What's that?"

"Spaghetti Bolognese. It's a meat sauce."

For Cam, a home-cooked meal consisted of frying bacon and toasting bread for a BLT. She had never heard of putting milk in spaghetti sauce unless it was the white kind.

I'm not going to question it. Jack seems to know what he's doing.

He motioned her to the counter next to the sink. "I'll show you how to make your own salad dressing."

Like I'm going to give up Wishbone.

He measured vinegar, olive oil, and a seasoning packet. "Now beat it until it's emulsified. Use this." He handed her a gadget they bought.

"Do I stir it with the beater?"

"It's called a whisk and here's what you do." He demonstrated the whipping action for her. "Stop when it looks thick and cloudy."

He mixed garlic with softened butter and slathered it on a split loaf of Italian bread. Cam got busy cutting a tomato, cucumber, and red onion for the salad. Jack preheated the oven.

A few minutes later he sniffed the air. "What's that smell?" He followed the odor to the oven. "When was this last cleaned?"

"Uh, never."

He opened the door. A cloud of gray smoke hit him in the face and rose to the ceiling. He waved his hands to clear the air. "Bloody hell."

Cam peered into the heated cavity. "So, that's where they are. I remember now. One day I put all my dirty dishes in there because I didn't have time to wash them."

Inside the oven were several plates, bowls and cups with blackened, ashy blobs and smears on them.

She reached for one, and Jack pulled her hand back. "Be careful. They're hot. Do you not have—? Of course, you don't."

He turned off the heat, grabbed a handful of paper towels, and folded them into a thick pad. He used it to pull a plate from the oven and set it in the sink. Cam brought a fan down from upstairs and plugged it in to get the burnt smell and smoke out of the kitchen.

When the oven-baked dishes cooled, Jack filled the sink with hot water and detergent. "I may not be able to save them all."

She smiled. "I guess it's a good thing I bought more."

#

Cam was awakened Saturday morning to the roar of her father's voice. "Who the fuck are you, douche bag? And what are you doing in my daughter's house?"

Her eyes snapped open. "Oh, shit."

She jumped from bed, pulled on a sports bra and shorts, then ran downstairs. In the kitchen she found her father glaring at Jack who was frozen in place.

Thank God, Jack's wearing his boxer shorts. Fuck. He's only wearing his boxer shorts.

Zane Coleman turned to his daughter. "You want to introduce me to this pile of monkey turds standing here in his skivvies?"

Cam learned early on with her father to show no fear. She padded across the kitchen and poured herself a cup of coffee that Jack must have just made. "Dad, this is Jack Reynolds. Jack, this is my father, Zane Coleman."

When she turned around, the scene had not changed. Jack stood statue-still, although the mug of coffee in his hand trembled slightly. Her father was ramrod straight, a menacing glare directed at him.

Cam leaned back against the counter and shot her father a warning look. "Dad, don't."

It appeared Zane's internal battle of being a protective parent warred with acceptance of his adult daughter's sex life. Finally, he put out his free hand. "Nice to meet you."

The words *I want to kill you* could have easily been substituted with the tone of his voice. Jack nodded and shook his hand.

Her father eyed the man in front of him. "Don't tell me you're sleeping with a goddamned mute? He hasn't said a word. What kind of strays are you taking in now?"

Cam pushed off the counter and stood next to Jack. "Say something to him."

"'Allo."

Zane's chin lifted. "Where you from?"

"Sydney, Oztralia."

"You're an Aussie." Her father smiled. "You got some fierce men in the Australian Defense Force. You ever serve in their military?"

"No, sir."

"Well, if you break my daughter's heart, I'll hunt you down and cut yours out."

"Dad, stop it. What are you doing here? I thought you and mom were in Columbus until tomorrow."

Jack put his coffee cup on the counter. "'Scuse me. I'll get dressed."

Zane watched Jack leave the room. "Good idea, *mate*." Then he turned back to his daughter. "We came back because I couldn't stand sitting around another day. How many hours of TV can one person watch? I painted Ed's damned garage yesterday just for something to do."

"How was Mom with coming back early?"

"Oh, she kicked up a fuss in front of her sister. But in the car she said she was tired of talking to Marjorie about zucchini recipes. They had a bumper crop, and now *we* have a bagful. God only knows what your mother's going to do with them."

Jack returned in his painting clothes. "I'll get started on the windows."

Her father said nothing until Jack walked out the kitchen door. "Don't fucking tell me you're sleeping with one of your employees?"

"Nope, he's my unpaid apprentice."

Chapter 7

"LET ME GET this straight. Jack is your apprentice, and he spent the night with you. Where did he sleep?"

"Well, there's only one bed. Where do you *think* he slept?"

"Don't get smart with me, Cameron."

"Dad, he's the first man I've wanted to get close to in four years."

A look of concern creased Zane's face. It was obvious he remembered the emotional wreck she had been after Oliver left.

Cam stepped closer to her father and touched his arm. "Jack's a recent college graduate, a nice guy who cooks for me, and he returns to Australia at the end of the year."

"I don't want you to get hurt again."

"Don't worry. I'm just having a fling." Cam put her coffee down and put her arms around her father. "Have you had breakfast? Jack makes a killer omelet."

She put on a pair of sneakers and went outside with her father. Zane headed to the carriage house for the riding lawn mower. Jack was on the scaffolding with a brush and a bucket of the window paint. She climbed up and kissed him good morning. His eyes darted around like he expected to be ambushed by a paternal commando.

Cam lifted the brush from his hand. "How about I take over, and you cook the three of us an omelet?"

"The three of us?"

"You would win my dad over. I learned everything I know about cooking from my mom."

#

On the patio, they ate spinach and feta omelets with rye toast and cantaloupe slices. Jack gathered up the plates and silverware to carry into the kitchen.

Zane looked at his daughter. "Aren't you going to help him?"

"Nope. One of his apprentice duties is to wash my dishes every morning."

Jack's lip curled. "She lets them sit in the bloody sink all day."

"Yeah, I know." Her father shook his head. "She's a soaker, just like her mother."

"So, that's where she learned it." The screen door slammed shut behind Jack.

Zane waited then leaned forward toward Cam. "You know, this guy might be a keeper."

"I'm keeping him for six months. It'll be like having a hamster. He'll be real cute for a while until I have to start cleaning up after him."

"I don't know, Cameron. In this relationship, *you* might be the hamster."

#

After breakfast, her father cut the remaining acres of weed-ridden grass. Cam and Jack worked on the windows until they were no longer in shadow. For lunch, he cooked turkey burgers spiked with cheddar cheese, sautéed onions, and bits of jalapeno peppers. Cam opened a bag of potato chips.

In the afternoon, they moved to the back of the house. Zane attacked the overgrown flower beds with a spade, weed whacker, and a small tiller. Cam helped him while Jack continued to paint windows.

She sat back on her heels and pulled off her gardening gloves. "Let's call it a day. It's two o'clock."

Zane continued to dig. "Why are we quitting?"

"I'm tired. I promised myself I wouldn't work full days this weekend."

Jack remained on the ladder. "I can keep working. You go crash."

"Yeah, take a nap, Cameron." Zane dug the blade of the shovel into the dirt. "We can handle this."

Cam pushed off her knees and stood. She had planned to have Jack take a nap with her but now couldn't say anything in front of her father. After wiping her brow with her forearm, she headed inside.

Her father's voice called out. "So, Jack, are you cooking supper tonight?"

#

Cam took a quick shower and lay down on the bed. She fell asleep in minutes.

Her mother's voice awakened her. "It's time to get up, honey. Jack has supper ready."

Her eyes flew open. "Mom? What are you doing here?"

Abigail stood beside the bed. "Jack told your father he'd cook pawn on the barbell. So, I brought our grill and some of your Uncle Ed's zucchini."

Cam brushed hair away from her face. "I think it's called shrimp on the barbie."

Abigail frowned. "He didn't say shrimp. I'm sure we'll find out what it is as soon as you get down there." Her mother headed for the door. "Hurry before the food gets cold."

When Cam stepped out onto the patio, the table was set with a red and white checkered cloth and her emergency candles. A piece of paneling from the basement rested on two sawhorses for a makeshift buffet. On it was salad in a plastic bowl and ears of grilled corn laid in a row on a cookie sheet. Jack smiled at her as he put down an aluminum pan of barbecued shrimp, zucchini, and pineapple.

He must have gone home to change because he wore a pair of Bermuda shorts, a polo shirt, and deck shoes. Her mother had on a sundress which Cam hadn't seen in ten years. Even her father wore a clean pair of jeans and a short-sleeved shirt. She glanced down at her tank top with a bleach stain near the hem and her clean, though paint-spattered cutoffs. She turned to go back inside and change.

"Where are you going?" Jack grabbed her arm. "Everything's ready." He handed her a plate, and she got in line behind her father.

Her parents oohed and aahed over the food like they had never eaten barbecue before.

Zane held up a large shrimp. "So, you call this prawn on the barbie?"

"It's our term for grilling it."

Cam picked up one from her plate and bit into it.

Jack smiled at her. "Howzit?"

"Great." She speared wedges of fresh-cut pineapple. "I didn't know you could cook fruit on the grill."

"The heat brings out the sugar."

"Can you do it with any fruit?"

"Wait and see."

Midway through the meal when Zane came up for air, he turned to Jack. "Where'd you learn to cook like this?"

"My dad is a chef. He owns a restaurant in Sydney. I learned by hanging out in the kitchen. My parents divorced when I was six. During the summers with Dad, he would bring me to work. At first, I just watched and asked questions. Later he had me bussing tables and helping out on the line."

Zane wiped his mouth with a napkin. "Why didn't you become a chef?"

"If I had, my Mum would have killed me. I like to cook, but I like designing and creating buildings more."

"What do you think about Cameron's project here?"

Before he could answer, Cam jumped in. "He did a research paper in college on the restoration of The Harte Estate. I read it. It's one of the reasons I agreed to his apprenticeship."

Zane pointed his fork at Jack. "Do you agree with her plans to restore the place and sell it as a single-family residence?"

"Of course, he does," Cam interrupted. "Many of his ideas for restoration were right in line with mine. Dad, I know you think I won't make any money when I sell, but the right buyer will want a property this size. Isn't that right, Jack?"

Her apprentice was fixated on the plate in front of him.

She ducked her head to catch his eye. "Jack?"

He looked up. "I hope you find the right buyer when you finish the restoration."

Cam's breath caught in her throat. It was like a concrete block had been thrown at her chest before she was ready to catch it. "What do you mean?"

Jack put down his knife and fork and leaned back in his chair. "I wrote the paper more than a year ago. The figgers were based on a homeowner who was willing to live here long-term to recoup his or her investment. That's not what you're going to do."

"I told you, Cameron." Her father now jabbed his fork in her direction for emphasis. "This place is going to take a while to go up in value."

She ignored him and remained focused on Jack. "So, you don't think I'll be able to make a profit when I sell in a year?"

"You might. But you'll make a healthier return if you create an enclave."

"What the fuck are you talking about?"

"Cameron." Abigail swatted her daughter's arm. "Jack, I did not teach her to talk like that." She gave her husband a frosty glare.

Cam leaned back with her arms crossed. She raised her eyebrows and cocked her head at Jack.

He took a breath. "You're going to spend a bloody fortune clearing the acreage 'round the two houses and landscaping them. The money's not recoverable based on the cost of land in this area. The only other restored, private residence in this neighborhood has three acres, not six, and that homeowner didn't care what he had to spend. You do."

"So, what's this *enclave* you mentioned?"

"The property is uniquely situated for a private development of four to five houses. Imagine the gatehouse is the first and the smallest residence. You can have another house on the north side, then the main house, and to the south one or two more. A common park could be built in the center for the use of the homeowners."

"You're talking about turning this is into a goddamned condominium complex?"

"No. No. Each house has its own lot. They just share what is now the front yard of the main house and the backyard of the gatehouse. But a condominium ideer is ace. Rules could be put in place to maintain the architectural integrity."

Cam's fist hit the table which caused the silverware to jump. "The integrity is maintained by keeping the place as a single-family property. It's what Morrison Harte wanted and the way it's been for a hundred years."

Zane snorted. "How do *you* know what Morrison Harte wanted?"

"I may not know what the original owner wanted, but I do know what Susan Gardiner told me. She did not sell to me so cookie cutter houses can be built on the land."

Color rose in Jack's cheeks. "That's not what I'm suggesting. I'm talking 'bout a private enclave or compound, possibly for a large extended family. If you repurpose the estate as such, you stand to make a much bigger profit. By selling the subdivided lots or contracting to have the houses built, you could make several hundred thousand more."

Cam stared at him as if he had morphed into a monster, like a developer or city building inspector. Her perfect apprentice who believed as much as she did in the restoration had turned into someone who proposed a mini-subdivision. Instead of The Harte Estate, Jack's property could be called *Laughing Cow*, wedges of houses in a circle.

She folded her arms on the tabletop and leaned forward. "Who are you?"

A look of unease passed over Jack's features. An instant later, he was the sweet, smiling Aussie who worked without complaint, cooked without a recipe, and made her wet without effort. His voice lowered into a soft, easy tone. "I'm the bloke who wants you to succeed because there are so many more places needing your help. I'm the apprentice who has learned more working here the past three weeks than I did the last three years in school. I'm the architect who wants to preserve the past but recognizes not everything can be saved in its original state."

A long, uncomfortable silence wrapped itself around the table.

Zane twitched his head to the side to catch his wife's eye. He glanced at his watch. "Look at the time, Abigail. We should be going."

Her mother glanced down at the food on her plate. "But Zane—"

He wiped his mouth, put down the wadded napkin, and scooted his chair back. "Up."

Cam sighed. "Let Mom finish eating, Dad."

Jack smiled at everyone. "Besides, you haven't had dessert."

"Dessert?" Her father's face lit up like he was about to belt out a Disney tune.

"I'm making grilled Bananas Foster."

"I don't know what that is," Zane sat and moved his chair closer to the table. "But I know it'll be good."

"Cam." Jack waited for her to look at him. "I wanted to talk to you about my enclave ideer. Just think about what I proposed. I'll draw up a plan to show you how it could look. I can also run some cost estimates and a current market analysis. It can be your Plan B if something happens to Plan A. Howzit sound?"

"I'll consider it." Her voice was a monotone.

When they finished dinner, Jack brought out a hot cast iron skillet with an amber sauce bubbling in it.

Cam pointed to the pan. "Where did that come from?"

Jack placed it on the still-warm grill. "I made the sauce in the kitchen."

"No, I mean the skillet. I don't remember buying one."

"I found it in the basement and scrubbed off the rust."

Jack added a splash of rum to the bubbling liquid and, with a flourish, lit it afire. Abigail scooped out four bowls of vanilla ice cream. Jack topped them with cut pieces of grilled bananas. When the flames died out, he stirred the sauce to cool it a bit, then spooned it over the ice cream. Cam's mother and father gushed about the meal.

"That was some of the best barbecue I've had in a long time." Zane rubbed his stomach.

Abigail stacked the dirty dessert bowls. "I loved your Bananas Foster. That seemed like an easy dessert to make. You'll have to give me the sauce recipe."

Both Cam and her father caught Jack's eye and mouthed, *no*. The effusive praise was followed by everyone pitching in with the cleanup. After her parents left, Cam and Jack stared at each other for several awkward seconds.

He draped a damp bath towel used to dry dishes over the handle of the oven door. "Shall I leave now too?"

She cocked her head at him. "I don't know. *Shall* you?"

He grabbed her around the waist. "Are you mocking my proper grammar?"

"I wouldn't dream of it. I love it when you and your grammar are all stiff and proper."

Chapter 8

ON SUNDAY, SHE and Jack ate leftovers from the previous night for lunch.

"Cam, may I take you out to dinner this evening?"

She put the corn cob down and wiped her lips. "Tired of cooking?"

"I want to pay for a meal we can eat somewhere other than this patio."

Many of her dates with Oliver involved schmoozing with an investor he tried to interest in one of his get-rich-can't-lose schemes. She often found herself making small talk with a wife or girlfriend who didn't know her ass from a butt joint.

She narrowed her eyes at Jack. "No dinner at the country club, right?"

"You pick the restaurant."

Jack had only seen her in work clothes or nude. When she had a business meeting or showed one of her houses for sale, she would spruce herself up.

Cam envisioned his reaction to her in a dress with makeup. "Sure. Let's go out tonight."

#

They finished painting at four o'clock. Jack went home to change. After he left, Cam showered, dried her hair, and wrapped it around hot rollers. She put on makeup, a black tube top dress, and high-heeled sandals. She wore a turquoise medallion necklace, bangle bracelets, and dangly earrings. When the arrival of a vehicle sounded, Cam descended the stairs with caution in her skinny heels, holding onto the bannister. Jack entered from the unlocked kitchen door. Her heart skipped a beat.

He was dressed in tan chinos and a pale pink polo shirt. His tousled, dark blonde hair was brushed back from his forehead. His broad smile made his azure eyes squint.

"Are you—" He stopped as if an invisible wall was just inside the door.

"Am I what?"

"Sure you want to go out?"

Cam moved toward him in a languid, sexy stroll. "It was your idea."

She picked up her purse and dangled the house key in front of him.

He slipped it off her finger and kissed her cheek. "You look wonderful."

"Thank you. You look very nice, too."

Cam led the way out and waited while Jack locked the door. She climbed down the porch steps and halted. A dark gray Mercedes sedan was parked in the driveway.

She pointed to the car. "Where did you get this?"

"It's my mum's. She leaves it here." He opened the door for her.

Once he got behind the wheel, Cam twisted to face him. "Why does your mom leave a car in Akron?"

He started the engine and adjusted the AC vents. "She's here two or three days a month. Where's the restaurant?"

"In the valley. I thought we'd go to the Mexican place."

"What about Papa Joe's? It's down there too."

"Mariachi Loco is cheaper."

Jack drove out to the street. "I can afford a nice restaurant."

"Not on what I pay you." As they traveled the steep, windy road into the Cuyahoga Valley, Cam studied Jack's profile. "Why does your mother come here from California every month?"

"She and her brother are partners in the firm my grandfather started. She attends the monthly board meeting."

"Where does your mother stay?"

Jack stopped at the red light and turned to look at Cam. "She owns a condo at Northside Lofts. It's where I'm living."

The high-rise building was within a block of downtown Akron. The prices for some units were close to a million dollars. The light changed, and Jack drove toward the restaurant. Cam stared out the windshield.

How rich is his family?

They have a membership at the city's premier country club. His mother flies in monthly from San Diego to stay in her condo and drive her Mercedes. As a recent college graduate, Jack has a new Ford F-150, nice clothes, and can afford dinner at Papa Joe's without collecting a paycheck.

He parked in the restaurant's crowded lot. When he came around and opened her car door, Cam didn't move.

He bent down with an amused smile. "Are you not getting out?"

She gave him a hard-eyed stare. "Who's paying you?"

He looked taken aback by her question. "Eh?"

Cam swung her legs out but didn't stand. Instead she squinted up at him in the early evening sunlight. "How can you afford dinner at Papa Joe's? Who bought your truck? Where do you get money for gas and groceries when you're working with me for free?"

He gave her a long, shrewd look, then his face crinkled into a smile. "I have my own money. You never asked why someone my age had just graduated from uni."

She shrugged. "I thought maybe you were a slow learner."

"Funny lady. I took three years off and played professional soccer. I was paid well and invested it."

"So, you're not a trust fund baby?"

"Sorry, no. Do you not want to have dinner with me now?"

She rose to her feet and kissed him. "No, now I do."

They went into the restaurant only to find themselves at the back of a crowd in the front entryway.

Jack rose up on his toes and peered ahead. "I didn't think there'd be a mob on a Sunday. I'll find out how long is the wait." He moved through the throng.

After he disappeared from view, a woman squealed. "Jackson. What are you doing here?"

Shit. I knew we should have gone to the other restaurant.

When Jack finally worked his way back to her, he wasn't alone. A young woman about his height hung onto his arm. She had brown hair with artful streaks of highlights and wore a body-hugging dress that barely covered her private parts.

Jack looked pained. "Cam, this is my cousin, Amelia."

Ah, the pain in the arse he mentioned. "Hello."

Jack's cousin viewed her from head to toe. "I can't believe you're Jackson's boss. I expected some Amazon dyke."

"Behave, Amelia." His tone was sharp.

"What?" The young woman raised her shaped eyebrows. "You hear about a woman working in construction and you picture this hulk with boobs. Anyway, it's nice to meet you. I'm here with some friends and invited Jackson and you to join us."

He cleared his throat. "I already told her we have to discuss work."

Amelia's eyes shifted from her cousin to Cam. "You don't look like you're dressed for a business meeting. You look like you're on a date."

A guy in tight jeans and a designer tee-shirt poked his body-builder frame between two people. "Amy, our table's ready."

"Come on." Jack's cousin tugged his arm. "We already told them a table for six."

Jack looked at Cam with a pleading expression she couldn't read.

Is he asking me to agree or begging for a way out?

The muscle man grabbed Amelia's hand and dragged her into the restaurant. Jack followed as his cousin still clung to his arm. He reached out and snagged Cam. The conga line bumped people aside. They followed the hostess to a room lined with booths along the wall. A party of three elderly couples sat at one long table which ran down the center of the room. The hostess walked past them to the second table and laid leather-bound menus in front of the six chairs.

Jack tried to maneuver Cam into a chair next to him, but Amelia slid into the seat. She pointed to the other side of the table. "You sit over there. Everyone, this is my cousin, Jackson, from Australia, and this is Sam."

"Cam," Jack corrected her.

The guy who came to get them was Amelia's boyfriend, Jason. The other two were Courtney and Vaughn. While the two couples discussed whether to get wine or order individual drinks, Jack caught her eye and mouthed, so*rry*. The waitress came to take drink orders.

Jason raised his index finger. "I'll buy the first bottle of *vino*. Make it a Merlot."

Jack looked up at the waitress. "I'll have a beer instead. Do you have Foster's?"

"Not that one." The waitress rattled off the names of several American beers and Jack chose Michelob. Then the woman turned to Cam. "And for you?"

"Water's fine."

Amelia pursed her lips. "You don't drink, Pam?"

If you can't get my name right, I don't have to answer you.

Jason crossed his beefy arms on the tabletop, thrust out his chest, and squinted at Jack. "So, you're the cousin from Australia."

Courtney leaned forward, dreamy-eyed. "I love your accent. It's so sexy."

Amelia barked a harsh laugh and smirked at Cam. "All he does is open his mouth, and he has to fight women off with a stick."

Jason settled back in his chair with exaggerated casualness. He bumped Cam's shoulder. "So how did you meet this dude?"

Amelia leaned across the table toward her friends like she was about to impart tantalizing information. "Get this. Jackson works under her."

"Lucky dog." Vaughn laughed. "You ever get to be on top?"

Everyone chuckled except Jack and Cam.

The waitress returned with an ice bucket, uncorked the bottle, and poured wine into four glasses. She pointed to Jack. "I'll be right back with your beer."

Cam buried her face in the menu. Jason and Vaughn ordered stuffed banana peppers and fried calamari appetizers for the table to share. Jack added zucchini fretto. Cam listened without interest to talk about who was dating whom, who broke up with whom, who was cheating on whom, who was going where, and who was doing what.

I guess I should be thrilled to hear about their exciting lives.

Cam studied Jack's cousin. The younger woman posed like a high-fashion model. Her every gesture and facial expression was angled as if for an invisible camera. She was as polished as a Barbie doll with the unnatural skin tone of a self-tanning product.

The appetizers arrived, wine glasses were refilled, another bottle was ordered to replace the empty one, and Jack signaled for a second beer. Cam sipped her water and passed the appetizer plates from Jason to Jack or vice versa.

"Have some calamari." Jason pushed back the plate Cam handed him.

"No, thanks, I'm not crazy for it." *I also don't want to eat food you ordered.*

Since everyone had appetizer items on their small plate, Cam covered hers with a slice of Italian bread and a packet of butter.

Jack handed her the zucchini fretto. "Here, *Cam*." He said her name loud enough for everyone at the table to hear. "I know you like zucchini."

She took a spear and passed it to Jason. The waitress returned with more wine. She asked if they were ready to order. Cam was but no one else. Menus were opened again and dishes discussed in the too-loud voices of the almost drunk.

Amelia snapped her menu closed. "I'm hungry for regular spaghetti and meatballs."

Jason leered at her. "After dinner, you can meet my balls, baby."

The waitress took Cam's order first. "I'll have the chicken parmesan and your white French dressing on the salad."

Jack asked for the same entrée. The others announced their selections then changed their minds. After the orders were finally placed, wine glasses were emptied, and the bottle was passed around the table again.

The talk among the four friends became more raucous. Two of the older women at the nearby table frowned when Amelia said in a shrill voice, "Are you shitting me?"

The appetizer plates were removed, another bread basket was brought, and the empty wine bottle in the ice bucket was replaced. Jack shook his head when asked if he wanted another beer. Cam's water glass was topped off.

After the salads had been eaten, Amelia turned to Cam, somewhat glassy-eyed. "Have you found Jackson to be a *hard* worker, Tam?"

Courtney giggled. "Why wouldn't she? He's such a stud."

Jack leaned over and whispered into Amelia's ear. She reared back, her shoulders rigid.

Jason appeared unaware of the whispered argument between the cousins. He drained his wine glass and set it down with a clunk. His cannonball-sized shoulder bumped against Cam's.

Fermented fumes leached from his mouth as he spoke. "So, if you do construction work, you must know something about erections."

He and the other couple laughed in a drunk-funny manner. Jack sat upright, chilliness in his blue eyes, his mouth set in a grim line. A nasty expression tightened Amelia's features. She directed a hard-eyed stare toward Cam.

Vaughn said, "Hey, Jackson, do you like working in old houses because they have a lot of tongue and groove?"

His girlfriend smacked his arm as the rowdy laughter drowned out the other diners' conversations. Jack glowered but remained quiet.

Cam looked down the table at the four friends, three who snickered and Amelia who sported a humorless smile. "Are you guys drunk or naturally crude?"

Amelia's voice was glacial. "Why would you say that, Cam?"

"Because in a nice restaurant like this with other adults and even families around, you guys are acting like you're at a kegger. But, at least, you got my name right this time, Amelia."

Jason's lip curled with a snarl. "Who are you? The booze patrol?"

Cam laid her napkin on the table and rose to her feet. "No, I'm the one who doesn't want to eat at the kiddie table."

As she walked away, Amelia snapped, "What a bitch."

Their waitress exited the kitchen as Cam walked by. She handed her a twenty-dollar bill. "I'm leaving. This should more than cover my bill and your tip."

"Do you want to wait for your order? I can put it in a container to go."

Cam shook her head. "You keep it."

Before the waitress took the money, Jack pushed Cam's hand back. "Why don't you wait for me outside? I'll take care of the bill." He glanced back into the dining room. "There's something else I need to do too."

The waitress cast nervous looks at the two of them.

Cam laid her hand on Jack's arm. "Just pay and let's leave. There's nothing you could say or do that would make a difference with those guys. Okay?"

Her eyes drilled into his with an unspoken message. At last, he heaved a sigh and nodded. She walked out the front door. It was still light out as she headed to where the Mercedes was parked.

Soon Jack came around the corner of the restaurant. He shook his head as he drew near. "I'm sorry. We should have left as soon as I saw Amelia. She and her friends are such whackers. What do you want to do now?"

"I'm still hungry and you promised to feed me. How about we head to Mariachi Loco?"

He smiled and put his arm around her shoulders. "Good ideer."

Chapter 9

ANTHONY LAID THE last metal frame from the dismantled scaffolding onto the pile. "What's next, Boss?"

Cam pointed to the aluminum-sided double garage. "We're going to tear down the god-awful prefab. I think Lavinia Harte had it built because the wood sliders on the carriage house got to be too hard to open and close. This piece of shit must have been cheaper to build than replacing those old doors."

She demonstrated to Anthony and Jack how to take apart the structure. When they took a break for lunch, a jet-black Lexus sedan entered the property.

Cam rose from the kitchen porch step and ambled over to her friend and realtor, Jeanine Switzer. "Hi. Come to see our progress?"

Jeanine closed the car door and looked around. Her statuesque figure was shown to perfection in a white eyelet sundress with a wide, red leather belt. Dark, almost-black hair spilled down her back, and her chocolate-brown eyes were highlighted with liner and mascara.

She hugged the much shorter Cam. "Wow. You've been busy."

"Let me show you what's been done so far. You won't believe how great the inside of the gatehouse is now. That awful cigarette smell is gone."

As Jeanine turned in a slow circle, she stopped dead. "Hel-lo? Who do we have over there?"

Cam glanced over her shoulder at Jack and Anthony who were headed back to the garage demolition. "You remember Anthony, don't you? He's been working with me since last year."

"I'm talking about the blonde. Is he your Australian apprentice?"

"Yeah, that's Jack."

Jeanine's eyes lingered on his backside as he strolled away. "He looks like a good worker."

Cam smirked. "You can tell by watching his butt?"

"Does he have an accent?"

"Of course."

"My God, how do you keep from jumping his bones?"

Cam bit her lip and remained silent.

Jeanine peered at her, eyebrows furrowed. Then she grabbed Cam and hugged her tight. In a sing-song voice, she chanted, "You-have-a-boyfriend. You-have-a-boyfriend."

Cam wiggled loose from the embrace. "I didn't say that."

"You didn't have to. It was written all over you."

"No, it wasn't. I was being inscrutable."

Jeanine raised her eyebrows despite how high they were already plucked. "That's a pretty big word for you, girlfriend."

"*I* have an extremely well-rounded vocabulary for someone who says fuck a lot."

Jeanine slung her arm around Cam's shoulders. "Let's go look at the gatehouse. While we're there, I want to hear all the down and dirty details about you and Jack."

After the tour and the interrogation, which rivaled ones Cam received when she broke curfew in high school, they returned to the main house.

Jeanine scanned the front façade of the once glorious mansion. "Have you tackled the inside yet?"

"Jack removed wallpaper in all the bedrooms, but I want to get the exterior work done while the weather's good. I figure I'll have the fall and winter to finish the inside."

Jeanine approved of the wisteria removal on the patio and the landscape clearing so far. "Are you sticking with your original idea to sell the property to a single buyer?"

Cam came to a sudden stop. "Why the hell would you ask that?"

"Since you've been here a few weeks, I wondered if you have the same plan in mind. Why? What's wrong?"

"Sorry. It's just that Jack also brought that up recently."

Jeanine glanced toward where pried loose nails screeched and aluminum clattered as it was thrown into piles. "I've got to meet this apprentice of yours."

"Sure. Let me introduce you."

They approached the garage as the last piece of siding was thrown into the trailer. The roof and walls had a definite cant toward a large pin oak just a few feet from the rear of the structure.

"Hey, Boss." Anthony removed his baseball cap and wiped his brow. His dark hair was creased around his head where the hat band had pressed against it. "Looks like the Leaning Tower of Pisa, doesn't it? The only thing keeping it from falling to the ground is the tree. Hi, Ms. Switzer."

Jeanine stepped forward with an outstretched hand. Anthony put out his then pulled it back to remove the glove.

She flashed him a dazzling smile. "Call me Jeanine. How's your mom doing?"

"Better with the warm weather. Thanks for asking."

Cam opened her palm to indicate her apprentice. "Jeanine, this is Jack Reynolds. Jack, this is my friend and realtor extraordinaire, Jeanine Switzer."

"G'day. Nice to meet you." His accented voice was low and husky.

Jack slipped off his suede work glove and wiped his hand on his shirt before he extended it. He gave Jeanine one of his quirky closed-mouth smiles. His eyes flashed with amusement as if he knew the two friends had discussed him at length.

Jeanine appeared calm, but there were telltale signs of fluster. The tall woman's bosom jutted forward. A fine sheen of perspiration sprang out on her upper lip which had nothing to do with the temperature. Her smile was a bit too wide and toothy.

Cam stepped in before her friend asked Jack to father her children. "She was admiring all the work you guys have done since she was last here."

"A-mazing." Jeanine remained focused on Jack.

He nodded. "Cam worked right there beside us. Didn't she, Anthony?"

"Yep. She gives orders then gets her hands dirty doing the same job."

"A-mazing."

Jack turned to look at Cam. His smile deepened which created slight dimples in the creases of his cheeks. "She is bloody amazing. I'm right lucky to be her jackaroo until the end of the year."

When the thrall of his eyes moved off Jeanine, she seemed to recover her equilibrium, like a hypnotist had snapped his fingers and brought her out of a trance. "Anthony, it was great seeing you again. And, Jack, I'm glad you're interested in saving this old house with my friend. I'll let you guys get back to work."

She slipped her arm through Cam's and spun them back toward her car. When they were twenty feet away, she heaved a deep sigh. "He is so hot and crazy about you."

"I agree he's hot but not crazy."

Jeanine halted. "That man looks at you like you're a cold beer on a hot day."

"He's just my six-month fling. I can't afford him to be anything more."

At her car, Jeanine opened the door and sat down sideways in the driver's seat. Her mouth twitched with a rueful smile. "You know, it's okay to open up your heart again. Not all men are like Oliver."

"I know. Jack's a good guy, but he's only here for the short-term. I won't leave Akron, and he's got a life back in Australia. I can't let my heart get involved."

Jeanine swung her legs inside and put the key in the ignition. "I almost forgot to tell you why I stopped by. Mrs. Underwood's house is going on the market."

The vintage home was a classic Queen Anne Victorian near the University of Akron campus and owned by a lady in her late eighties. Cam always admired the lone holdout on a block of converted and demolished houses. She hoped to have first dibs to buy the property one day.

A blip of excitement tempered by sadness ran through Cam. "You said the house wouldn't sell until the woman died. Has she?"

"No, but she did fall and break her hip. It doesn't look like she'll be able to manage the stairs to return home again. Right now, she's at Manor Care."

Jeanine's mother was a registered nurse at the skilled nursing and rehab facility. Tina didn't trawl for real estate prospects among her patients, but if one expressed concern about their home, she would ask if they wanted to talk with her daughter.

"I met with Mrs. Underwood over the weekend. She's like the woman who inherited this place. She doesn't want to see *The Grand Lady*, as she called it, reduced to rubble for parking or trashed for student housing. Are you interested?"

Cam looked back at the main house where the balance of her money was slated for the restoration. "I don't have cash reserves for another house right now."

"We can propose that Mrs. Underwood hold the mortgage with a nice down payment. Then rent out the house and convert it after The Harte Estate sells. I actually know a professor who wants a place within walking distance of the university for a year."

"Let me think about it."

"I told Mrs. Underwood I would meet with her again on Saturday. Why don't you come with me? Bring pictures of the houses you've done."

Cam agreed, and they set a time. Jeanine beeped a goodbye to Anthony and Jack as she drove away.

#

After everyone left for the day, Cam walked around the property. Tires crunched on the gravel driveway. She rounded the corner as her lanky brother, who towered over everyone in the Coleman family, exited his minivan.

He spotted Cam, and his face tightened. "What crazy thing are you up to now?"

"How was Chicago?"

He glared at her. "Answer the question."

"Okay. I don't know what you're talking about."

"I'm talking about the guy who's living with you."

"I'm not living with anyone. How was Chicago?"

"It was a weekend lost in translation."

His wife's Russian parents spoke little English. Adam probably smiled and nodded most of the time while he waited for Sasha or her sister to translate.

Adam put his hands on his hips. "Dad said you're sleeping with some guy."

"Right. He sleeps with me but doesn't live with me."

"Same thing."

"No, it's not." Cam jabbed her brother.

"Hey, that hurt." He rubbed his arm.

"If sleeping together and living together is the same thing, then you lived with a bunch of women before you got married."

"You still shouldn't be having sex with an employee."

"He's not an employee, and look who's talking. Wasn't Sasha your cleaning lady when you hooked up with her?"

"That's different."

"Why? Because you married her? Jack will be here for only a few more months. We're attracted to each other. Besides I'm having fun for the first time in a long time."

Her final statement softened her brother's expression. He put his arm around her shoulders and hugged her to his side. "I don't want you to get hurt again."

"Don't worry. He's nothing like Oliver."

Adam heaved a sigh and released her. "Okay, if you're sure."

His frown conveyed his concern. An observant childhood spent in the company of her grandfather, father, and brother gave Cam insight into the false reassurances males often expressed to females they loved. Adam would reserve judgement about Jack and keep an eye on him.

Cam cocked her head. "So, did you stop by just to give me grief about Jack?"

"No. Dad sent me to check out the carriage house doors and what we'll need to take them down. We got a call from a guy in Medina who wants them for an old barn he's converting into his house."

"Perfect. I've got new ones and automatic openers being installed next week."

Chapter 10

ON SATURDAY, CAM met Jeanine at Manor Care. They stopped at the nurses' station where Tina Switzer worked at a computer.

Jeanine leaned over the counter. "Mom, we're here to talk with Mrs. Underwood."

Tina pulled off her reading glasses and let them dangle from a beaded lanyard. She rose from the desk chair with a smile and open arms. Like Jeanine, she was a tall, curvy woman. Her long, dark hair was fastened into a tight bun at the back of her head. There were more silver strands than the last time Cam saw her.

After hugging her daughter's friend, Tina stepped back. "I'm so glad you're going to meet with Mrs. Underwood. She has worried too much about her house. I hope you can come to an agreement."

Cam and Jeanine found the frail woman seated in a wheelchair in her room.

After introductions, Mrs. Underwood marked the page of her book. "Let's go outside. They keep this place too cold to suit me."

Jeanine pushed the wheelchair to a patio area with beautiful flowers and shrubs. The sounds from a nearby fountain created a peaceful, Zen-like atmosphere. The two young women sat on a wooden bench across from the elderly resident. Cam turned toward a shuffling sound.

A stooped, old man in a grey sweater and baggy brown pants approached. A big, dentured smile creased his raisin-wrinkled face. "Hiya, girls."

Mrs. Underwood shooed him. "Lawson, go away. These *ladies* are my visitors."

The rebuke did nothing to divert him, and he directed his smile to Cam. "Hey, cutie, do you know how old I am?"

Jeanine sat up taller and answered in a loud voice. "You're ninety-six years old, Mr. Bates."

The nonagenarian's eyes widened. "How did you know?"

"You told me last week." Jeanine stood and walked behind the bench to grasp his arm. "Let's get you some coffee and maybe a snack. Cam, tell Mrs. Underwood about C.C. Restorations."

Just before they went inside, Lawson Bates stopped and eyed Jeanine up and down. "You're a real looker too. Ya know, I still have sexual relations."

She gave his arm a gentle tug to move him forward. "That's nice. When was the last time they visited?"

Mrs. Underwood waved a dismissive hand at the old man's back. "I know I should be nicer to him, but he's such a pest. So, tell me about what you do."

Cam explained her mission to preserve and restore homes for families. On her cell phone, she flipped through before and after photos of the properties she had done in the last four years. "Right now, I'm working on The Harte Estate on Portage Path."

"I knew Lavinia Harte. We were members of the Akron Junior League for many years. She never married and cared for her parents in that house until they died. She was sweet but strange."

Cam shared her vision for the property. "I could do the same thing with your house."

"I'm sorry, dear, but you're wrong." Mrs. Underwood gave a sad shake of her head like she was reluctant to explain the facts of life to a woman who should know them by now. "I'd like to think my house could be what it once was, but that is no longer possible. Just like my old body can't do what it used to. My neighborhood was once filled with families and children. Now its college students, who come and go, play loud music, and drive too fast. I just want to make sure *The Grand Lady* isn't torn down or falls into disrepair. She deserves to have a second chance as something new and different."

"Are you sure?"

Mrs. Underwood grew pensive. "The University of Akron is now the driving force in that area. They will tear down anything standing in the way of what they call progress. I remember when the school was just a small municipal college. The neighborhood was never the same after they started expanding the campus."

Jeanine returned. "How's it going?" She frowned at the look of regret on her friend's face. "What's wrong?"

Cam shrugged. "Of the three of us, it seems I'm the only one stuck in the past and won't let it go."

The women negotiated and Jeanine wrote up a sales contract. Mrs. Underwood agreed to the purchase price Jeanine proposed and only a five-thousand-dollar deposit. She would hold the mortgage with a balloon payment after ten years or in the event of her death.

Her rheumy blue eyes looked off into the garden. "If I have the money in the bank, whatever nursing home I end up in will just take it. I'd rather know my house is safe from the wrecking ball."

Cam and Jeanine promised to keep Mrs. Underwood informed of the restorations with regular visits. The closing was scheduled for the following week. After that, her family would have thirty days to remove the contents before C.C. Restorations took possession.

Next to their cars in the parking lot, Cam sighed as a film of tears clouded her eyes. "It must be so hard to see your old life change and disappear. Her treasured home will be gone forever."

Jeanine bent to look into her friend's face. "How many times do I have to remind you? Don't marry your house. It's a box to live in. Hopefully, you make a profit on it when you sell. If you fall in love, it'll break your heart every time."

#

Two weeks later, Jack was driving them home after Sunday brunch at a local hotel's restaurant.

Cam put her hand on his thigh. "I want to show you something."

His eyes twinkled. "I think I've seen everything you have to show."

She smacked his leg. He followed her directions to the north side of the university campus. They passed a fraternity house closed by order of city inspectors and the health department. Across the street was a rundown boarding house for students with a *Room Available* sign in the window. Next came an empty, weed-filled lot. In the center of the block was the jewel in the crown. The Grand Lady showed minor signs of neglect with peeling paint, sagging porch steps, and a chimney in need of repointing.

Cam tapped the passenger window. "What do you think of this place?"

Jack leaned forward to view the house. "Looks like a peacock in a cage full of buzzards. I wonder if it would be worth moving to a different location."

"Why the hell would it have to be moved?"

"Look at what's 'round it. There's no value in preserving it here."

"I disagree. Maybe it could have a coffee shop on the first floor and an apartment above. Or it could be another business catering to students and employees of the university."

Jack's eyes narrowed. "You're not considering it, are you? It's not for sale."

"I bought it on Friday." She flashed him a self-satisfied grin.

Jack stared at her like she relied on the Psychic Hotline for real estate advice.

Cam told him the story of Mrs. Underwood and Jeanine. "I don't take possession until next month. I'll fix it up a little, and Jeanine says she can find a good tenant. When I finish The Harte Estate and sell it, I can rehab The Grand Lady. Could you come up with possible options for what I can do with it?"

He stared out the windshield and didn't answer.

"Jack?"

"Eh?"

"Will you help me?"

"With what?"

Cam tousled his hair. "Earth to Aussie. Will you put on your architect's hat and design some conversions of this from a single-family residence to some other use? You heard me say it. I'm willing to restore a house to have a different function. Can you do that?"

"Uh, right."

#

Her apprentice was not his usual cheery self during the rest of the week. He arrived for work every morning but didn't linger after Anthony went home for the day. Cam was back to dinners cooked by Marie Callender.

On Thursday, she stopped him when he headed to his truck. "Is anything wrong? You seem preoccupied."

He looked at her with a somber expression, his eyebrows knitted together. "I'm a bit snowed under. I'm across it but."

"Jack, don't worry about Mrs. Underwood's house."

His head turned in her direction. "Eh?"

"I just wanted your input since you're working on my Plan B for here. You don't have to come up with options for the university house right now. I won't be doing major work on it for at least a year."

"That's not what's on my mind. It's some personal issues."

"Can I help?"

He glanced to where Anthony cleaned tools with a hose next to the carriage house. His back was to them, and he whistled off-key. Jack gave Cam a quick hug and kissed her temple. "Thanks. I have to handle this myself but."

When he released her, she put one hand on his cheek. "You've been a blessing to me, Jack Reynolds. You are just what I need, and I'm not only talking about your apprenticeship. If there's anything I can do to help, please tell me."

He gave her a sweet smile, but there was no twinkle in his eyes. "I don't deserve to be your bloody apprentice or anything else."

After Jack and Anthony left, Cam was walking back from the gate house when Jeanine's Lexus drove up.

Her friend powered the passenger side window down. "Get in. We need to talk."

For once, Jeanine was not her usual put-together self. There were purple shadows beneath her eyes, and her clothes were rumpled.

Cam opened the door and entered the cooled interior. "What's the matter? You look like shit."

Jeanine lowered the visor and checked her reflection in the mirror. "It's the client I've been showing houses to for three days. This woman couldn't make up her mind if a gun was put to her head, and she was given one choice. But I came to tell you my phone has gone crazy this week."

"What's the problem?"

"Gus Varsamis."

Cam shook her head. "Never heard of him. Who is he?"

"Akron's most notorious slumlord and the owner of the other properties around your new place. He just found out you bought Mrs. Underwood's house and is threatening to make you regret it."

Chapter 11

CAM REARED BACK in her seat. "Threatening *me*? Why? And how did this Gus guy know the house had been sold?"

Jeanine put the car in gear and drove to the front door of the main house. "Mrs. Underwood's granddaughter, Robin, was there with her sons loading a van. He stopped and accosted her. She told me her boys came outside when they heard him yelling. I guess they're football players and pretty intimidating."

"Why'd he call you?"

"Robin told him I brokered the sale but wouldn't say who the buyer was. The first time he called I hung up on him. His language was so offensive."

Cam laughed. "Worse than mine?"

"He called me a—never mind. So, I wanted to find out what was going on." Jeanine looked in the mirror again. "God, I need a facial and a good night's sleep." She flipped the visor back in place. "Some of this I know for sure, and some I just suspect. At each end of the block are those townhouses, but in the middle are eight properties, four on your street, and four on the street behind you. Gus owns seven of them. You own the eighth. Now this is the part that's only rumors. I was told a developer offered Gus top dollar for his properties. But the holdup was the Underwood place which sits smack dab in the middle of the block. Whatever is planned needs all eight lots."

"What does this developer want to build?"

Jeanine shrugged. "I'm not sure. The person I talked to said he heard it was going to be a multi-level storage facility. Can you imagine building a warehouse with lockers within two blocks of the campus? It would be a goldmine."

Cam winced. "And just as ugly."

"The deal can't go through without your property. I took great pleasure in telling Gus the house was now owned by C.C. Restorations. He asked what you were going to do with it, and I told him your plans. I wish I could have seen his face." Jeanine's sported a devilish expression.

"Well, I'm not going to sell the house so it can be torn down. I promised Mrs. Underwood that wouldn't happen."

"My source could be wrong. Maybe the deal has fallen apart already. Let's see what happens. If we get an offer, the developer's still interested."

"Do you think Mrs. Underwood knew about this?"

Jeanine rolled her eyes. "I'd bet my pink Louboutins she's been hounded for the last year. I think she decided to hand the problem off to someone like you."

Cam nodded. "A preservationist."

"Or as Gus called you, a fucking old house fanatic. I spoke with Mrs. Underwood yesterday. She's agreed to allow you access to install some security cameras inside and out. I don't know if Gus would do anything, but his financial situation is shaky right now. He may be banking on this sale. One of his properties is in foreclosure, and the rest either owe back taxes or have major code violations. We both know desperate men will do desperate things." Jeanine checked the clock on the dashboard. "I've got to go. I have one more appointment today."

"I'll be careful. You take it easy too."

The women stretched over the center console for one-armed hugs. Cam hit the speed dial on her phone before Jeanine reached the end of the driveway. Her brother answered on the second ring.

Cam told him about her concerns with the Underwood house. "Can you rig up a couple of cameras over there?"

"Where do you want them?"

"I think one outside at the front and another in back. Nothing'll happen during the day, because there's too much traffic, but they definitely need good night vision. Then I think one should be in the main hall of the house. Can you have them feed back to your computer?"

"Sure. How soon do you want it done?"

A chill ran through her. "Yesterday."

In the past, Cam had done rehabs in neighborhoods frequented by crime and shady characters. However, the house itself was rarely targeted unless a druggie was looking to score some quick cash by ripping out copper or stealing tools. Even in less than desirable areas, residents liked seeing a property restored. They banded together to drive off the riff-raff. Cam ensured their cooperation and rewarded their vigilance by helping out with free repairs. The little jobs created her own neighborhood watch and didn't cost her much in time, effort, or money.

#

The following weekend, Jack invited Cam to his condo for dinner and to spend the night. The August weather was hot and muggy. She looked forward to good food, great sex, and cool air conditioning. On the way, Cam purchased a bottle of wine. She drove past her parents' house and spotted her brother's van parked out front. She pulled into the driveway.

Everyone was in the kitchen. Adam, Sasha, Zane, and Abigail worked their way through a KFC bucket. The baby sat in a bouncer seat in the middle of the table.

Cam stood between her parents to coo at her three-month-old nephew. "AJ, you're getting to be such a big boy."

The baby's bright, blue eyes sparkled, and an open grin split his mouth behind the pacifier.

Her father inspected her in the white halter dress. "You look nice, Cameron. Where's Jack taking you?"

"He's cooking dinner at his place." Cam caught her brother's eye. "Have you looked at any of the video from the security cameras at the Underwood house?"

Adam put the chicken wing down and wiped his fingers on a paper napkin. "I check every morning. The family seems to be focused on clearing out the attic and second floor. The dumpster's less than half full."

Her father frowned. "Adam told me about the threat. You be careful, Cameron. Don't go over there by yourself. Who knows what the asshole who wants the house gone will do. If Anthony or Jack can't be with you, call me or Adam."

Cam sighed. "I'll make sure someone is with me."

"And have your Glock on you, too."

She knew better than to argue with him, so she turned to her brother. "What kind of activity have you seen around the house at night? Is there anything suspicious?"

Adam glanced at his parents and wife but didn't speak.

Sasha cocked her head. "Vhat wrong? Answer Cam."

He sighed. "The other night there was a guy and girl going at it in the backyard."

"Vhat going at eet mean?"

Adam's ears turned red. "You know."

Sasha shook her head, and her straight white hair waved back and forth. "No, I not know."

Cam laughed. "They were fucking, Sasha."

"Oh, dat I know."

#

The lobby of the Northside Lofts condominium was all glass, metal, brick walls, and stained concrete floors. As Cam rode the elevator to the third floor, she wrinkled her nose at the modernity of this urban building. When Jack opened the door of his mother's unit, he was wearing an apron which read, *Kiss the Cook, But Don't Touch the Buns.*

He grabbed her and pulled her close. "You can bloody well kiss and touch anything you like."

To her relief, no one walked down the hall to find them *going at it.* She pulled away from his marauding mouth. "You can't kiss me into liking the design of this place."

He pointed to the plastic shopping bag she carried. "What's in there?"

"My toothbrush and clothes for tomorrow."

He smiled at her overnight bag courtesy of Walmart then lifted the wine bottle from her hand. "I'll show you 'round after I get the steaks."

The condo was a corner unit. The floor to ceiling windows had views of Howard and Main Streets, the central plaza, and a corridor of buildings through downtown.

She pointed outside. "Nice view."

All the furnishings were leather, metal, or glass. There was no natural wood of any kind in the open concept kitchen, living room, or dining room. She strolled to where Jack pulled a glass dish with two thick steaks out of the refrigerator.

Cam studied the black metal cabinets, quartz countertops, and stainless-steel appliances. "So, this is where the magic happens."

Jack flashed her a crooked smile. "No, luv, let me show you where that is."

He had started calling her *luv* in the last week. It was a casual way of saying *I like you* by Aussies and Brits. Cam didn't fuss at him as long as he didn't say it in front of Anthony or anyone else on the job. She had never used pet names in personal or friendly relationships. She always called Oliver by his first name until he jilted her, then he became that son of a bitch among other colorful epithets.

Jack took her hand and led her to a room across from the kitchen. It had a queen-sized bed and a long black dresser. A computer station sat in front of a tall window.

He opened his arms wide. "This is where I sleep."

Cam gazed upward. Two of the four walls ended several feet shy of the loft ceiling where ductwork ran through. "Your room is open to the rest of the condo. Is that a problem?"

"Only if you get too loud when my mum is staying over."

She smacked his arm. He laughed and ducked away. Across the hall and behind the kitchen was a bathroom with a large glass shower.

Jack pulled her inside and pinned her against the tiled wall. "Plenty of room." He gave her a quick smooch on the lips. "Let me show you the master suite, my mum's space."

French doors with frosted glass panels opened to reveal an over-sized room with a king-sized bed decorated in feminine colors of cream and blue-grey. An ensuite bath was tiled in Carrera marble.

When they returned to the kitchen, Cam picked up the wine she brought. "Do you want to open this?"

He pointed with his chin to the Walmart bag lying on top of the counter. "Did you buy it there or at a bottle-o?"

"I bought it at a store by my parents' house."

It was a corner market where they knew her well. She had been shopping at E-Z Mart since she was ten. When she added a big Hershey bar to keep in her purse, the motherly clerk leaned toward her and whispered, "Is it that time of the month, dearie?"

Jack took the Merlot from her and put it aside. "Let's wait." He grasped her waist and, in a fluid move, lifted her onto the end of the island. "I like this dress."

His eyes swept down her neckline to her waist. A multi-colored scarf was cinched around it. His perusal continued to where the short, pleated skirt ended inches above her knees. He spread her legs apart and stepped between them. His hand slid under her skirt until he reached her panties.

"Jack?" She cocked an eyebrow.

"I've been looking forward to this all day."

He pulled her panties down and lifted her bottom to slip them off. She raised her legs to help him. The lacy thong was dropped onto the floor. They exchanged languorous kisses. Jack's hands glided over her body. Spirals of ecstasy surged through her. When they broke apart, Cam leaned forward to capture his lips again. But Jack scooted her away until the backs of her calves were against the wall of the island. He lifted her skirt.

His smile was both roguish and delighted. "You look very tasty, luv."

He bent toward her and hooked her legs over his shoulders. He lowered his head and nuzzled her with the warm wetness of his mouth. When his tongue speared her, she moaned through tight lips. He continued with gentle strokes as he inserted a finger. Soon an orgasm quaked through her.

Jack stamped a row of kisses across her abdomen then rested his chin there. A crooked smile creased his moist lips. "Luv, you'll being driving me crazy when I'm old and gray."

For Cam, any endearment or talk about the future was hindered by his impending return to Australia. "I love what you do to me."

He held her hand as she sat up and hopped off the counter. While Jack washed up, she retrieved her panties and put them on. Cam opened the wine and poured out two glasses. Jack took a sip then checked the bottle.

"Is it okay?" *I shouldn't have bought wine where they sell lottery tickets and condoms.* "It's from Australia. See, there's a kangaroo on it."

"It's fine."

She assembled the Caesar salad according to his instructions. Jack heated the grill top and checked on the baked potatoes. Twenty minutes later, they sat down to a scrumptious dinner.

Jack cut into his steak. "Did you work on the house today?"

"No. I cleaned, did laundry, and paid bills. Then I stopped at my parents' place before I came here. My brother was there with his wife and baby."

"Your sister-in-law is from Russia, right?"

"She's been here for five years. Sasha's so afraid the baby won't learn to speak English properly because of her."

"What does your brother say?"

"He wants her to teach AJ Russian. He thinks it's cool if his son is bilingual."

Jack put down his knife and fork. "Would you like to have a child someday?" He waited with an open, guileless expression.

Cam blinked. *Where the hell did this come from?* "I would. I just worry what kind of mother I'd be."

"Why?"

"Because I'm not your typical woman. I do construction work. I can't cook. I'm not, you know, girly."

"Cam, you have nothing to worry 'bout. You work harder than anyone I know. You drive men wild whether you're in overalls or a skirt. You're kind and loving, loyal and authentic. I can't think of any man who wouldn't want those qualities in a wife or a mother for his children."

A melting spread through her chest, and her eyes moistened. She lowered her face and focused on cutting her ribeye. "I do find my nephew fascinating. He changes every time I see him. AJ is like a construction project that gets bigger and more functional as the days go by."

Jack laughed. "I like that analogy."

After dinner and the cleanup, Cam wandered into the living room and sat on the lounge end of the white leather sectional. A deep sigh escaped her lips as she leaned back against the cushions and stretched out her legs. Jack dropped to the seat and put her feet in his lap. His palm brushed the top of her arches where a multitude of the sandals' straps crisscrossed. He unfastened the buckles on her shoes and slipped them off.

He *tsk*ed at the indentations. "I love how sexy your shoes are, but look what they've done to your pretty feet." His strong hands began to massage her left sole, heel, and toes.

"Ahhh. That feels so good." Her head lolled against the cushion. She covered her mouth when a yawn escaped. "Sorry."

Jack worked on her right foot. "Just relax, luv."

She closed her eyes to the sublime sensations. Without intending to, she fell asleep. When she opened her eyes, Jack was beside her. His arm held her against his chest. A soccer game played on the flat screen TV with the sound muted. He raised the remote and clicked off the device.

Cam stretched. "You can watch the game."

"It's almost over. Are you ready for dessert?"

"What is it?"

Jack stood and pulled her to her feet. "Strawberries, whipped cream, and my body parts."

Chapter 12

JEANINE CALLED CAM on Monday afternoon. "You're not going to believe this. I guess because I brokered the sale of the Underwood house, I've been contacted with an offer to buy it from a company called Castle Construction. I looked into them. They've built thousands of apartments and homes around the Great Lakes region, but for the last twenty years, their focus has been hotels and office parks. They might be buying up the whole block, including the townhouses at each end and building something for the university."

"Well, it doesn't matter because I'm not selling."

"Don't you want to hear how much they're willing to pay?"

Cam gasped when Jeanine told her the amount. "That's insane."

"As your friend and realtor, I think you should consider it. You don't have much invested beyond your down payment."

"But I promised Mrs. Underwood that her beautiful house wouldn't be demolished."

"There are two options. You could have your dad salvage the place and sell what's left. Or you can move the house to a different location. Better yet, sell it to Castle Construction for less if *they* move it. After all, it's the land they want. You have twenty-four hours to make a decision."

The next morning Cam called Jeanine. "I'll sell, but Castle Construction has to buy a lot I approve of and move the house to it."

She said goodbye still conflicted about her decision. The value of the property was its location close to the campus.

Jeanine called at three p.m. "They're not interested. I was told you can move the house to your own empty lot with the additional money you're being paid. However, you have to do it within thirty days of closing."

"Then forget it. I've got too much going with The Harte Estate to deal with a project like that right now."

#

With the muggy summertime weather, Cam had been spending nights at Jack's condo after work so they could sleep in air conditioning. At three a.m. his cell phone rang on the cabinet beside the bed. He rolled away from her and slapped the tabletop for the device.

"'Lo." He listened. The sheet was pulled tight when he sat up and swung his legs to the floor. "Bloody hell. When?"

The sharp edge of panic in his voice made her sit up and rub her eyes. The bow of his back was defined in the moonlight as he bent forward.

"I'll be there as soon as I can. Tell him I'm coming, and I love him." He waited as the caller spoke. "I know, but tell him anyway." Jack removed the phone from his ear, and his head slumped.

Cam waited several beats. "What's wrong?"

Her words galvanized him into action. He leapt to his feet and turned on the bedside lamp. Cam shielded her eyes against the sudden light. Jack picked his shorts off the floor and stepped into them.

He rounded the end of the bed and headed to his computer desk. "That was my uncle in Oztralia. My father was in a motor vehicle accident. He's in surgery now with a ruptured spleen." Jack sat on his desk chair and booted up his laptop. "He has a broken leg and is still unconscious. They don't know how severe the head injury is."

His fingers flew across the keyboard. A travel website popped up. His face was a mask of fierce concentration in the bluish glow of the backlight.

This is it. Instead of six months, I had him for two. Cam pinned her arms against her stomach. *This isn't about me. He may lose his dad.*

She slid from under the sheet and stood. Without a word, she dressed. The metallic hiss of the zipper on her purse made Jack swivel his seat toward her.

She laid a hand on her breastbone. "I'll get out of your way. I'm really sorry about your dad. I hope you have good news soon." She headed for the door.

"Cam, wait." He came to her and wrapped her in an embrace. They stood still for several moments, then Jack stepped back. "I'll contact you as soon as I can, luv."

"If there's anything I can do, call me. Take care of yourself, Jack."

He returned to the computer. She stared at his back with moist eyes to imprint one last image of him in her memory then let herself out of the condo. In the elevator, she knuckled away the fugitive tears which escaped down her cheeks.

Dammit, I was afraid of this.

In high school, one of her friends said the only way to know if you really loved a guy was if he made you cry. When did her fling become so much more? Perhaps it was when she began to daydream about a future with Jack. She had envisioned them working side-by-side, not as boss and apprentice but as partners. They could buy an old house together and fix it up just the way they wanted for their personal use. It was at that point she berated herself for imagining marriage and a family.

When am I going to learn that daydreams are a waste of time?

#

Two days later, Cam received a phone call from Jeanine. "I've got the keys to the Underwood house for you."

"I wasn't expecting them to have everything out until next week."

"I guess they hustled." Jeanine paused. "I also received another profane voice mail from Gus Varsamis. Castle Construction must have told him you won't sell and the deal is off the table. Please be careful, Cam. Don't go over there to work by yourself. Make sure Jack or Anthony is with you."

"I appreciate the warning, but I can probably take better care of myself than Anthony. As for Jack," she heaved a sigh, "he's gone back to Sydney."

There were several beats of silence before Jeanine spoke. "I thought he was here until the end of the year."

"His father was in a car accident. He flew back either yesterday or today."

"Have you heard from him?"

"Not yet."

"What about your relationship?"

"His father may not make it or he'll have a long recuperation. Either way, I doubt Jack will be back." Tightness constricted her chest. "His dad's family is all in Australia and his mom is in San Diego. The only thing here is an uncle and a cousin he can't stand and a family business that doesn't interest him. Why should he return?"

"To be with you."

"I don't think that's a possibility." She straightened her shoulders and smiled into the phone. "Do you know anyone who wants to work for free? I need another apprentice now that I have two houses."

"Sorry, girlfriend. If I find someone who looks like Jack and will work without pay, I'm keeping him."

#

The next day, Cam received an email from Jack.

> *Sorry it's taken so long for me to get in touch. Dad is out of intensive care. He has a bad concussion but no other head trauma. The surgeons removed his spleen and casted his broken leg. He'll be in hospital a while longer. I'm spending as much time as they will allow by his bedside. I miss you. I even miss the bloody work. As soon as I have definite plans, I'll let you know.*

Cam covered her mouth with her hand and closed her eyes. She feared Jack would be greeted with news that his father passed away while he was enroute. Now that Mr. Reynolds would recover in time, she expected one or two more updates before the one that would say he wasn't coming back to the States.

> *That is great news, Jack. I was so worried. Anthony and my parents want you to know they're thinking of you and wish your father a speedy recovery.*

The work has started on the Underwood house. I had to hire another temporary helper who, unlike you, isn't willing to work for free. I miss you too. I know you'll take good care of your dad.

#

A week after Jack's three a.m. phone call from Australia, another cell phone rang in the middle of the night. Cam sat up in bed, squinted at the screen, and clicked it on.

"Hello."

She was told her newest property, the Underwood house, was on fire. Cam dialed her dad's number and threw on clothes as she listened to the rings.

"What's wrong?" Zane's voice was hoarse and sleepy.

"I just got a call that my house by the university is on fire. I'm on my way over there."

"Wait for me, Cameron. Don't go by yourself. It might be a hoax."

"I'll swing by and pick you up. Be ready in ten minutes."

#

When they arrived at the scene, they found it was no crank call. The street was blocked by fire trucks and police cruisers. When Cam saw the extent of the damage, her father's arm was the only thing keeping her upright.

All that was left of the stately Victorian were portions of two side walls. The brick chimney rose above a pile of smoldering rubble. It looked like a fiery wrecking ball had crashed through the house and destroyed everything in its path. The smell of burnt wood and smoke stung Cam's eyes along with tears she couldn't hold back.

How could this have happened? Everything was fine on Friday.

Her father left her side and returned with a gray-haired firefighter introduced as Captain Panetta.

"I'm sorry about your property, Ms. Coleman," the captain said. "We weren't able to save anything. By the time we got here, it was pretty well engulfed."

"Do you know how it started?"

"Not yet. I've already contacted the lead investigator. He'll be in touch with you after my report is filed. I understand you were renovating the property."

She sniffed back another spate of tears. "I was here on Friday and made sure everything was properly sealed and stored. No one worked on Saturday."

"If it wasn't carelessness, then maybe an electrical short or arson caused the fire."

"Arson?" Cam stared at Captain Panetta. *Desperate men do desperate things.*

"It happens, especially with vacant houses."

Her father nudged her. "Tell him, Cameron."

Cam recounted the storm caused by the sale of the house and the threats made by Gus Varsamis. "I had security cameras installed inside and out. I wonder if—"

Her father's cell phone rang and he pulled it out of his pocket. "It's Adam. Before we came, I called him. He's checking the video footage from tonight."

The fire captain and Cam waited until Zane ended the call.

"What did he say, Dad?"

"Around one a.m., a figure wearing a hoodie came in from the back porch. Adam could see him doing something in the kitchen and by the front door before going upstairs. The shitbag was inside for about a half hour. He left and fifteen minutes later the picture went cloudy. Then the signal was lost."

"We'll need a copy of the video." Captain Panetta reached into an inside pocket. "Here's a card with my email address. Have your son send it to me. I'll let the arson investigator know."

Some of the emergency personnel packed up and wheeled away. Cam and Zane stayed until dawn with the firefighters who checked for hot spots.

As the morning sun chased away the night, the extent of the destruction was even more devastating.

Cam laid her head on her father's shoulder. "There's no way to rebuild what little is left. You should have seen the crown moldings, the oak mantle, and staircase. There were gorgeous leaded glass windows in the dining room and on the landing. Now there's nothing for you to even salvage." Sooty tears coursed down her cheeks.

Her father turned her away from the ruin and squeezed her tight. "If I get my hands on the douche bag who did this, I'm going to nail his balls to the floor, put a bucket of water just out of reach, then set the room on fire."

Chapter 13

LATER IN THE morning, Cam contacted Jeanine. "Should I call Mrs. Underwood? I don't want her to read about the fire in the paper."

"Let me check with my mom first." When Jeanine called back, she said, "Mrs. Underwood had a stroke two days ago and was transferred to the skilled nursing section. I called her family. They said if she recovers, they'll tell her what happened."

The State Fire Marshal's Office and the Akron Fire Department collected debris from what remained of the house for forensic analysis. Cam received a copy of their report which confirmed arson. She submitted it to her insurance company. The video was not able to identify the intruder. Gus Varsamis was ruled out because the figure caught by the camera was at least half a foot taller and fifty pounds lighter.

The arson investigator, Jose Nunez, called Cam. "If Mr. Varsamis is responsible, he hired out the job. Unless we find the actual fire setter, we can't charge him."

"But he made threats and wanted the house gone."

"I'm sorry, Ms. Coleman. There's nothing more we can do at this time."

#

Every two to three days, Jack would email or text her with updates on his father's condition. He gave no hint as to his plans except to say he had moved into his father's apartment and would care for him there after his release from the hospital. One of his emails read:

> *Lucky for me, my dad's flat is in a building with an elevator. Otherwise, he would need to stay at a physio center. He would have a blue with me and the doctor about that. I'm happy I can nurse him at home. When I was a kid, I spent my school holidays with Dad in a much smaller place. Mum had a beautiful home in California with a pool and lots of time to mother me. With Dad, I slept on the chesterfield, had to cook, and clean for myself. We spent time together mostly when I helped out at the restaurant. Now I look back and realize my childhood made me a more balanced adult.*

Cam responded to his messages with short replies of generalities and well-wishes. She longed for his company, both on the job and in private. He was not only her apprentice and lover but had become a friend as well. She missed him with a deep, visceral ache which caught her unawares at times. Her greatest fear was that he would return to finish his apprenticeship then leave again at the end of the year.

#

Over the next two weeks, Cam met with a claims adjuster. Following his approval, she rented a bobcat to knock down the chimney and remaining walls. Her father and brother loaded up bricks for A to Z Salvage. The remaining fire debris was hauled away in several dumpsters, and the basement pit filled with truckloads of soil. Now the property looked like any other vacant lot. Cam threw grass seed over the large rectangle of dirt where the house once stood. A drizzle started which was forecasted to send heavy thunderstorms for the next two days. She crumpled the empty seed bag and surveyed the area for any rubbish left lying on the ground.

A car door slammed. Jeanine came toward her with a large golf umbrella. Her friend climbed the concrete steps from the sidewalk.

She looked at the cleared land. "I thought this is where you might be. It's hard to believe a house stood here a few weeks ago."

"I got busy as soon as I was given the go-ahead by the insurance company. I didn't want anybody poking around and getting hurt. At least, the bastard who did this waited until all of Mrs. Underwood's belongings were out."

Jeanine moved so Cam was under the umbrella with her. "She died last night. Mom called me this morning."

Cam's shoulders slumped. She grieved for the gracious woman who fought to save her house from a rapacious developer and an unscrupulous slumlord.

Jeanine hugged her. "I also came to tell you Castle Construction has submitted another offer."

"Let me guess. This one's way lower than the original."

"Even though the house would have been torn down, the offer is for the land only. They figure you have no choice but to sell."

Anger stiffened Cam's face. "Gus and Castle Construction have no idea who they just fucked with. Now I have no reason *to* sell. I'll just pay the taxes every year, mow the grass, and sit on this property as long as I want. If Gus thought burning down my house would save his ass, he's dead wrong. Maybe I'll make this into a park in memory of Mrs. Underwood."

"Cam—"

"I can see it now. I'll put in flower beds and a bench under the maple tree." She gestured to an area a few feet away from where they stood. "Over there can be a sign that says this is The Underwood Memorial Garden. Then I hope Gus shits his pants every time he drives by."

Jeanine frowned down at her. "Don't go psycho on me, girlfriend. This is business, plain and simple. There's no reason to blow off a perfectly good offer for vengeance."

Cam stepped back into the rain and thrust her chin forward. "Maybe for you there isn't. For me, it's personal when someone destroys *my* property to make a buck for himself."

"Okay, okay. I understand. Take it easy." Jeanine's voice had the calm, reasonable tone used to deal with a mental patient. "Do you want me to tell them you're too upset to think about selling right now?"

"I don't fucking care what you tell them. No, wait. Tell them I won't sell until I regrow my hymen or the Cleveland Browns win the Super Bowl, whichever comes first. Is that crazy enough for you?"

She stomped to her truck, started the engine, and drove away. During the ride home, the afternoon sky had darkened. The street lights lit up. Tree branches swayed, and leaves swirled in little tornadoes. Thunder boomed and rocked the truck. Rain fell in silver sheets which taxed the wipers. When she arrived at The Harte Estate, only Anthony's vehicle was in the driveway.

Cam sat with her wrists draped over the steering wheel and waited before she made a run to the porch. Her thoughts drifted to Jack. She had not responded to his last several emails. Every night she crawled into bed too exhausted to think straight.

With all the shit I'm dealing with, I don't want to hear he's not coming back.

Her phone rang.

It was Jack. "Cam, are you not all right?"

"Where are you?"

"I'm in Sydney."

"How's your dad?"

"He's doing better." Jack sounded impatient. "That's not why I called. What's going on? I haven't heard from you for a week."

"Things have been really busy around here."

There were several seconds of silence from his end. "So, you're too bloody *busy* to write me a goddamn email or text?"

She answered in a slow even tone. "You could say that."

"I'm taking care of an invalid who's driving everyone crazy, and I have to worry 'bout what's going on in Akron. What the bloody hell is wrong with you?"

Cam gripped the phone until her fingers hurt. "An arsonist burned my house by the university to the ground."

"What?"

"Yeah, Jack, I've been a little busy. I'm glad your father is doing better. You don't have to worry about me. Bye." She ended the call and ignored the phone when it rang a minute later. Regret flooded her, and she put her head in her hands. *What the fuck is wrong with me? Maybe Jeanine is right, and I am a little psycho.*

#

At nine o'clock that night, Cam's cell rang. "Hi, Jack." Contrition laced her voice.

"Please, don't hang up, luv."

"I won't."

"I'm sorry 'bout the earlier call."

"Me too. You caught me at a bad time."

"Tell me what happened."

"You're dealing with enough. I don't want to bitch to you about my problems. Besides it would cost a fortune in roaming charges."

"Don't worry 'bout my bloody bill. I want to hear you tell me what's wrong."

She recounted her tribulations since he left.

"So, the whacker is going to get away with it?"

"He will unless the police or fire investigator finds the actual arsonist. I've secured the site, and I'm waiting for the insurance check. Most will go to pay back the mortgage. I told Jeanine, I'm not selling. The taxes are paid until January, so I can just sit on the land. I don't want Gus to think he succeeded." She sighed. "How are things in Sydney?"

"Dad has been home for five days now. He seems to be on the mend. His doctors say he'll make a full recovery, if I don't kill him first."

She laughed for the first time in days.

He didn't. "It's not funny, luv. I think he was sent home from hospital early at the request of the nursing staff. He was as mean as cat piss while there."

A shout sounded in the background.

"I have to go. I miss you. As soon as I get things settled here, I'll let you know my plans."

"Don't worry about me. If my dad was sick or injured, I would take care of him before anything else too. I'm fine except I miss you. Bye, Jack."

Cam looked around the stark bedroom. Except for her bed, and it was only a mattress and box spring on a basic metal frame, the only other furnishings were stacks of plastic bins containing her clothes and two laundry baskets. Since she started C. C. Restorations, her home was either at a house undergoing restoration or in the loft at A to Z. Until she met Jack, her solitary, minimalistic lifestyle gave her a certain freedom.

In contrast, Jeanine, who was the same age as Cam and worked just as hard, lived in a beautifully furnished, red brick Colonial. As Cam sat cross-legged on the mattress, her head dropped into her hands.

I'm twenty-seven years old, and I live like a homeless person. How pathetic.

#

After her last phone conversation with Jack, Cam scheduled the installation of cable TV and internet services at The Harte Estate. Once she was connected, she emailed Jack that they could now Skype each other. Since there was a fourteen-hour time difference between Sydney and Akron, their online video chats took place in the evening for her and mid-morning for Jack.

The first time he appeared on the screen of her laptop and she heard his voice, her eyes filled with tears. "It's so good to see you again."

"You too, luv." He wore a broad smile which crinkled his eyes.

Without warning, another face with laughing blue eyes topped by curly gray-blonde hair slid in front of Jack's image and filled the picture. "So you're the girl my boy's been moonin' over the past weeks. I guess us Reynolds men still have a thing for Seppo women."

Sappho women? Lesbians?

The video picture bounced as Jack walked away with his laptop. A voice called out. "Nice seeing you, Cam-er-on." This was followed by smooching sounds.

A door slammed shut. Jack once again filled the Skype box. "That was my dad."

Cam laughed. "I guessed. What kind of women did he say Reynolds men like?"

"Seppo. It means American, like you and Mum. I offered to let him talk to you if he behaved himself." He shook his head. "I should have known better."

The rest of their first video chat consisted of updates on his father's progress and discussions about the work at The Harte Estate. A half hour passed.

Cam's recitation of the exterior drain replacement was interrupted by a wide-mouthed yawn. "Sorry." She clamped her teeth together to stifle the next one. Her eyes watered, and she used the back of her hands to wipe away the dampness.

"You're tired, luv. Get some sleep. Dad has physio tomorrow morning, so IM me first. I may not be available to chat."

"I will. Take care, Jack." She leaned forward and placed her lips on the screen.

When she sat back, he pursed his lips and pantomimed a return kiss. "G'night."

#

From that day on, the pattern of their Skype conversations was twice during the week and on the weekends. Cam was asleep by the time Jack brought his father home from therapy on Mondays, Wednesdays, and Fridays.

Several times, she and Mr. Reynolds, who insisted she call him Hank, talked for a few minutes. "So did my boy ever tell you about his childhood with me?"

Cam chose her words with care. "He said you taught him how to cook."

"Yeah, well, I was workin' long hours so I had to bring him to the restaurant. His mum wasn't too happy 'bout that. But I had to give him jobs to keep him busy. He couldn't run 'round while customers were eatin' and my staff was workin', now could he? You know, Cam-er-on, I bloody well hate when people say to let kids be kids. It's just an excuse to raise assholes. There's nothing wrong with teachin' 'em to fend for themselves and do honest labor, no matter their age."

"It's how I grew up." She told Hank about working with her grandfather and father doing restoration work from the time she was old enough to hold a hand tool.

"I knew I'd like you. Jack told me you're a conchy kind of girl."

Jack wrested the laptop away from Hank. "It's my turn to talk with my conchy girl." He went into another room. After he settled in a chair, he stared into the camera lens. "You know, Cam, hearing you talk with my dad reminds me how you're not like any other women I've ever known."

Is that good or bad?

"You're so grounded. What's important and matters to you isn't what other women care 'bout, like my cousin, Amelia. You intrigue me. I want to know what makes you laugh, makes you cry, makes you silly, makes you sad."

In a soft voice, she said, "You do."

"I make you sad?"

"Yeah, when you're almost ten thousand miles away from here."

"I feel the same way, luv. Being with you has been a revelation." His eyes scanned her features with intensity. It was as if he was burning them into his memory. "To me, the most beautiful woman in the world is wearing a tool belt, covered in plaster dust, and asking me what the hell is taking so long because time is money."

Each time they video chatted, it seemed Jack picked away at the tough scab she had formed over her emotions in response to Oliver's desertion and theft. Only Jeanine was privy to all the feelings of pain and humiliation which had turned Cam into a sobbing lump of jelly after the wedding debacle. Everyone else, including her parents and brother, praised her stoicism and bounced-back attitude.

During one conversation, Jack recounted the previous night's birthday party that Hank's employees threw for him after hours at the restaurant. "I could tell he was really touched. Everyone wanted to know how he was and told him they missed having him 'round to yell at them."

To her surprise, Cam burst into tears. She jumped to her feet and ran to the bathroom. She sat on the toilet seat and wept. Her chest constricted with a painful tightness. She rubbed her breastbone with soothing circles.

In the bedroom, Jack's voice rose in volume from her laptop. "Cam. What's wrong? Cam?"

She returned after blowing her nose and drying her eyes with toilet paper. "Sorry."

"What did I say?"

She shook her head, embarrassed by her unexpected outburst of emotion. "It was nothing you said. I'm just a little lonely tonight. I really miss you and wish you were here. Sometimes I need someone who'll tell me I'm doing the right thing and to not be afraid."

His voice softened. "I can still do that, luv."

She sighed. "But not while holding me."

"No. I can't hold you in my arms right now, only in my heart."

Chapter 14

AS SEPTEMBER CAME to a close, the weather turned cooler. The first real cold front in October started the Crayola coloring of the trees. The house was cool inside but comfortable enough without firing up the boiler. Cam switched her work attire to hoodies, flannel shirts, and jeans. She added a comforter to the bed at night.

Jeanine presented another, slightly higher, offer for the Underwood property. "It's above market value. You should consider it. They've given you two weeks to respond."

"I'll think about it."

Jack began their nightly chat with his usual question. "I have some news for you. But first, how was your day, luv?"

"The weather was nice, so Anthony and I worked outside. I also got another offer from a company called Castle Construction to buy the lot where my house burned down. That makes three so far."

Jack's gaze shifted to his left. "Were you and Anthony doing yardwork?"

"We replaced the old covers on the basement window wells. I wanted to get some custom polycarbonate ones made, but my budget can't afford them. I ended up buying some cheap-ass ones at Home Depot." She sighed. "I'm wondering if I *should* sell the Underwood property. I could use the money but hate to think Gus Varsamis will have gotten what he wants."

"Have you any word from the arson investigation?"

Cam crossed her arms and sat back in the chair. "No, and it pisses me off every time I think about it."

Jack said nothing for long seconds. He licked his lips and leaned in closer to the camera. "I feel like I'm letting you down." His eyes were downcast, his expression grave. "You're a battler, Cam. I don't want you to ever doubt I'll always have your best interests at heart, despite anything that may appear to the contrary. Oliver was a weak man who preyed on others. You're still healing from what he did to you. But soon you'll be able to love again. I'm doing my best to be there when that happens. Trust me."

A memory of Oliver's false smile and promises flashed in her memory like a silverfish darting in a pond. Cam reached out with her fingertips. She touched the screen where Jack's face was. It was as if she needed some sort of contact, even with an illusory video image.

"I do trust you, Jack. What's your news?"

"Eh?"

"You said you had some news."

Jack cleared his throat. "Dad's cast came off today. He's been cleared to go back to work for four hours a day."

"That is great news."

Jack launched into a story about Hank wanting to have his cast mounted on the wall because of all the humorous things written on it. He especially liked the one that said, *I do my own stunts.*

When the Skype call ended, Cam hadn't asked, and Jack hadn't shared any information about his return to the States, soon or ever.

#

A week before Halloween, Cam awoke on a beautiful autumn morning. The trees which lined the northern edge of the property glowed in splendid hues of gold and scarlet. She watched leaves drift to the ground one at a time or in groups of three or four. It had been over eight weeks since Jack returned to Australia. He hadn't confirmed when he would come back or for how long. They were both in limbo, dependent on his father's recovery and the rapidly closing window of his apprenticeship's conclusion.

At noon, Anthony left to check on his mother and eat lunch at home. Cam worked on cracks in the dining room plaster prior to painting the walls and ceiling. Soft music played from an old radio plugged into an outlet. She hummed to herself as she worked.

"Where's that sonofabitch?"

Cam spun around. A man stood just inside the wide doorway from the front hall. He had a stocky build and swarthy skin.

"How did you get in here?" Cam put the mud pan on the floor and slipped the four-inch taping blade into her back pocket.

"The front door was open."

The heavy oak door may not have been latched tight, but the storm door was closed. "You can't just walk into someone's house without knocking or ringing the bell."

"Well, I did." The man advanced to the middle of the room. "Now tell me where Coleman is."

"Which one?"

"Fuck. There's more than one?"

"There are four of them."

The man shook a finger at her. "I want that bastard and pain in my ass, Cameron Coleman."

"Who are you?"

"You don't need to know, Blondie. Just tell me where Coleman is."

She fumbled for the phone in her side pocket to speed dial her dad. "He was around here a minute ago. Let me call him."

The intruder rushed toward her faster than she anticipated. He slammed her hard against the wall. The back of her head bashed the plaster. Black dots and bright flashes danced before her eyes. The phone dropped from her hand. Instinctively, Cam jerked her knee up, aiming for the man's crotch.

As if he sensed her intent, he turned and most of the impact landed on his thigh. "Nice try, bitch."

He raised his open palm. The blow landed on the side of her mouth and cheek. She blinked to clear her head. The attacker twisted Cam to the side and pushed her left shoulder and arm against the wall.

His voice was low and menacing. "You give him a message. I've had it with him and the old lady. Tell him—"

While he spoke, Cam hunched her shoulders and reached into her back pocket. She grabbed the taping blade. Her assailant, who she guessed was Gus Varsamis, continued his rant. His breath was hot on her face. Spittle hit her cheek like acid. Her body shifted from cowed to coiled. She bunched the muscles in her wiry bicep. With a tight grip on the handle, she thrust the sharp knife upward.

The taping blade jammed deep into the sagging skin under his chin. Gus howled. He tugged it out, a mad glaze in his eyes. Before Cam could move, a hand latched onto Gus's shoulder and spun him around. The sound of a bone-crunching punch echoed in the empty room. Gus's heavy body thudded onto the hardwood floor where he curled in a fetal position. His hands covered his face. Booted feet stood next to him. Cam raised her eyes from the writhing man and gaped.

Jack rushed to her side and stared at her mouth. "He hit you?"

"Oh, my God. You're here."

He pulled her to his chest and held her tight. Gus groaned.

Jack scowled and dropped his arms. "Do you not have duct tape handy?"

She nodded. "There's a roll in the kitchen drawer."

"Watch him and call the coppers."

They bound Gus's wrists and ankles together. He spewed invectives at Jack whom he still called by Cam's name. They had not corrected him.

Because of his swollen, bloody nose, Gus's voice had a bad-cold quality to it. "I'm going to sue you, Coleman, until everything you own is mine."

Cam checked her face in the half bath mirror. Her lip was swollen and her cheek was darkening with a bruise. While Jack stayed with Gus, she waited at the front door for the police. Two cruisers arrived, lights flashing. Three officers exited the vehicles. One remained next to his patrol car.

She held open the glass storm door. "I'm Cam Coleman. I live here. The guy who attacked me is in the dining room. My boyfriend is watching him."

"Wait here, miss." The older patrolman indicated the front hall. He nodded to his partner who looked like he was just out of high school. "You stay with her."

No lunch and the adrenaline drain made Cam a little dizzy and nauseous. "Can I sit down on the step?" She pointed to the main staircase. "I don't feel good."

The officer escorted her over. She sat and put her head between her knees. From this vantage point, she could hear, if not see, what was happening in the dining room.

Jack's voice was angry. "Where's my girlfriend? She was alone when this bounce came in and attacked her."

"She's fine, sir. My partner is with her. I need you to wait in the kitchen. We'll get your statement in a few minutes."

"Arrest the cunt. She stabbed me," Gus shouted. "And cut this fucking tape off."

"I need *you* to settle down. Paramedics are on the way."

"The asshole broke my nose. I'm pressing charges. Arrest him too."

The officer with Cam left her side to open the door for the EMT's. While one examined Gus, another checked out Cam.

"I'm okay except my head hurts. It hit the wall when he pushed me." She felt the hair behind her head and froze, open-mouthed.

The EMT studied her. "What's wrong?"

"I don't know."

Her fingers were wet and sticky. She moved them in front of her face. Instead of being red with blood, gray matter coated her fingers. She laughed.

The EMT frowned. "What is it?"

"Joint compound. I was repairing cracks in the plaster."

The technician cleaned the small cut on her lip and pronounced her cheekbone bruised, not fractured. He inspected her scalp with gentle fingers. She had a bump but no broken skin. Using alcohol pads, he cleaned the worst of the goop out of her hair. From the conversation in the dining room, she surmised Gus was going to be taken to the emergency room for stitches and a tetanus shot due to the damage inflicted by her taping blade.

He was loaded onto a gurney. His tirade against Cam and Jack continued until the ambulance doors closed.

A detective arrived to take her statement. She reported the verbal threats Gus made and provided Jeanine's contact information. She retrieved a copy of the arson investigation report from the upstairs bedroom. He wrote down the file number and the investigator's name. Her face and the cracked indentation in the plaster were photographed.

The young patrolman, who had waited with Cam, walked up to where she and the detective sat on the staircase. "There's some guy outside claiming he works here."

Cam followed him to the front door. Anthony was beside his truck. She gestured with a thumbs-up sign then signaled for him to wait. Her father's panel van skidded on the gravel driveway and came to a halt behind one of the cruisers. An unknown silver Cadillac was also parked out front.

She returned to the detective who was on his feet. "What's going to happen now?"

"Based on your and Mr. Reynolds' statements, Varsamis will be arrested and charged with trespassing and assault. By the time he's done at the hospital, bond court will be closed. He'll likely spend the night in lockup."

"Jack and I aren't going to be charged with anything, are we?"

"No."

"How can I be sure Gus won't try this again?"

The detective's lips curled with a wry smile. "There's no guarantee, Ms. Coleman. You could file a restraining order against Mr. Varsamis. If he comes near you, call us."

I will, right after I shoot the bastard.

Jack entered the foyer with the officer who had taken his statement. He rushed to Cam and enfolded her in a tight hug. The police called for Gus's car to be towed off the property. They left fifteen minutes later and allowed her father and Anthony into the house. Cam sat on a kitchen chair with an icy gel pack against her face. Jack sat next to her.

Zane stormed into the room. "What did that sack of monkey shit do to you, Cameron?"

"I'm okay, Dad."

He squatted in front of her and lifted the ice pack as he turned her face to the light.

"Don't worry, Mr. Coleman." Jack gave her father an uncertain smile. "The mongrel is in much worse shape."

"He better be fucking dead." Zane rose to his feet and stared at Jack. "You're back?"

"I was on a redeye flight that landed this morning. I wanted to surprise Cam. Then I walked in and found some guy bailing her."

Zane looked even fiercer. "Was he trying to tie her up?"

"No, he had her pushed against the wall."

"Cameron, did you kick the waste of sperm in the nuts like I taught you?"

"No, I stabbed him with a taping blade, then Jack punched him. It was a team effort."

Zane's jaw muscles clenched. "That shitbag may have no problem burning down a house with someone in it after today. You better come home with me. I don't want you alone here."

Cam shook her head. "I'm not going to let Gus run me out of my own house. He wouldn't dare try something now. Anyway, the police said he would probably spend the night in jail. I'm pressing charges."

Jack stood and faced her father. "I'll take care of her, Mr. Coleman. She can move in with me, or I'll stay here."

Zane drew a deep breath. "Neither of you can be on guard all day and night. Cameron, you better get Adam to hook up a good security system as soon as possible."

She sighed when she calculated the additional cost of exterior security lights, cameras, and an alarm system for a place the size of the main house. "Okay, I'll call him."

"Never mind. I'm headed back to the warehouse. I'll tell him."

While Cam and her father discussed what kind of equipment Adam should buy and install, Jack checked her refrigerator and cupboards for food.

He kissed the top of her head. "I'll be back with my clothes and groceries."

Anthony followed her father and Jack outside. By the time her assistant returned, Cam had scraped the loose plaster from where her head cracked it. She picked up a fresh taping knife and mud pan.

Anthony lifted both from her hands. "Let me finish and clean up. You need to take it easy."

Since her head still throbbed, Cam acquiesced. She put on a jacket and headed outside to the patio.

Thirty minutes later, Anthony joined her. "I'm all done, Boss. What else should I do?" The unspoken *until Jack gets back* hung in the air.

"Tomorrow I'm going to show you how to use the electric drywall sander. Bring it in from the carriage house along with the shop light stand. You and I, and now, Jack will take turns with it. We'll do the corners and edges with sanding blocks." She rose from the plastic chair. "I'll bring up more drop cloths and the roll of plastic sheeting from the basement."

Anthony put out a hand. "I'll get everything. You rest until Jack gets here."

"I guess you figured out he and I are involved in more than just his apprenticeship."

"I already suspected it." Anthony smiled at her. "I know when two people are hot for each other. It was kinda cute. Are you glad he's back?"

"I am. Of course." Her words sounded so lame and unconvincing she winced. "But he'll be returning to Australia at the end of the year."

"Maybe he'll stay. He told your dad he came back because he loves you."

Chapter 15

JACK ARRIVED NINETY minutes later with his suitcase, laptop, and groceries.

Cam took the plastic food bags out of his hand and began to empty them. "I have a surprise for you. Anthony clued me into buying used furniture from Craig's List. I fixed up a room upstairs. I'm no longer a squatter."

After they put the food away, Jack pulled her against him. "I was gobsmacked when I saw Gus with you. I thought he was more of a standover man."

She leaned back. "What's that?"

"He has other blokes threaten or hurt people who get in his way." Jack placed his hands on her cheeks and tilted her head up. "If I kiss you, will it hurt your lip?"

"I don't know. Let's find out."

Jack gave her a gentle kiss.

Cam touched her fingers to her swollen mouth. "It's a little sore but not too bad." She wrapped her arms around his back and squeezed. "Hugging won't hurt at all." *But how painful will it be when you return to Australia for good?*

Cam helped Jack carry his personal items upstairs. She sat on a futon as he hung his clothes in the closet. "Jack, did you tell my father you love me?"

He turned around with an unreadable expression. "Yes. I'm in love with you."

She grimaced and rubbed her forehead.

"I don't expect you to say it in return."

She glared at him. "Of course, you do. No one says *I'm in love with you* without wanting to hear it back. This wasn't supposed to happen. You were my six-month fling."

He laughed. "I've been called worse things."

Cam leaned forward, elbows on knees, and put her head in her hands.

Jack sat next to her, thigh to thigh, shoulder to shoulder. "When I became your apprentice, I wasn't looking for a serious relationship either. In no time, I found you're a woman worth loving. I know you're not ready yet to love me back."

She turned her head to look at him. "That's the problem."

"Eh?"

Her words tumbled out in a rush. "Dammit, I love you too."

Jack put his arm around her. "You're supposed to look happy when you say it, luv."

"Just so you know, I'm *never* moving to Australia."

He shook his head. "Whatcha mean?"

"If we love each other, you must think or hope I'll go back with you."

Jack slid a lock of hair behind her ear. "Things have changed."

He kissed her forehead, temple, the tip of her nose, avoiding her sore lip and cheek. She waited for him to enlighten her with this new development. Instead Jack's lips slid along her jawline. He nibbled on her earlobe. His warm breath streamed a path along her neck. He nuzzled her hair aside.

Her shoulders hunched with a delicious shiver when his tongue flicked against a sensitive spot. His fingers danced on the back of her neck. Her heartbeat throbbed under her ear. His lips zeroed in on that pulse point. Cam turned, breathing hard. Unable to stop herself, she pulled Jack's face to hers and covered his lips with her tender mouth.

He nipped at the uninjured corner. "Say the words again."

She closed her eyes and wrapped her hand around the back of his neck. "I love you, Jack Reynolds. God help me, I do."

#

After he was settled in, she took him on a tour of the projects which were completed in his absence, from a clean, well-lit laundry room in the basement to remodeled bathrooms on the second floor.

When Jack saw the new four by six, white tiled, and glass-walled shower built to replace the cheap acrylic one, he gave her a broad smile. "Let's practice conservation and shower together."

"You're concerned about my water bill?"

"We must all do our part to protect the planet."

Sometime later, Cam wrapped a towel around her wet hair. "We aren't saving anything if you keep me in there for an extra fifteen minutes."

"You shouldn't have bent over to wash your feet, luv."

She rolled her eyes and giggled. "Yeah, it was all my fault."

He flashed a grin which dimpled his cheeks and creased his eyes. Jack used the second bath towel to dry her off. She flushed with a warm sensation when he paid more attention to her bottom and the backs of her thighs than was necessary.

He stood and hung up the towel. "I need to get cooking. You look like you haven't had a good meal since I left."

Her stomach growled. "I'm starving. With all the excitement around here, I didn't have lunch."

Jack frowned. "Why did you not say something before this?"

She grabbed him around the waist and rubbed against him. "I had other appetites I wanted you to take care of first."

In the kitchen, Jack insisted Cam eat cheese, crackers, and grapes while he prepared their supper. They sipped glasses of white wine he bought.

Cam picked up the bottle. There was no yellow kangaroo on the label. "Tell me why you've decided not to go back to Australia at the end of the year."

"I'm taking a position with my family's business." Jack poured rice into a pot of boiling water. "My grandad and Mum hoped I'd help run the company someday. But I wanted to work as an architect, not a manager or CEO. Anyone with good business sense can do that."

"So, what's different now?"

"I've negotiated with the board of directors 'bout creating two new departments. One will provide designs, so we won't just be building others' plans. The other department will focus on preservation or restoration of existing structures." He plucked a grape from the cluster and held it to her lips. "I was determined to find a way to stay here, not only to work, but to be with you too."

Her heart expanded in her chest until her ribs hurt. It was as if a pneumatic blast broke apart the shell she built around it four years ago.

#

Jack and Cam were together all day, every day. She was thrilled to wake up with him in the morning and go to bed with him at night. He cooked and cleaned the kitchen. She did laundry and kept their living quarters tidy.

By the end of the third week, she was taking long walks in the neighborhood or around The Harte Estate while Jack prepared supper. During this needed alone time, her thoughts zeroed in on her parents. They worked at the warehouse during the day and went home together for more than thirty years.

How do they do it?

One day on her way to pick up tile mortar, she stopped at A to Z. In the office, her mother sat on a stool at the counter. "Hi, honey."

"Is Dad around?"

"No. He went to the bank."

"Good. I want to talk to you."

Abigail stood, on alert. "What's wrong?"

"Everything's fine." Cam laid her forearms on the wood counter. "How are you able to work and live with Dad every day? Do you ever get tired of him?"

Abigail eyed her as if this was a trick question.

Cam sighed. "I love Jack and I'm so happy he's back. It's just—"

"You're not used to that much togetherness."

"What's wrong with me? Jack is so easygoing and pleasant to be around. I should be thanking my lucky stars. Instead I'm walking the streets or running unnecessary errands for time alone. I keep telling myself it's only until the end of the year. Then he'll be working at his new job."

Abigail patted her daughter's hand with a motherly benediction. "Honey, you need to tell him you're not used to both living and working with someone. Who knows? He might be feeling a bit closet-phobic too."

Cam smiled. "I hadn't thought of that."

Abigail pointed to the closed door marked *Private*. "Why do you think your father's office has a lock that I don't have the key for? When two people love each other, they find a way to make it work."

#

The next day Jack and Cam had lunch in the little town of Peninsula and drove home through the Cuyahoga Valley National Park. The fall foliage was nearing its conclusion. Piles of dried brown leaves littered the ground. Many trees were almost bare.

Jack said, "Well, looks like the beautiful part of autumn is 'bout over. Still, I'm a lucky bloke. I saw the changing of leaves twice this year. The fall season in Sydney was March, April, and May."

"It's not the same as here?"

"The seasons are reversed in the northern and southern hemispheres."

Cam turned to look out the passenger side window. A rush of self-consciousness made her squirm. Her life experiences weren't in the same league as Jack's. He lived in two different countries, on two continents. He travelled the world with his professional soccer team. He told her he had been to almost every country in Europe and south America, although most involved only hotels and arenas.

She didn't even have a passport. *Hell, the farthest I've gone from home is a sixth-grade field trip to Washington D.C.*

When they arrived at The Harte Estate, Jack parked the truck but didn't turn off the engine. "Cam, I need to tell you something."

He's feeling closet-phobic just like Mom said. "I know what you're going to say."

He blinked. "You do?"

"I understand it's going to take some time, but we'll work it out. I'm just happy you're staying in Akron."

Jack leaned back in his seat and laughed. "You always surprise me. I've wanted to tell you for quite a while. I thought you'd be upset."

She reached across the center console and laid her hand on his thigh. "I didn't say anything because I didn't want to hurt your feelings."

Jack squished his eyebrows together. "Why would it hurt my feelings?"

"Because you left your dad and Australia to come back to me."

"Cam, what are you talking 'bout?"

She sighed. "I know we're both a little overwhelmed by having to spend all day, every day with each other. I'm sorry, but I've never lived *and worked* with someone before. I know it'll be better with time, especially after you start your new job in January."

Jack ran his hands through his hair with a pained expression. "My new job is with Castle Construction."

It took several seconds for his revelation to sink into her brain. When it did, Cam shot him a look of fury. "Why did you *really* become my apprentice? Was it to get me to sell the Underwood house?"

His nostrils flared. "I did no such bloody thing. When I became your apprentice, you didn't even own the house."

Oh, yeah. "Did you tell them you were sleeping with the new owner and could get me to sell?"

Jack's voice verged on anger. "Is that what you think I'd do?"

Cam covered her mouth with her hand as if to prevent any more impulsive and regretted words from escaping. "I'm sorry I said that. It's just—"

"You still expect me to screw you like Oliver did."

She stared at her feet. "I-I'm sorry—"

Jack's voice softened. "I didn't know Castle had made offers on your property until you told me during one of our Skype talks. I was afraid if I told you then—"

"I would shut down and not talk to you."

"I wanted to wait until we were together."

She sniffed. "Obviously you had good reasons to be worried about my reaction. Look at what I just did."

"As far as us living together, I think you're right. We need a little space. It's hard to go from being apart to twenty-four-seven." Jack reached across the center console and laid his hand on her leg. "Can we talk about

Castle another time?" When her head bobbed in silent agreement, he opened his door. "Let's give each other a little space for now. I'll get my things and leave the key."

Cam sat in the truck and mulled over the implication that Jack's family business wanted to buy her fire-bombed property. When she entered the kitchen, his house key lay next to the stove. Footsteps sounded on the floor above and filtered down the back stairs. Cam sat at the kitchen table and waited.

When Jack came down with his arms laden, she stood. "Do you want some help?"

"I left my laptop case at the top of the stairs."

"I'll get it."

She retrieved the last item and went outside where Jack waited by his truck. He placed the bag on the bench seat. When he turned around, she held the house key in front of her face. He raised his eyebrows.

She lifted his hand. "You're right. I just need a little time and space."

The corners of Jack's mouth turned up. She laid the key in his palm. He kissed her forehead and climbed into the truck. Cam stepped back when the engine roared to life.

The driver's window lowered. "I love you, Cam."

"I love you too."

She waited until his red taillights disappeared before she entered the house, armed the security system, and went to bed alone.

Chapter 16

WITH SHORTER DAYLIGHT hours, the crew of C.C. Restorations began work at seven in the morning and ended at four p.m. When Jack packed up and left after the workday, Anthony looked surprised but said nothing. Despite the estrangement in their personal relationship, they worked together without a problem. Meanwhile, Cam had several long, lonely evenings to reflect about Jack and Castle Construction.

At quitting time on Friday, six days after moving out, Jack walked over to her, his hands in his pockets. "Want comp'ny this weekend?"

"Well, I am getting low on groceries."

Jack waited.

Cam licked her lips. "So, maybe you can come over tomorrow, and we can go shopping."

He stepped closer until he stood within arm's reach.

She gave him a tentative smile. "Then you can cook."

He removed his hands from his pockets and wrapped them around her upper arms like velvet bands.

She cocked her head at a jaunty angle. "And we can eat what you cook."

Jack smiled back but kept quiet.

"Then we can talk."

"Those are all good ideers." His mouth lowered and teased hers with feather-light kisses.

She waited for his lips and tongue to become demanding, to delve inside.

Instead, he raised his head and took a step back. "I'll pick you up at noon." He headed to his truck.

"Damn you, Jack Reynolds," she whispered to herself.

#

On Saturday after their return from grocery shopping, Jack assembled ingredients while Cam put laundry in the washer. When she emerged from the basement, a large pot simmered on the stovetop.

Cam lifted the lid and wrinkled her nose at the contents. "What's this green stuff?"

"You Yanks call it split pea and ham soup, but in Oztralia its pea ham."

Cam's phone rang with her mother's cell number. "Hi, Mom."

"Hi, honey. Is it okay if your father and I stop by? We're coming back from a job estimate in Stow."

"Hang on." Cam covered the speaker and turned to Jack. "It's my parents. They want to visit."

He shrugged. "It's fine with me. Do you want them to eat with us? We have plenty."

Cam eyed the bubbling swamp again. "Mom, Jack made soup. Are you guys hungry?"

Fifteen minutes later, a knock sounded at the same time a key unlocked the kitchen door. Cam's father entered.

Her mother squeezed past him and sniffed the air. "What do I smell?"

Jack straightened from where he had been bent over the hot oven. He held a cookie sheet with a mound of baked dough on it.

Abigail stared. "What's that?"

He placed the sheet pan on the stainless-steel counter. "Damper bread. It's like Irish soda bread because it has no yeast. You eat it with lots of butter or sop up gravy with it."

Cam's parents looked like children with their noses pressed to the window of a candy store.

She kissed their chilled cheeks. "Before you take off your coats, let me show you the new storm windows we built out of low-E glass."

Abigail shrugged off her jacket anyway. "Show your father. I'll stay inside where it's warm."

Cam smiled at her mother's outfit. She wore a white turtleneck sweater, covered by a bright yellow cardigan, and pumpkin-orange corduroy jeans. "Are those pants new, Mom?"

"I got them on sale at TJ Maxx."

I can see why.

Jack took her mother's coat and hung it on a hook by the back door. "You look very autumnal, Mrs. Coleman."

Abigail's green eyes went wide. "Abdom-nal?"

"Autumnal. It means fall-like."

"Au-tum-nal." She rolled the word around her mouth like a wine connoisseur tasting a new vintage Chardonnay.

Zane growled. "She looks like a damned piece of candy corn."

Abigail gave her husband a sweet smile. "You know it's your favorite." She turned to Jack. "I have to buy him a bag every year."

Cam grabbed her jacket and pulled gloves from the pocket. After she and Zane walked the perimeter of the house and viewed the completed projects, they headed toward the kitchen porch.

Zane stopped with one foot on the bottom step. "Have you heard anything about the dirtbag who attacked you?"

"Gus was released without bail the day after he was arrested. The prosecutor won't make a final decision on charges until after the preliminary hearing."

"What the hell is taking so long?"

Cam shrugged. "I don't know. Jack and I filed restraining orders, but I'd be surprised if Gus gets more than probation. I wish there was some way to find the arsonist, so he could tell the police who hired him."

"The fucking criminals have more rights than law-abiding citizens. At least, I sleep better at night knowing Jack's here with you."

"You don't have to worry, Dad. I can take care of myself, and the new alarm system works fine." She sidestepped her father to climb the stairs.

"Cameron, stop." Zane's hand snagged her elbow. "Jack is still staying with you, isn't he?"

She licked her lips. "He moved out last weekend. We needed a little time away from each other."

"What happened?"

She took a deep breath then blew out into the cold air. "Remember me telling you about the offers from Castle Construction to buy the house before and after the fire."

Zane gave a curt nod.

"Well, Castle Construction is the company Jack's family owns."

"Yeah, so what?"

Cam voice rose. "Well, why didn't he tell me?"

"Did you ask him?"

"No. But he didn't say anything when we were skyping, and I let him know an offer came from Castle Construction after the fire."

"Was that when he was still in Australia?"

Cam emitted a squeal of female exasperation. "What does it matter where he was?"

"He probably wanted to wait and tell you eye-to-eye." Zane gestured with forked fingers from his face to hers.

"We were on Skype. I was looking right at him."

Her father shook his head. "Not the same thing. Something important you want to say it in person, not over the damned internet. Jack is still working with you and cooking for you, among other things, right?" Her father shifted his gaze when he alluded to her sexual relationship.

She smiled at his discomfort. "We planned to talk about our relationship when we had dinner tonight, but now you and Mom are here."

Zane gave her a flinty look, stomped up the steps, and opened the kitchen door. "Abigail, get your jacket. We're leaving."

Cam hustled after him. "Dad, wait."

Her mother sat at the kitchen table with a soup spoon halfway to her mouth.

Cam tugged on her father's coat sleeve. "Let Mom finish eating."

Jack nodded towards a steamy bowl with crisp diced ham floating on top. "I've got soup ready for you, Mr. Coleman."

Zane's shoulders relaxed. "Okay. We'll eat then go." He handed his coat to Cam, picked up the bowl, and joined his wife at the table.

Tentative at first, Cam ate her pea ham soup with soaked chunks of the damper bread. Although, she found the color off-putting, it tasted delicious.

After her first spoonful, Jack smiled at her, his eyebrows raised. "Whatcha think? It's chunkier than my dad's. You don't have an immersion blender, so I couldn't puree it."

Puree? "It's good. I like it."

Her father finished his serving and plopped the spoon into the ceramic bowl. "Is there enough for seconds?"

Abigail frowned. "I thought you wanted to leave."

Jack grabbed the empty bowl and scooted his chair back. "There's plenty, Mr. Coleman."

Abigail lifted her empty bowl. "I'll take a little more too."

After her parents finished their second helpings, Zane went to the coat rack. "C'mon, Abigail, time to go. Thanks for the great soup, Jack."

Her mother placed their bowls in the sink. "What's your hurry? We should help clean up."

Zane put on his coat, walked to Abigail, then steered her toward the door. He tossed her coat around her shoulders. The fur-lined hood flopped onto her head and partially obscured her face. He opened the door and ushered his half-blinded wife through it. The hollow echo of their footsteps sounded across the wooden porch.

Jack shook his head. "What was that 'bout?"

"It's Dad's subtle way of giving us time to talk."

"Your dad is 'bout as subtle as a bloody bomb in a barrel of oatmeal."

They put away the food and washed the dishes. Cam made hot tea for them to take upstairs. She carried the mugs while Jack opened the hallway door to the back staircase. There was a noticeable drop in temperature. The heat from the Aga stove kept the kitchen warmer than the other rooms on the first floor.

As she climbed the steps, Cam shivered. "I can't wait until I get the new HVAC systems installed."

Jack opened the door into the room with the TV and futon. A space heater pumped out warm air. "How many units are you installing?"

"One on the third floor, two on the second, and two on the first." When he sat down next to her, she handed him a mug of tea. "Now tell me about your family's business."

Jack took a deep breath. "Castle Construction was started by my grandfather after World War Two. He decided to cash in on the housing boom in the fifties. From early on, my Uncle Carl was expected to take over when Grandad retired."

Cam turned to face him with one leg bent on the seat cushion. "Then why does your mother fly to Akron once a month for board meetings?"

Jack's voice was like a whip. "'Cause my uncle is a lying, cheating bludger, both in business and his personal life. Carl is only happy when he's doing something shonky or illegal. It's the reason Granddad worked up until the day he died. He couldn't trust his only son to not destroy the company he built. His will stated Carl would have a job at Castle until the age of fifty-five, but his duties and decisions were at the discretion of the board and the majority stockholder, my mother."

Wow, he really hates his uncle. "What kind of *shonky* things has he done?"

"He was a serial philanderer while he was married. He bragged 'bout faking an injury on a cruise ship with his wife to get a second free trip with his mistress."

"You're kidding."

"Most of his underhanded schemes affected the company. My mother was put in control when an independent auditor caught him funneling money from Castle's accounts to a phantom company to pay his gambling debts. Remember when I showed up here on July Fourth?"

A wistful smile touched her lips. It was the first time she had ever had *al fresco* sex. "I do."

"'Cause of Carl, I left the club."

"And yet, you've agreed to work with him now."

"No." Jack's hand sliced the air. "A condition of my employment is that we have little or no contact with each other. He turns fifty-five in the spring and the board is planning to force mandatory retirement on him.

Carl's not much more than a figurehead who collects a generous salary and benefits."

Both of them sat without speaking and sipped their tea. Jack set his mug on the scarred coffee table and studied her under his lowered brow. "Are we done talking 'bout Castle?"

"For now."

Jack leaned sideways on the futon. He turned his azure gaze up to her as a smile dimpled his cheeks. "So, do we stay together on weekends like before I went to Oztralia? Or do I move back in here with you?"

Cam opened her eyes wide with false sincerity. "*Or* you can just be my apprentice?"

He smiled like a game show contestant on a winning streak. "Want to wager how long before you have a naughty with me?"

Cam's heart thudded behind her breast bone. She put her empty mug on the table then pushed him back against the side pillow. "That would be a sucker bet." She straddled his body. "I plan to be naughty with you all weekend."

Chapter 17

JACK'S MOTHER AND stepfather issued an invitation to spend Thanksgiving with them at their condo in Breckenridge, Colorado.

He turned to Cam after ending the phone call. "Would you be able to get away, luv? It'd be a grand vaca for you."

She shook her head. "I can't go. I promised Jeanine I would be at her party."

For the last five years on the Saturday following Thanksgiving, Jeanine threw the first Christmas party of the season. She invited co-workers and anyone who had bought or sold a property with her in the past year.

"Then I'll get us a flight back on Friday or Saturday."

Cam bit her lip as he booted up his computer. It wasn't only her tight schedule and Jeanine's party that concerned her. She would be forced to stay in the same house with his mother whom she had not yet met. She had never skied, snowboarded, or done any winter sport in which Jack's family were probably proficient athletes. The airfare was bound to be expensive, and her budget didn't need the unnecessary expenditure.

Besides, I've never flown on a plane before.

After searching various websites, Jack slumped toward the keyboard. "There's bloody nothing available to get us back in time for Jeanine's party."

Cam was propped against pillows in his bed. "That's too bad, but you can still go."

Jack swiveled his desk chair around. "What 'bout the party?"

"I've gone alone the past four years. I can go stag again."

He walked over to the bed, put one knee on the mattress, and kissed her. "But I want to be your date *this* year." He sat down and put his arm around her shoulders. "And next year." He lifted her hand and put it against his lips. "And the year after that." He rose and straddled her. "And the one after that." He pulled her sweater over her head.

She smiled at the look of intent on his face. *I want that too.*

#

Jack parked at the curb in front of the Coleman house on Thanksgiving Day. "It looks like we're the first ones. What other rellies of yours are coming?"

Cam ticked the names off on her fingers. "My brother, Adam, and his wife, Sasha. My nephew, AJ. My mom's sister, Marjorie, and her husband, Ed."

"They're the zucchini growers, right?"

"Uncle Ed loves to garden. Don't be surprised if we go home with jars of canned food. The last three are my dad's brother, Zach, his partner, Peter, and their thirteen-year-old daughter, Hayley. They live near Cleveland."

Jack's eyebrows arched. She waited for him to comment on her rough-edged father having a gay brother, but he didn't. She loved her family with all her heart. They were like a plain, gray overcoat from JC Penney on a hot male supermodel, dependable but quirky, sensible but unexpected.

"What time is the meal?"

"One."

Jack checked his watch. "It's eleven now. Why did we come so early?"

"So you can help my mom if she needs it."

Every time her mother hosted Thanksgiving dinner, there was some kind of kitchen catastrophe. Once it was a grilled turkey burnt to a crisp. Another time, the overfilled pumpkin pies spilled out into the hot oven. The dessert had a distinctly smoky flavor that year.

For this holiday dinner, Abigail told Cam, "I decided to order a pre-cooked bird and stuffing from the grocery store. It'll make things a lot easier for everyone."

Probably a lot tastier too.

Cam opened the car door.

Jack hit the switch to raise the trunk lid. "Let me get my dish from the boot."

He lifted an aluminum pan of roasted root vegetables and joined Cam on the sidewalk. The front door was unlocked. No one was in the rarely used formal living room. Cam led the way through the dining room where the table was set with her great-grandmother's English bone china.

In the kitchen, Abigail stared into the built-in oven's window. "Oh good, you're here, Jack. Would you take a look at the turkey I'm warming up?"

He shot a worried look at Cam. "You're not cooking it, Mrs. Coleman?"

Abigail tittered. "It's pre-cooked, but it seems awfully cold."

Jack put his pan of vegetables on the counter. He hung his jacket on the back of a wooden barstool. Abigail handed him oven mitts.

He pulled out the roaster pan. "How long has it been in the oven?"

"Over an hour."

Jack removed a glove and poked at the bird with a fingertip then laid his bare palm against the lightly browned skin. "It's still frozen. Were there directions with it?"

Her mother spun in a circle and headed to the trash container. She fished out a printed wrap.

Jack pieced the cut edges together and bent over the counter to read. "Well, it needed to be thawed for a couple days first, but we can fix this. We'll cut the bird then cook it. It'll have to be dismantled to serve anyway."

Abigail hugged Jack's arm and rushed to the dining room. "I'll get you the electric knife."

Under his breath, he muttered, "I may need a chain saw too."

Abigail bustled into the kitchen and waved the corded knife above her head like a sword. "Jack, you're my unstung hero."

"It's unsung, Mom."

Abigail ignored her. "Where do you want me to plug this in?"

Cam hung their coats in the front hall closet and went into the enclosed back porch which doubled as her dad's office. Zane was seated at his desk in the knotty pine-paneled room and studied an open checkbook register. Cam leaned down and kissed his cheek.

Her father removed his reading glasses and leaned back in the antique wooden chair. "You're here early."

"I brought Jack in case Mom needed help."

"Does she?"

"She and Jack have it under control."

"You know, Cameron, when I married your mother I knew she couldn't cook worth a damn. But I decided I'd rather spend my life with someone whose company I enjoyed more than eating good home-cooked meals with someone I couldn't stand to face across a table." He slid his glasses back onto his nose and picked up his pen. "Keep that in mind."

#

An hour later Aunt Marjorie and Uncle Ed arrived from Columbus. They came in with a gust of chilly air. Cam took a box filled with clinking Mason jars out of her aunt's hands. She kissed Marjorie's soft cheek which smelled like creamy vanilla candy. Her relative was as different from her small, pleasingly rounded, blonde mother as possible. Marjorie was a lean woman with narrow shoulders and wide hips. From the rear, she resembled a cello. She was a brunette when she was younger but had gone auburn with age and Clairol.

Her uncle came inside with another cardboard box. The spring-loaded storm door closed behind him. Ed had frizzy gray hair which circled his head in a corona. He was slightly taller than his wife, had watery blue eyes and a paunch.

"It's colder than a witch's tit out there." Ed's breath huffed from his lips. "It was fifty-five degrees when we left Columbus."

Marjorie stripped off her gloves. "I told you it was going to be that way. He never listens to me. Look at him. He's got on his golf jacket, for goodness sake. Maybe Zane can lend you a heavy coat to wear home."

"I'll be fine. We have a heater in the car."

Marjorie shook her head in obvious disgust. "If we get a flat or break down, I'll be the one outside with the tow truck driver."

In the kitchen, Jack washed dishes while her mother dried them. Cam laid the box she carried on the counter and relieved Ed of his carton as well.

Abigail came over and hugged her sister. "Let me introduce you to Jack. He and Cameron, well, he's—"

Jack came forward as he dried his hands on a dishtowel. "'Allo. Nice to meet you. I'm Jack Reynolds, a friend of Cam's." He shook their hands.

Marjorie cocked her head at him. "Are you English?"

"'Strayan."

"I should have known. You have blonde hair."

Ed scowled. "What the hell are you talking about? Just because he's blonde doesn't mean he's from Australia."

"Well, Crocodile Dundee is blonde. Olivia Newton-John is blonde. Wasn't the other crocodile guy—"

"So, you're the gardeners," Jack interrupted. "I had some of your zucchini this summer. It was bloody amazing."

Her father walked in and welcomed his in-laws with a handshake and a hug.

Marjorie lifted various Mason jars of pickles, banana peppers, beets, and green beans from the box to show Jack. "We brought some for everybody."

Cam's mother unfolded the flaps of the other box and lifted out two foil-covered ovenproof dishes. "We don't need two green bean casseroles, Margie."

"One is corn. I used the last of what we canned a year ago."

When Cam returned to the kitchen after hanging up coats, Zane and Ed were gone. Her mother and aunt sat at the table in the breakfast nook with cups of coffee.

Jack pulled her into the living room. He eyed her long cream sweater, the wide leather belt cinching her waist, the calf-length, coffee-colored skirt, and her leather boots. "Luv, you look tastier than anything in your mother's kitchen."

He drew her against the steely length of his body, his lips smothering hers. His tongue tantalized her mouth with capricious flicks. Cam's arms locked around his waist as he pressed his growing rigidity against her.

"Anybody home?"

Cam and Jack sprang apart. Her brother, Adam, stopped just inside the front door. In his hand, he held a car seat carrier covered with a baby blanket. He frowned at Jack. His expression darkened more when he looked down at the bulge behind Jack's zipper.

"Adam? Vhy you stop?" A muffled voice spoke from behind him. Cam's brother moved aside, and his tall wife stepped past him with a diaper bag and a foil-covered pie plate.

Cam's mother and Marjorie hustled from the kitchen. Her aunt grabbed the carrier from Adam and cooed to the unseen baby under the blanket.

Abigail relieved Sasha of the plate and tucked it between her arm and body. She motioned the younger woman into the room. "Come in, come in. It's so cold out there."

"Vait. Der's more in van." Sasha turned to go back outside.

Abigail stopped her with a hand on her jacket sleeve. "Adam, you get the rest. Sasha, come in and meet Jack."

Her son had not moved. He was in a stare-down with Cam.

Abigail shooed in her son's direction. "Adam. Go. You can meet Jack when you come back."

Cam's brother pushed through the storm door and went down the sidewalk like he was stomping out little flames along the way. Sasha draped her coat over the back of a chair.

Cam grabbed it and flung it over her shoulders. "I'll see if he needs any help." She pushed her arms into the sleeves as she ran toward her brother. "Adam. I need to talk to you."

He opened the rear hatch of his minivan. "Are you able to speak now that your boyfriend's tongue isn't down your throat?"

Cam said nothing.

Her silence seemed to unnerve him. He glanced at her then reached inside the van. "You aren't going to hit me, are you? I'm holding Sasha's apple pie."

"I'm thinking about it."

"So, he's the guy you're sleeping with?"

"Yep."

"And you expect me to be nice to him?"

"Yep."

"And if I'm not, I'll be sorry?"

"Yep."

Adam exhaled a drawn-out Eeyore-like sigh which created a cloud of vapor in front of his face. "I'll give him a chance but only because Dad likes him."

A car horn beeped behind them. Through the windshield, Uncle Zach waved from the passenger seat. His partner, Peter, saluted. Only the top of their daughter's head was visible in the backseat.

"Give me the plate." Cam lifted the foil-covered pie from Adam's hands. "The gang's all here."

#

Once the turkey was heated through, the twelve Coleman family members and one guest sat around the extended dining table.

Cam's father rose to his feet. "Thank you all for coming today. Jack, we're not a religious family, so we don't say grace. Instead, everyone tells one thing they're thankful for. Since I'm the one talking, I'll start. I'm thankful to be blessed with a wonderful family."

Zane sat down and motioned to his brother.

Cam's uncle was a less wiry version of her father with better hair. He clapped a hand on Zane's shoulder. "Lord knows, I'm not a perfect brother, but I'm grateful I have one."

Everyone laughed or smiled, except his teenage daughter, Hayley. Cam had always been close to her young cousin from the time Zach and Peter adopted her at age three. Now she was torn between wanting to hug or smack the technology-obsessed teenager.

Zach held an open palm out to his daughter. "It's your turn, Hale."

The girl sighed and rolled her eyes. "I'm thankful for my iPhone."

Her other father sat on her right. Peter was a slight man with reddish hair brushed back from a high forehead. Unlike his Levi-clad partner, he was natty in gray suit pants, an open-collared dress shirt, and a navy-blue blazer.

With a droll expression, he placed his hand on his chest. "I'm grateful for a childhood without technology and for learning it's not *de rigueur* to comment on your kid's Facebook page."

Hayley wailed. "Dad, you're embarrassing me."

Peter shot her a jocular smile. "Welcome to the rest of your life, sweetheart."

Next to him, her Uncle Ed scooted back his chair and rose to his feet. "Well, when it comes to blessings, I have too many to count. Even though our sons were unable to make it home for Thanksgiving this year, I'm grateful to be able to spend the holiday with family. Also, this year my business has—"

"Yeah, yeah." Marjorie tugged on her husband's arm. "Sales are up, losses are down. We have to move it along. The food's getting cold. I'm thankful I wore stretch pants today. Your turn, Abigail."

Cam's mother reached out and stroked the wispy blonde hair on her grandson's head. He sat in a high chair next to her. "I'm so thankful for this little guy. Becoming a grandmother this year is another millstone in my life."

Millstone? Cam's eyes darted around the table. No one said a word.

Sasha smiled at her baby and mother-in-law. When she realized everyone waited for her to speak, her sunny expression faded. "My English so bad."

Adam patted her hand. "It's okay, honey. Your English is way better than our Russian."

She looked at her husband with shining eyes. "Vhen I come to America, I vant many tings. I tankful, now I haf everyting I need."

Cam's brother pulled his wife close and kissed her temple. Across the table, Aunt Marjorie sniffed and blinked back tears.

Adam said, "I'm thankful for my wife and son and that they have turned a house into a home."

Now everyone looked at Cam. "I'm thankful for my health, my family, my friends, and this food."

Jack was the last person to speak. He waited until Cam turned to look at him. "I'm thankful to have you in my life." After a pause, his face crinkled with a wide grin. "Let's eat, mates."

Chapter 18

AN HOUR BEFORE Jeanine's party, Cam slipped a black, long-sleeved mini-dress with a turtleneck collar over her head and smoothed it down her body. She pulled on black high-heeled boots. The only skin that showed was from knee to upper leg, her hands, and face. Her hair trailed in big curls down her back.

Jack arrived thirty minutes later dressed in dark chocolate pants, a camel-colored cashmere sweater, and his leather bomber jacket. "You look wonderful, luv."

"So do you." Cam's cell phone rang. "Jeanine's calling. I hope nothing's wrong. Hello."

"Cam, are you on your way?" Her friend sounded frazzled.

"Jack and I are about to leave. Why?"

"I thought the caterer was bringing ice. He thought I was buying it. We have enough in my freezer for about a dozen drinks. Would you stop and buy fifty pounds? Call me when you get here. I'll have some servers help you carry it in."

#

When they arrived at Jeanine's house, two women bustled out into the chill night air for the needed ice. They each carried two ten pound bags into the house. Jack handed the last one to Cam. "I'll go park."

She dropped off the ice in the kitchen and made her way to the dining room. Every imaginable finger food covered the table like a dazzling jigsaw puzzle.

Jeanine hugged her. "You're a lifesaver." She waited while Cam shrugged out of her red wool coat then handed it to a passing server. "Where's Jack?"

"He's parking the car."

Arm-in-arm, Jeanine walked Cam to where a bartender worked behind a linen-topped table. "This is my friend who brought the ice. Make Cam and her date when he gets here a *nice* drink."

Jeanine saved empty bottles of Stoli vodka, Courvosier cognac, Chivas Regal whiskey, Tanqueray gin, and Glenfiddich scotch. She refilled them with less costly liquors for the party.

She once told Cam, "People can't tell the difference no matter what they say. If they see the label, they think it's what they're drinking."

She had the bottles of the real stuff marked. If Jeanine brought a guest to the bar and told the bartender to make the person a drink, she wanted the expensive booze used. Cam ordered cranberry juice and vodka.

Drink in hand, she checked out the beautiful artificial Christmas tree in the living room. It was decorated with antique ornaments and old-fashioned bubble lights. After waving at one realtor she recognized from Jeanine's office, she turned toward a large archway and wide steps which descended into the family room. A soft-needled pine tree sparkled with white lights and silver ornaments next to the stone-clad fireplace.

Maybe one day I'll have a permanent home I can decorate for the holidays.

A hand grasped her elbow. An strange man grinned down at her. He was handsome in a mature, debonair way with thick gray hair swept back from a patrician forehead. With his lean face and body, ice-blue eyes, and capped white smile, he had all the warmth of a predator about to devour its prey.

A silver fox, she thought.

"Hello, there." He flashed a wintry smile. "You're the prettiest little thing to walk in here tonight." With an almost imperceptible tug, he pulled her closer.

Cam's arm was pressed against his body. Her small stature and blonde hair made stupid men misjudge her. But years of working in a male-dominated environment taught her how to deal with them. They were like any bully who needed clear, precise instructions.

"I don't know you, and I want you to take your hand off me."

Her gaze never wavered as she set her drink on a console table. A spill from the red cocktail would stain Jeanine's carpet.

The silver fox's eyebrows lifted, but his hand remained wrapped around her arm. "I was just making conversation."

"No, you weren't and we both know it."

"You're a prickly little thing, aren't you? I like the challenge."

This guy intimidated people. He touched without provocation. His condescension was intended to sound like a compliment or humorous observation. He imposed his height and body into another's physical space. The silver fox had no boundaries.

"That's the second time you've called me a little thing. How would you feel if I called you an old thing?"

His false geniality disappeared. He pushed Cam against the wall and leaned in close. "What did you say?"

Before she could answer or determine which of his body parts to injure first, a harsh voice spoke behind the man's back. "Hands off, Carl, before you bloody well get hurt."

The silver fox straightened, sniffed the air, and turned to face Jack with a feral expression.

Carl? This guy is his uncle?

Cam gazed past the tall man. Jack stood with his fists balled at his side, his face flushed. His narrowed eyes slid away to Cam. She nodded to convey she was fine, then she shifted her attention to Carl Townsend, and plotted which hand tools would hurt him the most.

The Silver Fox sneered at his nephew. "Are you going to be the one to hurt me?"

Jack shook his head. "Not me." He motioned with his chin toward Cam. "But I recently saw her hospitalize a man who messed with her."

Carl turned a startled look to Cam. He dropped his hand from her arm and took a step away.

Ever the vigilant hostess, Jeanine joined the tense threesome. "What's going on?"

Cam motioned Jack forward with her head. "This is Jeanine's mother, Tina, and her father, Ron. This is Jack Reynolds."

"'Allo. Pleased to meet you.

He and Cam set their plates and drinks on the table then sat. Ron asked Jack where he was from and about the Great Barrier Reef.

While the men conversed, Tina leaned close to Cam. "I'm so happy to see you with someone again."

Jeanine's mother had met Oliver and knew about his financial chicanery. She had comforted her at the Portage Country Club after her wedding fiasco while her parents dealt with the shocked guests.

Tina glanced at Jack again. "Is he more than just a friend?"

"We've been dating."

"Jeanine told me about the fire. It's sad you never had the chance to restore Mrs. Underwood's house."

"I'm glad all her belongings were out of it."

"You know, I think she was hanging on until she could sell it to someone like you." Tina stared down at her hands. "So many elderly people seem to be straddling this world and the next. They may be waiting until a loved one comes to see them or because of some unfinished business. In Mrs. Underwood's case, I think she wanted to see her house sold to someone who would love it as much as she did."

The corners of Cam's lips drooped. "And I let her down."

"No, you didn't. The fire wasn't your fault. Instead you helped a woman in a lot of pain leave this world in peace. It was a beautiful gift."

"I lost my temper with Jeanine when she asked what I was going to do with the land. I told her I would make it into a park and call it The Underwood Memorial Garden."

Tina laughed. "I can imagine my daughter wasn't too happy to hear that."

"She told me not to let my feelings get in the way of a business deal. I've already turned down three offers from Castle Construction."

"Really? I graduated from Old Trail School with a girl whose father owned that company."

Cam lowered her voice. "Brooke Townsend is Jack's mother."

No one spoke.

Jeanine scanned Carl's hard face. "You came with Margo Gentry, didn't you? She's in the living room."

He turned cold eyes on Cam. "I'm sorry if I offended you." He jutted out his chin and strode away.

Jack moved close and put his arm around Cam's waist. "Are you okay, luv?"

"I'm fine." She picked up her drink and took a sip. "So far, I've met your pain-in-the ass cousin and sonofabitch uncle. Anyone else I need to be aware of?"

"Just my mum but she's bonzer compared to those two."

I'll judge that for myself. Cam turned to Jeanine. "I haven't had a chance to tell you, but Jack's uncle and mother own Castle Construction. That was Carl Townsend, one of the owners."

Her friend's eyes widened. She turned to stare in the direction the Silver Fox had gone. "Margo didn't tell me his last name. I sold her house, and she asked to bring the man she's seeing."

Jack's lip curled. "Suggest to Margo she dump the bludger. It'll save her heaps of drama."

Jeanine arched her eyebrows. "One of you will have to tell me about him later. Let me take your coat, Jack, and thanks for the ice run."

After Jeanine left, he looked Cam up and down as if inspecting for injuries. "What did Carl do?"

"It was just typical male intimidation." She gave him a droll smile. "You know how well I react to that."

He laughed. "I should have let the bugger get what he deserves."

Cam took his hand and led him to the bar for *the good stuff.* They filled plates from the array of foods on the table. Every available seat in the family room was taken, including the raised fireplace hearth. They went into the enclosed sun porch. A wall-mounted electric heater kept the temperature comfortable.

Cam spotted Jeanine's mother and father seated at a teak patio table with two empty chairs. "Are you saving these seats?"

"No, please, sit down." Tina wore her dark hair around her shoulders. A silky white blouse topped black ankle pants.

Tina's eyes shifted to where her husband talked with Jack about the nautical hazards of sailing on Lake Erie with a fixed keel. "He looks a bit like her. I heard she married someone in Australia."

"Jack's father is still there. His mother has remarried and lives in California now. Did you know her brother?"

Tina inhaled sharply and looked surprised. "I was a freshman when he was kicked out of Old Trail in his senior year."

"What did he do?"

"Oh, it was kept very hush-hush."

"He's here."

Tina's nose wrinkled. "Who's here?"

"Carl Townsend."

Jeanine's mother twisted in her chair like someone behind her had just said, "Boo." Her sudden movement caused the table to rock, and everyone grabbed their drink glasses when they teetered.

Ron cocked his head toward his wife and gave her a quizzical look. "What's wrong?"

"I-I just remembered something I need to ask Jeanine." Tina stood, threw her napkin on the table, and hurried from the room.

Cam had never seen the woman so flustered. She gave Ron and Jack a don't-ask-me shrug. As time passed, Tina didn't return to finish her food. Cam pushed back from the table.

Jack looked up. "You need something, luv?"

"I'm going to check if Jeanine needs any help. I'll be right back."

Ron looked at his watch. "If you see Tina, remind her we have to let the dog out in an hour."

Cam looked in all the rooms on the first floor. She didn't see Jack's uncle, Jeanine, or Tina. She headed upstairs. Coats were piled on the bed in the first guest room. The master bedroom door was closed because Jeanine shut her cat in there during the party. When Cam reached it, she heard voices on the other side. One of them was in obvious distress.

She knocked. "Jeanine, its Cam. What's wrong?"

The door swung open. Tina sat on the end of the bed. Her eyes were swollen and red. She blew her nose into a tissue.

Jeanine sighed. "Maybe you can find out why she's upset. She won't tell me a thing." She turned back to her mother. "Please talk with Cam. I have to get back to the party."

"Go." Tina sniffled. "I'm fine. Remember you promised."

"I know. I won't say anything to Dad."

Chapter 19

CAM CLOSED THE bedroom door behind Jeanine. Her friend's cat, which resembled a white fluffy slipper with eyes, glared from a pillow in front of the quilted headboard. Cam sat on the end of the bed and wrapped an arm around Tina's waist.

The older woman heaved a deep breath. "Aren't you going to ask me why I've been crying?"

"If you want to tell me, you will. But I suspect it has something to do with Carl Townsend."

The only sounds were the hum of voices from downstairs and melodic strains of Christmas music.

After a time, Jeanine's mother sat up straight and looked Cam in the eye. "I am going to tell you something I haven't told anyone. I've never told Ron or Jeanine. In fact, I haven't talked to anyone about it in forty years, but hardly a day goes by that I don't think about it." She took a deep breath. "When I was fifteen years old, Carl Townsend raped me."

Cam did her best to not react with shock, but her body tensed and flooded with overwhelming rage. "I knew I should've kicked the sonofabitch in the balls."

There was moment of silence before Tina burst into laughter. She giggled, wiped tears of mirth from her eyes, then wrapped her arms around Cam. "That's why I love you." Finally, she folded her hands in her lap and stared at them. "After eighth grade, I was thrilled to attend Old Trail School, even on a scholarship. The other students were smart, sophisticated, and rich. But I was able to make several friends there right away. Carl was a senior, tall, blonde, and a star athlete. I was surprised when he showed an interest in me, a lowly freshman."

Tina paused. Cam watched a myriad of emotions from regret to pain reflect on the woman's face. She didn't press her to continue.

At last, Jeanine's mother raised her chin and with a blank stare gazed straight ahead. "I went with some friends to a dance but accepted a ride home from Carl. He had beer and marijuana in the car. Of course, I wanted to please him, so I drank a little and passed the joint back and forth. When he started kissing me, it was nice. But then, he pressed for more. When I said no, it was like a switch went on. He went wild, hit me, choked me." Tina breathed in and out in short bursts. "Anyway, after it was over, he took me home like nothing had happened."

"How did your parents find out?"

"They were waiting up for me. I said I had been in a fight with another girl to explain the bruises and torn clothes. Then my mother saw blood and semen running down my leg. When they tried to call the police, I became hysterical. In the end, they photographed my injuries and got in contact with Carl's father the next day at his office. I don't know what was said at their meeting, but a deal was worked out. Carl was sent away, and my tuition was paid, not only for Old Trail, but through nursing school too."

Cam frowned. "In other words, the Townsend money bought Carl out of a statutory rape charge."

"My parents said it was for the best, and I didn't want anyone at school to know or have to testify in court."

"So, he didn't claim it was consensual?"

Tina shook her head in weary resignation. "There were bruises and other marks. I know emotional trauma never truly goes away, but I was stunned when you told me he was here. In my daughter's house. I don't know what I'm going to tell Jeanine."

Both women sat in silence, until Cam lifted her index finger in the air. "I know. Let's say we were talking about Mrs. Underwood, and you became upset about her house burning down."

They rehearsed their story while Tina redid her makeup. When they went downstairs, Jeanine was in the foyer saying good-bye to several guests.

She closed the front door and turned around. "Well?"

Tina hugged her daughter. "Oh, honey, I'm sorry for worrying you."

"Mom, are you having another menopausal reaction?"

Tina's eyes lit up as she looked at Cam over Jeanine's shoulder. "I guess that's what happened." She stepped back. "I never know when these emotions will come over me. Cam told me about the house burning down. I thought about poor Mrs. Underwood and just lost it."

"It's okay. I understand." They hugged again then pulled Cam into their embrace.

"What's going on here?" Tina's husband came into the foyer.

"Nothing." All three women answered in unison.

Ron eyed them like a teacher who knows his students were up to no good while his back was turned. "Don't tell me it's nothing. I can see it was something."

Tina stepped forward. "If you must know, it's *The Change.*"

Jeanine's father batted the air and turned away like someone had just farted. "Oh, geez, that again? I thought you were over it."

Tina crossed her arms. "Apparently, I'm not."

After Jeanine's parents left, Cam found Jack in the family room. They spent the next two hours chatting with other party guests before thanking Jeanine and saying goodbye.

On the walk to the car, Jack patted her hand which rested on his bent elbow. "You and Tina were gone for a long time. I wondered if you met up with my uncle again."

"I didn't see him at all. He and his girlfriend must have left early."

Did Jack or his mother know about Carl's sexual assault on a young girl? If he could commit such a heinous act then, what was he capable of now?

#

The morning after Jeanine's party, Jack laid a plate of blueberry pancakes in front of Cam. "My mum would like to meet you next Saturday."

Cam lifted her eyes from the Sunday real estate section of the Beacon Journal. Even though his mother was in town once a month, the subject of meeting her had not been broached since they didn't go to California for

Thanksgiving. Jack had informed her that Brooke usually flew from San Diego to Akron on Thursdays, met with department heads on Friday morning, attended the board meeting in the afternoon, and flew home Saturday.

He sat down across from her. "She's staying over Saturday night, so we can have lunch or dinner. Mum said she'd like to see The Harte Estate and what I've been working on. What do you say?"

Jack looked like a little boy who had just found a puppy and was begging to keep it.

Cam smiled at his winsome expression. "I guess it's time your mom and I finally meet."

#

When the doorbell rang to announce the arrival of Jack's mother, Cam's heart raced. She leaned toward the mirror above the sink as she rushed to strip hot curlers from her hair. There was mascara and eyeliner on only one eye.

How the hell did that happen?

The last roller tangled in the long tress wrapped around it several times. The more Cam struggled to loosen it, the more it snarled. "Fuck it all to hell."

"Cam?"

Startled, she spun around. Jack stood in the doorway between the bathroom and bedroom. Her eyes darted behind him. "Where's your mother?"

"Looking 'round downstairs. What's wrong?"

Her teeth gritted. "I can't get this goddamned thing out."

She tugged to loosen the toothy grip on her hair then dropped it in frustration. The roller dangled on her shoulder like a spiny creature caught in a silken net.

"Let me help." With patience and gentle fingers, Jack unwound the tangled strands. "There." He laid the curler in her open palm. "Take your time. You look beautiful." He pointed at her face. "Except this one eye—"

"I know. I know." She shooed him toward the door. "I'll be down soon."

Cam finished getting ready and descended the wide main staircase dressed in a pair of pleated wool slacks and a turtleneck sweater. As she neared the bottom, Jack and his mother emerged from the hallway which led to the library and back stairs.

Brooke Townsend Reynolds Keller was not what Cam expected. She had pictured Jack's mother as a beautiful, fifty-something, petite woman who didn't look old enough to have a nearly thirty-year-old son. She had an image of someone with blue eyes in a tanned face courtesy of the California sun or a spray-on booth. The woman would have wavy still-blonde hair, cut and styled at a salon, not a beauty parlor, and a well-preserved face smoothed out with Botox and fillers.

Instead, his mother approached her with a wide smile that created deep ellipses from her nose to her mouth and creased the corners of her eyes. In high-heeled boots, she was taller than her son. A gleaming mane of grayish-white hair fell to her shoulders from a center part like icy twin waterfalls. She was a vixen, the female counterpart, to Uncle Carl's silver fox persona but without the menacing undercurrents.

With hands outstretched, she smiled with genuine warmth. "Cam, at last we meet." Jack's mother gave her a quick hug. She turned to her son who stood several steps behind her. "You're right, Jackson. She *is* gorgeous." Facing Cam once more, she cocked her head. "You are an amazing woman. I am so impressed with what you've done here. Susan had shown me old pictures of her family's home. Now I can't wait to tell her about it when I get back to San Diego."

Cam was disconcerted by his mother's gushing sincerity. The resemblance to Jack was evident in the woman's guileless enthusiasm, in how the one corner of her mouth rose when she laughed, and in her inquisitive azure eyes.

I like her. She's nothing like her brother or her niece. "Thank you, Mrs. Keller."

"Please call me Brooke. Jackson has told me so much about you I feel we've known each other forever." She pulled her cell phone from her pocket.

"Do you mind if I take some pictures of what you've done here to show Susan?"

As they continued through the house, Jack pointed out all the projects he'd worked on. They made a quick stop at the gatehouse to see the renovations there before heading to dinner.

Cam followed him and his mother in her truck to Northside Lofts. Jack drove the Mercedes into the condo's underground garage. Cam turned into the parking lot for Luigi's and waited for them to cross the street. Together they entered the restaurant.

Despite the construction of a Y-bridge and the rerouting of Main Street traffic above and around the restaurant, the landmark eatery continued to thrive. Patrons crowded the entryway and bar area.

While they waited to be seated, Brooke glanced around the dated restaurant. "This part hasn't changed since I was a girl."

Cam nodded at the original dining room with the long oak bar and wooden booths along the wall. "My family has been coming here as long as I can remember."

The hostess seated them and handed out menus. A waitress took their drink orders.

Brooke laid the one page menu on the table and tilted her head to the side. "So, Cam, tell me about the assault on you."

Do you mean Gus or your brother, Carl?

Before she could speak, Jack answered in a cautious voice like he was giving critical testimony at a trial. "A local slumlord tried to scare her into selling a property she owns on the east side of town. The bloke has houses 'round it and wanted to unload them as a package deal to an investor. He even threatened her after he had an arsonist burn the place down."

Brooke's eyes widened. "Mr. Varsamis hired someone to destroy your house?"

Clearly thrown by his mother's question, Jack spluttered. "Y-you know him?"

His mother asked Cam, "Was Gus arrested for arson?"

She shook her head. "Only for trespassing and hitting me. There's not enough evidence to charge him with the fire."

Jack put his elbows on the table and leaned forward. "Mum, how do you know 'bout this?"

Brooke smiled at her son with the indulgence of a parent whose child just asked a silly question. "I *am* the CEO of Castle Construction."

"But I thought Bill Riley handled all the property acquisitions."

"He does. But everything the managers handle is reported to me. I know we've made offers to C.C. Restorations for the property, and I know Cam's the owner."

The waitress came with three Luigi's signature Italian salads with cheese. Or as Cam's family called it *a bowl of cheese with salad.* As they ate, Cam and Jack told his mother the details about Gus's attack, his subsequent injuries at their hands, and his arrest.

Brooke speared a forkful of mozzarella and greens. "Has he gone to trial yet?"

"I haven't heard anything." Cam shrugged. "I don't even know if the prosecutor will file charges."

"Will you sue him?"

"No. It's not worth the aggravation. I just want him brought to justice for the fire."

After their individual pizzas arrived, Brooke stared at her son. "You know, Jackson, I didn't get to see you at Thanksgiving, and you were missed. Why don't you and Cam think about coming to California for Christmas?"

"Uh, okay." Jack flashed Cam an uneasy glance. "We'll have to check our schedules and get back to you."

When they exited the restaurant after the meal, Brooke hugged Cam. "Thank you for showing me the work you and Jackson have done on the house. It was a pleasure to meet you. Let's do this again."

Jack walked his mother to the condo lobby and said goodbye while Cam waited in her truck.

After he seated himself in the passenger seat, he twisted to face her. "Mum just asked again 'bout having us spend Christmas with her and Owen."

A couple hours in his mother's company was fine but for days or a week was too much, too soon. Cam sighed. "I'm sorry, Jack, I can't take off and go to California right now."

He settled back and buckled his seat belt. "We don't have to stay very long. Just a couple days."

"It's so close to the holiday. Remember when you tried to find a flight at Thanksgiving and there was nothing to get us back in time for Jeanine's party? Besides, it would probably cost more than I can afford to spend right now."

He remained quiet. When she looked at him, a tiny smile widened his gorgeous mouth. "I know better than to offer to pay for your ticket."

She laughed. "You're catching on. Listen, if you want to go, it's okay with me."

"I've only been back from Oztralia a few weeks. I feel like I owe you for the two months I went home to take care of dad."

"Don't. With your help, I'm ahead of schedule. Besides, it's the least I can do for someone who's worked all this time for free."

"I've been well compensated, luv." He waggled his eyebrows at her.

Chapter 20

TWO WEEKS LATER, Cam drove Jack to the airport in Cleveland. It was mid-morning, but the leaden sky made it appear the daylight was waning. Piles of crusty snow lined the road leading from the highway. A fierce, bone-chilling wind whipped off Lake Erie. People exited vehicles at the curb and hunkered into their coat collars, buffeted by icy, stinging tornadoes. Suitcases large enough to contain contorted bodies were dragged along pavements salted with Halite to the pneumatic doors of the terminal.

Jack released his seat belt. "I'll Skype you every day." He wrapped his hand around her neck and pulled her close for a long kiss. "Don't work too hard."

"I won't," she lied.

"Use the condo if the house gets too cold."

"I might," she fibbed.

"Do you still love me?"

"I do," she vowed.

#

In the afternoon, Cam received a call from the rep whose company was scheduled to install the new HVAC systems in January. "I have good news. All the equipment is here. We can begin the job on Monday."

"You mean, you can tear the place up during the holidays and before I'm ready." *C'mon, tell me how you're going to make it worth my while to save on your end-of-year inventory taxes.*

After Cam and Rick the Rep dickered for several minutes, she agreed to a six percent reduction of almost four thousand dollars.

When Cam went to bed that night, she laid her head down and sat up at once. "What the hell?"

She reached a hand under her pillow and found a gift-wrapped box. Before Jack left, they had agreed to wait to exchange gifts until he returned home. She called him.

As soon as he answered the phone, he said, "Before you say anything, it's a mutual gift I want you to wear when you pick me up at the airport."

"Mutual, my ass. Which is probably what this is supposed to cover but won't."

"I know you'll like it as much as me. Open it, think of me, and get a good night's sleep. I love you."

A feeling like warm honey sliding down a spoon ran over her. The present was wrapped like a set of Russian nesting dolls. She was down to the third box by the time she found a small bottle of Marc Jacobs perfume. It was a joke between them that her only two scents were sweat and Ivory soap.

I'll wear it when I pick him up, but it'll be somewhere other than my wrist.

#

At nine o'clock on Monday morning, the HVAC crew arrived with several trucks and off-loaded a ten-foot storage container onto the driveway between the main house and carriage house.

One worker with a large cardboard box on a dolly waited for the elevator when Cam squeezed by in the hallway. "Man, I wish every house we worked in had one of these."

Cam stopped. "Just don't break it. After what this job is costing me, I'll have to leave you in there until I can afford to call a repairman."

At noon, she turned off the thermostat to Big Bertha, the boiler in the basement. With all the coming and going, it was impossible to maintain a moderate temperature in the house. The interior soon matched the thirty-five degrees outside.

Jack skyped her at nine p.m. They talked for fifteen minutes during which Cam did her best not to shiver. She didn't tell him that she planned to patrol every night with a Maglite, her cell phone, and a loaded pistol. There was expensive equipment outside which she paid for and was unprotected.

#

The next day, on Christmas Eve, the temperature dropped ten more degrees. Cam met the job foreman at four p.m. to review the work. "We'll be back on Thursday, Ms. Coleman. You have a Merry Christmas and try to keep warm."

The Aga stove kept the kitchen at a just bearable forty degrees. After cleaning up debris left behind by the workmen and eating a peanut butter and jelly sandwich, she waited with her laptop for Jack to contact her.

He squinted at the screen. "Where are you, Cam?"

"At the house. But I spent most of the day at my parents' place."

"Are you going back there?"

"In a little while." *In the morning for Christmas breakfast, opening presents, and a nap.*

From the background, it appeared Jack was sitting outside. He was shirtless. The sky was blue and sunny. Palm tree fronds waved behind him.

She wrapped her hands around a mug of hot coffee. "Did you go surfing today?"

"It was bloody amazing. I didn't make a fool of myself out there with all the groms. There were a few shark biscuits on boogie boards with more wipeouts than me. I was a floater on the three to five footers until they got a bit mushy."

Okay, whatever that meant. "Well, tell your mother and stepfather happy holidays from me."

"I will, and let's not spend this time of year apart again."

At two a.m., Cam sat in the dark kitchen with her laptop open to a landscaping website. A flash of light sparked in the glass of the kitchen door. She switched to the security app and accessed the video feed from a camera mounted just under the front eave. A dark-colored pickup truck, with its headlights off, parked in the shadow of the gatehouse's garage. The interior overhead light in the cab remained dark when two men exited.

Cam grabbed her Maglite, gun, and moved into the dark library. From a front window, she monitored the men's slow and cautious approach toward the house. They remained in the shadow of trees lining the drive until the construction trailer blocked her view. She dialed 911.

"What is your emergency?"

Cam gave her name and address. "Two unknown men are on my property. I'm alone in the house, and I'm armed."

"Stay inside. I'll dispatch police."

If one of these guys was the arsonist, they might run off when they heard sirens. *I need them caught to testify against Gus.*

The figures were still fifty yards from the house and trailer. Slipping the phone into her jacket pocket, Cam ran out of the library, clumsy in her rubber-soled boots. She hustled to the rear of the main foyer and disarmed the alarm. After she unlocked the back door as quietly as possible, she re-armed the security system. A light dusting of snow covered the dormant grass. Cam tiptoed across the patio to the side wall of the house. Her head poked around the corner. She saw nothing but the bulk of the corrugated metal container.

At first, the only sound was the wind as it rustled through the pines, then came the scuffling of boots on gravel. The intruders were still walking toward the house but were out of the tree line and on the driveway. She took a deep breath, removed her glove with her teeth, and switched off the safety on the Glock. With careful steps, she moved to the side of the trailer.

"What was that? I heard something," a male voice uttered.

Everything stilled. Dead leaves, which had not yet fallen, rustled on the maple and oak trees. A soft snuffling noise sounded from the direction of the carriage house.

"Over there. It's a deer. Shit, it's a seven-point buck. Man, I wish I had my rifle with me."

A punch into a down jacket whooshed in the air. "You fucking idiot. Keep your mind on the job."

Cam inhaled freezing air through her nose and calmed her nerves. She waited against the side wall of the container, away from the end where the locked entry gate was located. Her gun and Maglite were readied at chest level. She pulled her neck scarf up to cover her mouth and nose. The men's footsteps drew closer. Cam cocked her ear for the sound of a police siren, but it was a silent night.

From the opposite side of the trailer, a gruff voice said, "Let's check her out."

"You're sure you can handle this?"

The voices moved to the end where the double doors were located.

"Yes." One of the men hissed in triumph. "It's a Master Lock. I got this."

Cam released the breath she had held. *These guys are just common thieves.*

"Hold the light right here." After a minute of jiggling the lock, there was the audible click of released tumblers followed by the scraping of metal against metal when the padlock's shank was pulled through the security hole. "Open her real slow. Don't make too much noise."

The padlock was tossed in an arc past the door and landed in the snow-covered grass a few feet from Cam. A slight squeal from the hinges resonated in the quiet night. The door closest to her opened and was stopped when it aligned with the side wall. When the clump of boots echoed inside the trailer, Cam put the Maglite in her left pocket. Holding the gun alongside her leg, she took three steps away from the metal wall and picked up the padlock.

"There's four, no five, units here," said an excited voice. "Hot damn. Let's try and get 'em all."

"Grab the handcart. We'll have to make a couple trips. I don't want to bring the truck any closer."

Cam put the safety on the gun and tucked it into her waistband. She placed her knuckled right fist which held the padlock on the container door. Then she laid her other gloved palm flat on the metal, taking care to not move it or make a sound. She positioned her feet to push off like a sprinter waiting for the firing of the starting pistol. The sounds of grunting and shifting of heavy objects sounded deep within the container. She inhaled and, with all the might in her one-hundred-and-ten-pound muscular body, she heaved the door toward its framed opening. This time there was a mighty screech of metal as the hinges turned.

The door banged shut. As soon as the security holes lined up, Cam jammed the padlock's U-shaped shank through them, twisted the body into position, and locked it. A second later, loud thumps slammed against the closed door and reverberated in the night air.

Muffled curses from inside were punctuated by banging fists and feet. A siren whooped in the near distance. Flashing lights bathed everything in a bluish hue as a police cruiser turned off Portage Path onto the property. The noises inside the metal box quieted.

Cam's gloveless right hand was numbed and clumsy with cold. She laid the Glock on the ground and stepped several feet clear of it. The police car skidded off the driveway as it rounded the pickup truck and headed her way. She removed the knit cap so her blonde hair tumbled to her shoulders and raised her arms.

It took the police nearly an hour before the padlock, jimmied so easily by the thieves, was opened. During the wait time, Cam sat in the front seat of a running patrol car.

The officer typed her statement into his laptop. "Yeah, we get lots of these kind of calls on weekends and holidays. For the bad guys, it's when their workday begins."

"That's why I live at many of my projects. They're magnets for thieves."

"You got that right, Ms. Coleman. Chances are the two bozos locked inside that trailer cased the place waiting for today. They weren't expecting someone to be in a house with no heat on Christmas morning."

When the men were finally removed from their temporary cell, a patrolman recognized one of them. "Still at it, I see." He handcuffed the man. "How long you been out this time, Bailey?"

The prisoner mumbled a reply, his head down.

"Since Thanksgiving? You didn't waste any time, did you? Looks like you'll be spending more holidays in lockup."

#

By six a.m., everyone had left and Cam was alone with a trailer full of valuable equipment no more secure than before the break-in. A weak sunrise crept over the horizon as she loaded one compressor onto the handcart and wheeled it across the hard-packed and frozen gravel drive to the front steps of the house. Once all five units were inside the foyer, she relocked the near-empty storage container.

At seven, her cell phone rang. *Shit, it's Dad. I'm late.*

Zane shouted. "Where the hell are you?"

"I'll be there in a few minutes."

"Hurry up. I don't know how much longer your mother can keep the food warm without making it totally inedible."

When Cam arrived at her parents' house, the family was still gathered around the table with the dregs of breakfast spread out.

Zane stood up when she walked into the dining room. "Are you okay?"

Her brother scowled. "What took you so long?"

"Let me heat up your breakfast in the microwave, honey." Abigail heaped scrambled eggs onto a plate.

Sasha reached for the carafe and an empty cup. "I vill get you coffee." She poured but only a small amount went into the cup. "Wait, I vill make more."

AJ banged a spoon on the table as he sat in his father's lap. "Da."

Cam dropped into a chair, still in her winter wear. She crossed her arms on the tabletop and laid her head down. "I'm beat."

Zane pulled the knit hat off and helped her out of her coat while Cam related the attempted theft.

Her father glared at her. "Goddammit, why didn't you call me or Adam?"

"The police were there in minutes."

Her sister-in-law put a steaming cup of coffee which looked like black tar in front of her. "Der you go, Cam. Careful. It hot."

She took a careful sip. "Most of the equipment should be installed by the time Jack gets back on Friday. Then I won't have to worry."

Her mother placed a plate on the table with an eggy pile of rubbery, yellow turds, dark greasy sausage links, and a Krispy Kreme doughnut cut in half. "Here. You need to get some food in you."

Cam's stomach recoiled with a gurgle. "Sorry, Mom. I'm too tired to eat."

Abigail frowned with maternal concern as she scanned her daughter's drawn face. "Just bite or two. You need something other than coffee. You can't keep treating your body like a machinist."

Adam said, "You mean, masochist, Mom?"

"Isn't that what I said?"

Her brother handed AJ to Sasha and spun his sister sideways in the chair to remove her boots. Cam bit into the glazed doughnut.

Sasha asked, "Vhat is dis mass-o-keys dat Cam is?"

Adam pulled off the second boot. "It's what you call someone who can't stop abusing themselves."

Sasha's jaw dropped. "Oh, my Got, she is addict? We do intervention?"

Cam's sister-in-law loved reality television. She claimed it helped her learn English.

Adam laughed aloud. "Yeah, that's what we'll do. An intervention. We'll send her to rehab." He laid the boots aside. "She'll be a *Rehab Addict*, like on HGTV." He stood and stared at his sister. "Actually, she kinda looks like the woman on the show."

"Vhat drug she taking? Crack? Oxy?"

Cam's father returned with a pair of fur-lined moccasins. "No one in this family is taking drugs, or I'll kill 'em."

"But Adam say Cam need rehab."

"She doesn't need rehab. She just needs to …"

The sound of voices receded. Her father called her name, but her eyelids felt like they had been fastened shut with toggle clamps. Someone lifted her out of the chair. Her head lolled against a hard shoulder.

The last thing she heard was her mother's voice. "Merry Christmas, honey."

Chapter 21

CAM AWOKE, ROLLED over, and with bleary eyes looked at the clock on the bedside table. It read five o'clock. She jumped to her feet and looked around for her phone.

Why didn't the alarm go off?

She ran downstairs and followed the sound of a TV to the family room. Her mother sat in her usual spot on the end of a plaid sofa. She knitted and watched Dr. Phil.

"Mom, where's my cell phone?"

Abigail looked up and smiled. "In the mailbox."

Cam had turned to head in whatever direction her mother's reply sent her. Instead, she faced Abigail again. "Why is it in there?"

"It's been buzzing for an hour. I couldn't figure out how to make it be quiet."

"So, you put it outside?"

"I tried sticking it under the sofa cushions and inside a cupboard, but I could still hear it. Don't worry, it's safe. The postman isn't delivering today. Besides, I didn't want it to wake you."

The back door opened and Zane bellowed. "Why the fuck is the mailbox buzzing?"

Cam hustled into the kitchen, passed her father, and reached into the black box affixed to the brick wall. She fished out the offending device and switched off the alarm.

"Your mother couldn't figure out how to turn it off, could she?" Zane tugged off his boots and laid them on a rubber mat by the door. He shrugged off his sheepskin coat and headed to the hall closet.

Abigail came into the room. "Is your father home?"

"He's hanging up his coat. I need to head back to the house."

"I think you should sleep here tonight. You need more rest."

"I can't, Mom. I need to—"

"I'll take the night shift." Her father entered the kitchen. "I saw the video of what happened on Adam's laptop. Goddammit, Cameron, what were you thinking? You were out there with those two shitheads long before the cops showed."

"I was armed."

"You could have gotten hurt. A few HVAC units aren't worth it."

Abigail chimed in. "I told you. You're a mas-masochist." She gave a self-satisfied smile. "Honey, you need to take better care of yourself."

"But, Mom—" A big yawn interrupted Cam's protest.

"That's it." Her mother latched onto her arm and dragged her toward the stairs. "I want you to take a hot shower." They climbed to the second floor. "I'll get one of my flannel nightgowns for you. Get in bed, and I'll bring a tray up. You haven't eaten today. Got that?"

"Yes, Mom."

After a hot shower, Cam was warm and toasty as she sat propped up in her childhood bed. Unlike other girls whose rooms were pink and girly, hers had been decorated with reclaimed vintage items. The bed was a tarnished metal frame when her grandfather salvaged it from a barn in southern Ohio. Now its brass shined with the monthly polishing her mother gave it. Every item had a story behind it from the small mahogany pedestal desk once used by a church secretary to the antique rosewood mirror which reportedly had been in a brothel.

She checked her phone. While she slept, Jack had called several times. Abigail entered with a bowl of soup, crackers, and hot tea on a tray. "Jack called to wish you Merry Christmas. He got worried when you didn't answer, so he called here. Your father told him about the burglars." Abigail laid the tray across Cam's lap. "He offered to come home on an earlier flight, but Zane told him to talk with you first."

"Thanks, Mom."

She crumbled crackers into her soup and finished the bowl of Campbell's best. After drinking most of the tea, she slumped down on the pillow with her phone on her chest and closed her eyes.

I'll call Jack in a minute. She was startled awake when her phone rang. She checked the screen. "Merry Christmas, Jack."

He sounded stressed. "Cam, are you okay?"

"I'm fine. I know Dad told you what happened last night but don't worry. Everything's under control."

"Why did you not stay inside and wait until the police arrived?"

"I didn't know the guys were just after the HVAC units. I thought maybe one of them was the arsonist. I was afraid they would take off if they heard the police sirens."

Jack gave a snort of exasperation. "That's all the more reason you shouldn't have confronted them."

"I didn't confront them. They never even saw me. As soon as they went into the construction trailer, I locked the door. That's when the police arrived."

"But, Cam—"

"Jack, I knew what I was doing. I wouldn't have tried to take them on. All I wanted was to make sure they didn't leave before the police got there. How was your Christmas in California?"

"It was fine except for worrying 'bout you in Ohio."

"Was Santa good to you? Did you get the pony you always wanted?"

At last, Jack chuckled. "No pony, but I can't wait to come home to our mutual gift."

"Thank you for the perfume. I'll wear it to the airport when I pick you up."

"Shall I come back early? I'm on my laptop right now. I can get a red-eye flight that leaves tonight."

"That's not necessary. Tomorrow the compressors start being installed. There'll be heat in part of the house by the end of the day. When you get home on Friday, everything should be up and running. Besides, how much would that ticket cost?"

"Let me check." Jack paused. "Seven hundred."

Cam gasped. "Dollars? That's crazy."

Jack's voice went low and velvety. "You and my peace of mind are worth it, luv. It would kill me if something happened to you."

Warmth like clothes fresh out of the dryer enveloped her. "I love you, Jack."

"I love you too. Why didn't you tell me you were spending the whole night at the house? I thought you were sleeping at your parents' house."

"I was but during the day when the workmen were here. Besides, until last night nothing happened."

"I know I can't stop you, so I want you to promise you'll stay inside the house, especially if there is anything suspicious outside."

Cam sighed. "All right. I won't patrol the perimeter, and I'll wait for the police to arrive. But if it's just an animal or something like that I can go out, right?"

"No. If the situation doesn't warrant law enforcement, then call your father or Adam to come over. Promise you will not go outside at night without someone with you, or I'm heading home."

"All right, I promise. I don't want your mother mad at me because you left early."

#

Two days later, Cam's truck crept toward the arrival area at the Cleveland airport. Jack leaned against a support column, his overstuffed backpack on the ground at his feet. He looked relaxed, tanned, and way too attractive for a man who had just flown more than six hours.

A knot of business people with wheeled overnight bags and briefcases exited through the pneumatic terminal doors behind him. Two in the group were women. One attractive brunette in a black wool coat stared at Jack's sun-streaked blonde head and lithe, well-muscled body in tight jeans and his leather bomber jacket. Her hesitation created a stutter-step in the synchronized formation of suits. This caught the attention of the woman next to her. The second business-suited female viewed Jack from head to toe.

It looks like she's leveraging his assets for a corporate takeover.

Unaware of the women's perusal, Jack's mouth tilted up in a roguish grin when he spotted Cam's truck. Like a missile from a drone, his smile came out of nowhere, and had the power to disarm her. She braked, shifted to park, and hopped out. After he threw his backpack onto the seat of the extended cab, he snaked an arm around her waist, pulled her close, and captured her mouth with his. Every cell in her wanted to be crushed against him, to have his body molded with hers, and never let go.

He sniffed. "I don't smell anything on your neck."

"Your gift isn't there."

A predatory look came into his eyes. "I love treasure hunts."

His low tone sent shivers up her spine. She headed to the driver's door. After Jack fastened his seatbelt, she concentrated on pulling into traffic without sideswiping another vehicle or running down a pedestrian in her haste to get him home. When she was on the expressway heading south, she relaxed her grip on the wheel. Jack described the beaches he visited in his search for good waves.

She smiled at his excitement with surfing again. "Sounds like you had a good time."

He was quiet for several long seconds. "The worst part was Christmas Eve. My Uncle Carl showed up. He and his girlfriend were headed to his condo in Maui."

"Was she the same one?"

"Eh? You mean the same girlfriend at Jeanine's party?"

Cam nodded.

"Was that woman named Debbie?"

"No, but I don't remember what her name was."

"This one looked like a stripper, which is more his style. Maybe Jeanine told the other one to dump the dickhead, and she did." Jack paused. "At one point, we were alone on the patio, and he asked me if … "

Cam glanced over when Jack didn't continue. His mouth was set in a hard line.

"It doesn't matter." His voice carried an undertone of hostility. "Owen and my mum walked out of the house and saw something was 'bout to happen. I told them what he said. Owen suggested it was time for Carl and Debbie to leave."

They were at The Harte Estate thirty minutes later. Before she left for the airport, Cam had set two of the four thermostats on the first and second floors to a toasty seventy degrees. After she showed Jack the new heating system, they ate the soup she'd bought at Panera's.

He dropped his spoon in his empty bowl and leaned back in his chair. "It's good to be home with you."

"I missed you, too." *More than I thought I would.* She lifted the bowl and slurped the remainder of the chicken orzo soup. Before she lowered the dish, she picked out an errant piece of meat and dropped it into her open mouth.

Jack grinned. "I love watching you eat. Most women pick at their food. You appreciate pleasures of the flesh."

She stuck out her tongue and bit it with a smile. Jack washed the bowls and spoons while Cam put away the uneaten loaf of sourdough bread. She laid a hand on his back. "Stay here. Five minutes." She kissed his cheek and hurried to the back stairs.

"Eh?"

"Five minutes." She ran to the second floor.

Chapter 22

JACK ENTERED THE bedroom with a large and small gift bag. Cam eyed them with suspicion. "What are those?"

"Presents for you."

"I already got one."

"No, that was *our* present. These are strictly for you." He pointed to the box wrapped in red and green plaid paper sitting in front of Cam. "But more importantly, what have we here?"

Her legs in black, high-heeled boots and her bare arms were wrapped around the rectangular present. She rested her chin on top, behind a stick-on bow.

Jack tilted his head. "What are you not wearing, luv?"

"A lot. Open this." She patted the box.

He removed the bow off the top and tore part of the wrapping paper away. After pulling apart the flaps, he revealed a metallic blue square.

A perplexed expression knitted his brows, then he broke into a wide smile. "You got me one." He lifted out a classic Trusco Tool Box. "It looks like yours, just brand-new."

Within days of his apprenticeship, he had admired the one Cam inherited from her grandfather. He had found it amazing that the box was designed by a Japanese man in the late nineteen-forties and still fit today's tools.

"Do you like it?" Cam asked.

Jack pushed the wrapping paper aside and sat on the bed next to her. He leaned sideways and kissed her cheek. "Thanks. I'll be a right worker with one of these." He eyed the empty box. "Can we get rid of this now?"

Cam pushed, and the carton tumbled to the floor. She wore black thigh-high stockings attached to garters on a strapless black bustier.

Jack's eyebrows rose. "No panties?"

Cam reclined on her elbows. "None needed."

In one fluid movement, he set his gift on the floor and stood. After stripping in record time, he lifted one of her booted legs. "Did you put perfume on your feet?"

"No."

"Good. We can leave the boots on." He sniffed behind her knees. "There's a faint scent here. Right?"

She nodded.

"Anywhere else?" he murmured.

Goosebumps broke out on her arms. "Two more places."

He crawled up her body like a sleek tawny lion on the prowl and nuzzled the space between her breasts. "Spot number two." He moved backwards down her body, and the width of his shoulders spread her knees apart. He chuckled with an intimate steamy breath. "Did you not think I'd check here?"

He opened her with his thumbs and his mouth was on her. Cam's back arched. Jack teased her with rhythmic thrusts of his tongue. Her core tightened.

She panted, "I want—"

He lifted his head. "This is *my* gift, luv. I'll decide what you'll get."

He put one knee on the mattress and hovered over her. Cam gripped his lean hips. She arched her back, to levitate her body up to his. He settled between her legs, rolled his hips, and pushed inside. Cam writhed and dug her nails into him as his features tightened.

Jack's weight pinned her to the mattress. "It may take me all night to love you."

Cam lost track of time, and Jack was true to his word. In the morning, they lay curled together in warmth and satiation. She wiggled deeper into his embrace. The two gift bags he had brought into the bedroom sat by the door.

She raised up onto an elbow. "What else did you get me for Christmas?"

"Eh?" His voice was husky with sleep.

She scrambled over his prone body and slipped off the bed. When she returned, Jack scooted back and lay on his side. Cam sat in the curve of his waist and pulled tissue paper from the larger bag. She lifted out a box labelled Milwaukee Tools and read the description.

Her breath caught in her throat. She held the gift to her chest, leaned down, and kissed him. "Oh my God, this is fabulous. With the rechargeable battery, I won't need a compressor anymore. Thank you so much."

As she studied the description on the back of the box, Jack laughed. "My mum thought I was bonkers to buy my girlfriend a nail gun for Christmas. That's why she insisted on the other present."

Cam picked up the second much smaller bag. From it, she removed a rectangular jewelry box. Inside rested a silver necklace with a heart-shaped pendant surrounded by diamonds. "Oh, Jack."

He sat up, lifted the necklace out of the box, and slipped it over her head. The heart rested between her naked breasts. "Beautiful. You'll always have my heart."

Cam touched it. "Thank you. I won't gripe about how much money you spent because I love everything and you."

#

For the next week, Jack, Anthony, and Cam sanded and stained the hardwood floors on all three levels of the main house. On the first Monday of the new year, Jack started his new job at Castle Construction.

Jeanine called a few days later. "Cam, I have news you'll want to hear. Can I stop by?"

"Sure. Come on over."

Jeanine arrived swathed in a winter-white coat with wool pants, leather boots, and a cashmere turtleneck sweater. Cam wore a quilted flannel shirt under a pair of brown Carhartt bib overalls and insulated socks.

Jeanine took off her coat, shivered, and shrugged it on again. "It's chilly in here. I thought you put in a new heating system."

"It's in, but I turn the temperature lower during the day when we're working. Let's go in the kitchen. It's warmer." Cam glanced down at her friend's high-heeled footwear. "We've just refinished the floors. Stay on the carpet squares or take off your boots."

When they were seated at the table, Jeanine opened her coat. "You've gotten a lot done since the last time I was here."

"I'm ahead of schedule. We'll be able to put the house on the market in the spring."

"Just let me know when you want to list it."

Cam arched her eyebrows. "What's your news I have to hear?"

"Gus Varsamis has only two properties left on your block."

"He sold the others?"

Jeanine had a wicked glint in her eye. "The banks foreclosed on two of them. Castle Construction is negotiating with the lenders to buy them since they acquired three others at the city's annual tax lien sale. I imagine Gus is trying to wring as much money as he can for the two he has left."

"So, once again, my property will be the lone holdout."

Jeanine leaned toward Cam. "You need to think long and hard about what you want to do. Don't play too tough and lose your advantage. Castle has clout. If what they're building is for public use, you may be forced to sell by right of eminent domain. In which case, you would only be given fair market value."

#

Jeanine called at the beginning of February. "I heard from Castle Construction this morning. Gus has reached an agreement with them on his last two properties. They're anxious to complete their acquisition of the block. I've received another offer."

Cam had already made her decision in the event this happened. "How much?"

"It's ten thousand dollars above market value. I think because they were able to get Gus's properties at bargain prices they could afford to be more than fair with you. What do you say? Will you accept?"

"If you have a contract, I'll sign it. Also, let's discuss putting The Harte Estate on the market. Maybe I'm in a selling phase right now. I might as well take advantage of it."

#

It took two weeks to close on the sale of the former Underwood property. Cam waited several days for Jack to say something.

One night at dinner, she made the announcement. "I sold the lot by the university."

He looked up from his bowl of white chicken chili. "Did you get a good price?"

"C'mon, Jack. You know Castle bought it."

"How would I know? It's not my division. Why did you decide to sell?"

Cam told him about Gus losing most of his houses and Castle buying them. "Since that fire-starting asshole isn't going to profit from my sale, Jeanine convinced me it was the right time to make a deal." She waited, but Jack said nothing more. "Did anyone at Castle ask you to feel me out about selling?"

"No, but if they would have asked me to feel you up, I'd have gladly volunteered." He reached over and caressed her breast. She giggled and batted his hand away.

#

Although C.C. Restorations' bank account was healthier with the money from the sale, Cam still worried about her finances until The Harte Estate sold. One evening, she walked around and admired all the completed work.

I love this property.

She often studied Jack's enclave plans. He created a layout for the six acres with two more houses, the restored clay tennis court, a playground, and future swimming pool. Cam daydreamed about the two of them living in the main house. She pictured Christmas with a massive tree in the living room. Her father and mother would hang the ornaments Cam inherited from her grandparents. Jack and his father would prepare restaurant-worthy food in the kitchen. She'd greet Brooke and her husband, Owen, when they arrived from California, ecstatic with the winter wonderland. In her musing, little AJ ran through the large rooms followed by several younger children. One little boy's hair had curls similar to Jack's. Cam's breath caught in her throat.

Stop it. This will be some family's home one day, just not mine.

#

The month of February was coming to a close with temperatures in the thirties and scant snow. As usual, Jack arrived on Friday evening with groceries and his work clothes for the weekend.

While watching TV, he turned to Cam at the start of a commercial. Lifting the remote control, he muted the sound. "I have something to ask you."

"What?"

"My mum's birthday is in two weeks. Some Akron friends of hers are throwing a party next Saturday. They sent me an invitation."

Cam waited. She tried not to show the sting of not being invited. It was tempered by the relief that she didn't have to attend.

"The invitation said I could bring a guest." Jack wiped his palm across his mouth. "My Uncle Carl and Amelia are going."

Now it made sense. Since Cam's initial encounters with his relatives did not go well, Jack was uncertain she would be willing to spend time with them again. She didn't look forward to seeing Amelia the Bitch or Carl the Rapist, but she would go to support Jack.

"Do you and your mom want me there?"

"It's a surprise fiftieth party for Mum. She doesn't know 'bout it, but I want you to go." Jack cleared his throat. "The party's at the Portage Country Club."

Cam inhaled sharply and let the air out in a slow stream.

Jack took her hand in his. "I understand if you say no. It's a lot to ask. Other than me and mum, you would only know Uncle Carl and Amelia, and the party's at a place you said you'd never step foot in again. I can go alone. If Mum asks, I'll say you had another commitment. I just wanted you to know 'bout it, that's all." With that, he unmuted the TV volume and turned to face the screen.

Cam studied Jack's profile. He was a good man, much like her father and brother. Jeanine had lamented one time, after a bad first date, that there were none left, or at least, none she had been able to find.

Jeanine had gulped the glass of wine in her hand. "I'm telling you, Cam, I think a good, decent, hard-working man is an urban legend. To find one is like hitting the lottery or discovering the last living member of an endangered species."

Jack is my winning ticket. With that thought in mind, Cam cast aside her fear of returning to the Portage Country Club, the site of her greatest hurt and humiliation, and the awkwardness of being with Amelia and Carl again.

She reached for the remote and hit the mute button. "I'd like to go with you to your mother's birthday party."

Jack's eyes lit up. "Really? That's great." He sobered and scanned her face. "You're sure 'bout this?"

Cam leaned to the side and kissed him. "With you, I can face anything."

Chapter 23

THE SURPRISE ASPECT of the birthday party was coordinated between Jack and his mother's friends. Since he started working for Castle Construction, Brooke had extended her monthly stay in Akron to include the entire weekend. She and Jack often used the time to discuss company business. Afterward, Cam joined them, and they dined together on Saturday evenings, either at a restaurant or the condo where Jack cooked the meal. As a cover story for the surprise party, he told his mother Cam had never been to the Portage Country Club, despite living within a few miles of the place all her life. So, he had made a reservation there for their Saturday night dinner.

Shortly before Jack picked her up, Cam was still relaxed and confident. She wore a deep purple sweater dress and her black suede boots. The drive to the country club took two minutes from The Harte Estate. Cam's heart skipped a beat when Jack pulled into the parking lot, but it settled back into a normal rhythm at once. When he opened the club's oak front door, Cam took a quick breath before walking into the dark paneled entryway. He led them to the party room. She was grateful it was not the same room which had been set up for her wedding reception.

She was introduced to the two women who were Brooke's friends since childhood. Unlike Jack's statuesque mother with her fashionable clothes and long hair, Judy and Rhoda more closely resembled Cam's mother. They wore short bobs, mature clothing, and had slightly overweight figures. They were more matronly than Brooke and less like the pretty girls they had once been.

"We're so glad you could come, Jackson," said Judy, the blonde. "And we were thrilled you could bring Cam with you. Brooke said that you've been seeing someone here in Akron. She's hoping this beautiful girl keeps you in the States for good."

Jack smiled. "Thank you for doing this for Mum. I hope she'll be surprised."

"She should be," said Rhoda, a woman of Italian or Greek origin. "We took her to dinner last night and gave her our presents. She told us you guys would be getting together tonight for your monthly dinner."

More guests arrived, including Uncle Carl and Amelia. After greeting their hostesses, Jack's relatives approached. Carl's nose wrinkled like he had just gotten a whiff of something unpleasant. Unlike her father, Amelia's face was as smooth and expressionless as polished marble. Her eyes appeared just as flat and glassy.

Cam affected a calm exterior despite the lightning zing of a warning alarm that made her stiffen her spine and set her nerves alive. Jack took half a step forward, as if to shield her from the Townsend onslaught.

"'Allo Carl. Amelia."

The Silver Fox nodded to his nephew. "Hello, Jackson. I see you brought your pretty lady friend."

Cam lifted her chin. "My name is *Cam*."

She added the extra emphasis for Amelia's benefit, but the young woman appeared oblivious. Her gaze was directed to where a wet bar had been set up on a side table.

At that moment, Jack's phone dinged with a text. He pulled it out of his pocket and checked the screen. "Mum's on her way." He clasped Cam's hand. "Let's head to the front door."

Without offering an excuse, they left Carl and Amelia. Jack stopped and told Judy about Brooke's imminent arrival so she could get everyone into position. Ten minutes later, his mother breezed through the main entrance in a tailored black suit, white turtleneck, black boots, and leather driving gloves. With her hair pulled into a tight bun on the back of her head, she looked every inch the corporate CEO.

Smiling, she came forward, hands outstretched. "I hope you two haven't waited long."

"Not long." Jack kissed his mother.

"Cam, darling, how are you?" They touched cheeks.

"I'm fine. You look wonderful."

Brooke glanced down her body. "I met with several bigwigs who are interested in building a resort near Sandusky. I had to dress to look the part of a successful businesswoman." She turned toward the hall that led to the main dining room. "Is our table ready?"

Jack held up his index finger. "In a few minutes. I was, I mean Cam was, we were going to—"

He's doing it again. Jack can't lie to his mother. "I just asked if we could look around," Cam said. "I've never been here before. My family has driven by this place thousands of times, but all we've ever seen is what is visible from the road. Do you mind?"

"Not at all." Brooke looped her arm through Cam's and cocked her head toward the dining room. "You can see the bar and dining room when we eat. Let's head in this direction."

After checking out a large reception room with a fireplace at one end, lead crystal chandeliers, and a parquet floor covered by a massive Oriental rug, Brooke directed Cam down a hallway. They passed an elevator.

Brooke pointed at the ceiling. "Upstairs are offices and guest rooms where members can stay for the night. Ahead of us are the party and meeting rooms. I've attended several bridal and baby showers here."

When they reached the one where the surprise party was located, Cam stopped. "Can we look inside?"

She opened the door and was taken aback to find the room in total darkness. A frisson of panic raced through her. *Is this the wrong door?*

All of a sudden, the lights switched on, and a crowd of people who were gathered several feet from the door shouted, "Surprise."

Either Brooke was a fantastic actress or she was taken completely off guard. Her hand flew to her mouth, the other to her abdomen as if she was about to hurl.

Judy and Rhoda rushed forward and ushered her into the room. Cam and Jack waited in the hallway as guests hugged and kissed his mother and wished her happy birthday.

Jack nodded. "We surprised her all right."

"No thanks to you."

His head swung in her direction. "What do you mean?"

Cam laughed. "You are the world's worst liar. Especially to your mother."

"I am not."

"Yes, you are. You get all fidgety and start stumbling over your words."

Jack put his arm around her shoulder. "That ought to make you happy, luv. I'll always have to tell you the truth, or you'll see right through me."

Once they joined the party, Cam was introduced to several more friends of Brooke's as well as a dozen people who were board members or employees of Castle Construction. Soon Judy and Rhoda herded everyone to tables in the room and dinner was served. During the meal, a number of people approached Brooke and handed her envelopes.

Cam leaned sideways and spoke into Jack's ear. "Were we supposed to bring a gift?"

"The invitation said a donation could be made to one of her favorite charities."

"Why didn't you tell me?"

"Because you're my guest."

"Did *you* make a donation in your mom's name?"

"A gift is strictly voluntary. Don't worry." He patted her leg under the table.

Cam was not reassured. "What are her favorite charities?"

Jack eyed her. "You don't have to do anything, luv. Your presence is Mum's gift."

She did not argue with him, but every time someone handed an envelope to Brooke, whether it might be a birthday card or confirmation of a donation, an uncomfortable feeling of being a party mooch hit her.

A large sheet cake was wheeled into the room, candles were lit, and the guests sang the obligatory birthday song. Afterward, people roamed around talking to others. Since Cam knew few of the guests, she remained seated when Jack was called away. At one point, she was the only one at her table.

Without warning, the chair next to hers was pulled out, and Amelia sat down. She plunked a glass in front of Cam, similar to one she held. Her voice had the unnatural cadence and louder-than-normal volume of the inebriated. "Here. I brought you a drink."

"What is it?" Cam eyed the lemony-colored beverage.

"It's called a John Daly."

"What's that?"

Amelia brayed a laugh. "Lemonade and vodka. Let's play a drinking game, you and me."

"I don't—"

"Every time I say your name, *Cam*, see, I got it right, I take a drink." She tipped her glass and downed a healthy swallow. "And every time you say my name, *you* take a drink."

"I'm not going to play. This is no game."

"Sure, it is, *Cam*." She drank another gulp. "According to my father, it's called alcoholism."

Cam looked around for Jack. He was engrossed in a conversation with several men across the room.

"*Cam*, do you remember Jason?" She lifted her glass and drank, more it seemed, because it had been ten seconds since the last swallow than because she said Cam's name. "We broke up. I found pictures of some naked girl on his cell phone. He says it was his old girlfriend, and he forgot to erase them. That's a lie, don't you think? I said I'd delete them for him, but he grabbed the phone away. He didn't really want to get rid of them, did he? In fact," she leaned in close with a slushy voice that was a poor imitation of a whisper, and said, "I don't think she was an old girlfriend, do you?"

Cam said nothing.

"Well, do you?"

"I don't know." *Where the hell was Jack?*

Amelia continued in excruciating detail about the breakup, ending almost every sentence with a rhetorical question. "He wouldn't give me back my key, so I had to change the locks on my apartment. I had no other choice, did I?"

By then, Jack's cousin had finished her glass of John Daly and started on the one she brought for Cam. The two women sat in silence for a minute. Then as if a switch had been flipped, Amelia's expression changed from pathetic, boozy confidante to the calculating look of a mean girl.

Her red mouth stretched into a grotesque slash. "You're probably sitting here thinking you're better than me, aren't you? You're too smart to let a man get away with being a dick. But guess what, Cam?" The woman drank a healthy swallow. "You think you know, Jackson, but you don't. He's not who you think he is. You know that house of yours that burned down—"

"Amelia. Shut up."

Both women jumped. The second John Daly in Amelia's hand erupted into a geyser which dampened her, and some splashed on Cam. Uncle Carl stood behind his daughter, a look of fury so intense Cam worried for the drunken girl's safety.

"Daddy." Amelia set down the near empty glass and dabbed at her clothes with a used napkin from the table. "Look what you made me do."

Carl wrapped his hand around Amelia's upper arm and lifted her from the seat. "Come, it's time to go."

The young woman stumbled after him. Carl stopped after several steps and turned back to Cam. "Please accept my apologies. My daughter becomes impolite when she has had too much to drink."

Impolite or indiscreet?

Without a word of farewell to anyone, they left the room.

"Sorry. I didn't see Carl and Amelia with you." Jack bent toward Cam with his palms flat on the table. He sounded somewhat breathless. A hint of anxiety made his words sharp. "Are you okay?"

"I'm fine." She shook her head. "It was weird what just happened."

Jack sat in the seat Amelia vacated. "What?"

"Amelia was drunk and talking about her breakup with Jason, the guy she was with at the restaurant. Remember him?"

"I do. Go on."

"All of a sudden she became nasty." Cam pointed to Jack. "She said you are not who I think you are. Then she brought up something about my house burning down. That's when Carl told her to shut up and hustled her out of here. How does Amelia know about the arson?"

Jack thrust out his bottom lip and shrugged. "Dunno. Maybe Carl told her Castle bought the lot where your house burned down."

"Does she work at the firm?"

Jack's lip curled. "Work? Amelia doesn't work. She's a professional student who changes her major every time she gets close to graduation. Her father and mother will continue to subsidize her party girl lifestyle until she can find a husband." Jack stood and held out his hand to Cam. "Come on, let's mingle so I can show you off."

Cam rose as Jack tucked her hand between his elbow and body. As she followed him across the room, one thought repeated itself.

What was Amelia about to say?

Chapter 24

ON THE FIRST Saturday in April, Cam and Jack were planning to have dinner with his mother. They had a seven o'clock reservation at Ken Stewart's Grille in the nearby town of Hudson. Cam had heard the food was great but had never eaten there. The upscale restaurant was too pricey for her or the Colemans who tended to patronize places with two out of five dollar signs on Yelp reviews.

Cam headed upstairs to shower when her cell phone rang.

The caller was an unknown woman. "May I speak with the owner of C.C. Restorations, Cameron Coleman?"

"Speaking."

"This is Detective Vickie Holmes with the Akron Police Department."

Cam stopped on the landing. *What is this about? Gus? The Christmas thieves?*

"Ms. Coleman, I work in the narcotics unit."

What the hell? Drugs?

"Recently an individual was arrested for selling controlled substances. He claims he has knowledge of a house fire caused by arson. In exchange for reduced charges, he will trade his information."

"One of my properties was burned down last year."

"Yes, I know. I've been in contact with Jose Nunez, the investigator assigned to your case. You named another property owner as the one responsible. The arson report lists a …" There was a rustle of papers. "… a Gus Varsamis as a suspect. But the name given by our felon is Jack."

A shock wave ran through Cam. Her knees turned to jelly. "Jack?"

"Do you know this individual?"

Cam couldn't speak. Her voice was paralyzed.

"Ms. Coleman?"

"I-I know someone named Jack." A thought flashed through her mind. "But he wasn't even in the country when the house burned down."

"He may still be responsible. Crimes of this sort are often arranged when the perpetrator has a solid alibi."

"No. No way. Jack wouldn't do that. He loves …" She couldn't speak for several seconds.

"Ms. Coleman? Are you there?" Detective Holmes asked.

"Sorry."

"What were you saying?" the detective continued.

I was about to say he loves me. "He loves old houses. Jack would never destroy one."

"What is Jack's last name, and how can I contact him? Maybe he has additional information."

"He doesn't. I'm sure of it. Besides Jack is a common name. Your drug dealer could have just thrown it out there, and it happens to be someone I know."

"I can assure you, Ms. Coleman, any investigation would be done with discretion. All suspects are presumed innocent until proven guilty. You needn't worry, especially if your friend's not had anything to do with the crime."

"I just …" Cam's voice cracked with emotion.

"Ms. Coleman, if you are afraid of this person, your identity will be kept confidential."

Cam blew out an angry breath. "I'm not scared of Jack. Don't you have anything else other than the name?"

"Our informant claims he was contacted by someone he's known for years to arrange the arson. Jack is related to that individual. That's all we know right now."

"What kind of deal does this guy want?" *I doubt I'm going to like what I hear.*

"He won't be arrested for conspiracy to commit arson and the distribution charges will be knocked down to simple possession."

When Cam had told her father that Gus Varsamis was going to get probation for attacking her, he said, *the fucking criminals have more rights than law-abiding citizens.* Now this arsonist or arson broker wasn't even going to be charged? She remained silent.

Detective Holmes's voice softened. "I understand your frustration. I don't like it either. This lowlife only arranged or committed the arson for the money. The real criminal is whoever paid him. That's the person you want behind bars."

"Fine," Cam spat out. "I want to know who's behind this because it can't be Jack. Offer him the deal."

"Don't worry. We'll investigate thoroughly. There will be no deal if his story is bogus."

#

Jack picked her up an hour later. They drove to Ken Stewart's Grille to meet his mother. Cam gazed out the side window. Her phone conversation with Detective Holmes played in her head.

Jack touched her leg. "Is everything okay, luv? You haven't said much."

"I'm fine."

"I know something's on your mind."

Should I tell him someone named Jack has been accused of burning my house down? He didn't do it, so what will it matter? "Jeanine called today. She's having trouble doing a market analysis for The Harte Estate. There are no other comparable properties that have sold in the last six months. Her suggested listing price is less than I was hoping for."

"Will you make a profit?"

"Yes, but not as much as I expected. The real value's in the land. It's the same problem Susan Gardiner had. She could afford to wait three years to sell. I can't."

At the restaurant, Cam tried to be more animated with Jack's mother.

Despite her best efforts, Brooke gave her an earnest look. "What's wrong? You seem off tonight."

"I had some disappointing news from my realtor." She related the conversation with Jeanine.

Brooke took a sip of wine and looked at Cam over the rim of her glass. "You made a healthy profit on the land Castle Construction purchased by the university."

"Yes, I did. But no amount of money will compensate for the willful destruction of a beautiful house."

"I understand, however—"

"No, I don't think you do." Cam fixed Brooke with a hard stare. "There were architectural elements in that Queen Anne Victorian no one can ever replace. The oak staircase was custom built using no power tools. There were hundred-year-old windows with hand-blown pieces of cut glass. The fireplaces were decorated with original Pewabic tiles from the early 1900s. I lost a piece of history, and it was deliberately destroyed for someone else's financial gain."

No one said anything for several seconds. Jack and his mother exchanged a glance that seemed to convey a secret to which only they were privy. The meal continued with a strain between the three of them. They all requested take home boxes and didn't linger. Cam and Jack waved goodbye to his mother outside the restaurant and returned to The Harte Estate.

#

The subject of the arson was not broached again that weekend. Cam was torn where Jack was concerned. One part of her held an absolute conviction in his integrity and innocence. The other half reminded her that, when she was in love, her judgement of men tended to be faulty. Was she being manipulated by another con man? She worried that, if Jack was truly innocent, would her doubts and suspicions wound him? Or would she be the one to suffer the deepest cut?

When Jack left on Sunday evening to return to the condo, he hugged her close. "Remember I'll be in Michigan most of the week."

"I know."

He leaned back and eyed her. "Still not telling me what's wrong?"

He knows me so well. Cam made a decision. Some drug dealer's shady testimony wasn't going to affect their relationship any longer, no matter what the detective said.

She kissed him. "We'll talk about it when you get back on Friday. I promise."

#

On Tuesday, Detective Holmes called Cam. "Ms. Coleman, would you be able to meet me and the arson investigator at police headquarters today?"

Cam swallowed. "Do you have more information?"

The detective sidestepped her question. "Can you be here at four p.m.?"

When Cam arrived at police headquarters, she was escorted into an interview room. Eighteen minutes later and two minutes before her screw-this-I'm-leaving deadline, a woman entered. She had short red hair and an hourglass figure holding firm in jeans, a button-down shirt, and suit jacket.

"I'm Detective Holmes."

A thirty-something man with thick dark hair, olive complexion, and chocolate brown eyes followed her in. He held out his hand. "Hello, Ms. Coleman. Jose Nunez. I'm sorry for the delay. I just got out of a meeting that could have been handled with an email."

Cam was mollified, but the wait had amped her apprehension.

Detective Holmes laid a pen and folder on the table. "Let's get right to it. The guy we have in a cell at the county jail alleges he was not the one who actually set fire to your house. He claims he was contacted about the job by an acquaintance. We think she is also one of his customers."

"What kind of customer?"

"The kind that buys weed and Ecstasy. At least, that's what was on him when he was arrested."

"Did he tell you the name of the woman?"

"Yes." Holmes opened a file she had placed on the table.

The detective gave Cam a hard-eyed stare. An icy chill ran down her spine and turned into a breath-stopping glacier that slowed her response time to a crawl.

Before she could open her mouth and claim her innocence, Holmes spoke. "Amelia Townsend."

Cam winced at the mention of Jack's cousin.

Nunez no longer sounded friendly and apologetic. His voice was crisp and precise. "The woman told him that the homeowner wanted the insurance money. It was a simple case of arson-for-profit."

Cam's heart stopped. Now it was clear why they asked her to come to police headquarters. This was why she was made to wait in an interview room so long. They thought she was in collusion with Amelia. She was going to be arrested for arson.

Cam put her palms flat on the table and glared. "What the fuck is going on? I did not want to burn down my house. If Amelia said I did, she's a lying sack of shit. I was trying to save it. I promised the previous owner—"

Nunez held up his hand like a crossing guard. "Hold it, Ms. Coleman. We're not accusing you of anything."

"But you said—"

"The person who paid for the arson is a male relative of Ms. Townsend's. He's the one who claimed to be the owner of the house."

Cam slumped back in the chair and shook her head with weary resignation.

Detective Holmes consulted her notes. "Our perp addressed him as Mr. Townsend when they met because he thought the man had the same last name as Amelia. The individual said to call him Jack." The woman lifted her eyes and stared into Cam's. "So, do you know a Jack Townsend?"

"No. My friend's last name isn't Townsend." *Just his middle name is.*

"Does the man you know have any connection to Ms. Townsend?"

A tension headache throbbed just above Cam's left eyebrow. "He's Amelia's cousin."

She told them about Jack's apprenticeship and his connection to Castle Construction that now owned her former burned-down property. Holmes studied her with intense regard.

Cam stared at a spot on the wall behind the detective's head. "Jack and I have also been seeing each other."

Holmes glanced at Nunez. "By seeing each other, do you mean you're involved in a romantic relationship?"

Cam licked her lips and nodded.

Nunez leaned forward and with a gentle, coaxing tone said, "Ms. Coleman, what is your friend's last name?"

Cam tried to swallow, but a lump of unshed tears clogged her throat. At last, she croaked, "Reynolds."

Holmes asked for Jack's address, phone number, and place of employment. She wrote the information in her folder. She thanked Cam for her cooperation then rose to her feet.

The detective opened the interview room door. "We'll meet with Ms. Townsend and get her statement first. Then we'll contact Mr. Reynolds. Please don't share information about the investigation before we've had a chance to talk with them."

"I'm telling you, Jack had nothing to do with this." *I can't say the same for Amelia.*

"You don't know that for sure. We'll confirm if he's innocent. But if he is culpable, your warning could give him time to cover his tracks."

Chapter 25

JACK CALLED HER Thursday evening from his hotel room in Michigan. "I'm freezing my bloody nuts off up here. How can people live and work in weather like this?"

"Are you able to evaluate the site?"

"There's still snow on the ground in places up here. I was able to get the measurements and photos I need. What have you been up to?"

"Anthony and I have been stripping the old varnish off the window frames on the first floor."

"That sounds better than what I've been doing."

"Except your work pays more."

Jack laughed. "I've told you, luv, your fringe benefits more than make up for the money. In fact, I could use some of those perks right now to warm me up."

"When you get home, I'll make you forget all about the cold weather."

"How?"

She lay back on the bed with a wicked smile. "Well, you know that red chair in the other room?" It was a low-slung, armless upholstered seat once used by a harpist. "Imagine you're sitting on it naked. I walk towards you wearing only my black boots."

Jack's breathing sounded louder.

"I straddle you and lower myself onto you inch … by … wet … tight … inch." A soft groan came from the phone. "I ride you face-to-face until you're about to explode. Then I stand and turn around."

Jack spoke her name in a long, agonized whisper. "Stop, luv. I can't take any more."

When the call ended, instead of feeling lonely and horny, Cam was miserable. *Why didn't I warn him that the police might question him?*

#

Jack did not come to her house or contact her Friday evening. She left him a message. By late Saturday afternoon, she was frantic because every phone call went right to voice mail. Cam couldn't wait at home any longer. She'd check to see if Jack was at the condo or, if necessary, go to the police station. Neither Holmes nor Nunez were answering her calls. After changing clothes, she went downstairs and lifted her coat off the hook.

The kitchen door opened, and Jack entered.

He looked like he had just completed an arduous journey. His face was unshaven, his hair matted down in spots, and he wore a rumpled suit under his overcoat.

"Oh my God. Where have you been? Are you okay?" She dropped her jacket and ran to him.

His arms wrapped around her middle as the weight of his head lay on her shoulder. They stood in silence, alternately swaying in place and squeezing each other tight.

At last, Jack's hands fell away from her, and he stepped back with a weary smile. "You're not going to believe it. I was arrested and spent the night in jail."

Relief flooded Cam. "But they found out you weren't responsible, right?"

Jack's face hardened. "Are you first not going to ask what I was arrested for?"

Shit. She took his arm to led him to the kitchen table. "Come sit down, and tell me what happened."

Jack remained in place. With another tug, he followed like his feet were weighted down. Once seated, he said nothing. Cam waited.

Jack blew out a breath. "On Friday arvo, a woman detective named Holmes and another bloke showed up at my office. They asked me to go with them to answer questions 'bout your house fire. I told them I had no information. When I refused to leave, they read me my rights and said there was a warrant for my arrest. I was cuffed and taken to the police station."

Cam rubbed the base of her neck. "I don't understand. The detective said the drug dealer's story would be investigated before they talked to you."

"When did you hear this?"

"Tuesday."

Jack glared. "You've known since then and never said a word to me."

"They asked me not to." She lowered her gaze.

"What did they tell you about this?"

"A guy they arrested for selling drugs said someone named Jack paid him to have my house burned down. I told them you would never do that. But the dealer would only give more information if I agreed to let them offer him a deal."

Jack flinched as if he had been struck. "I can't believe you said nothing to me all week."

"Actually, the detective called me for the first time the week before." Cam spoke in a rush. "She said if you didn't do anything there was nothing to worry about. But if I warned you and you were guilty, you could—"

"Bloody hell, Cam. I wasn't guilty."

"I know. I told them you weren't even in the country at the time of the fire. Holmes said that might be your alibi. She pressed me for your name, but I refused to say more."

Jack's eyes narrowed. "What changed your mind?"

Cam sighed. "They told me the person who contacted their informant was your cousin. Her relative, named Jack, paid for the arson. I've been trying to get in touch with you since yesterday. I decided you had a right to know Amelia was claiming you were the one who paid to have my house burned down."

Jack leaned forward and put his head in his hands. "I'm not surprised that girl would do something this underhanded then lie 'bout it. Like father, like daughter. What I can't get over is that you didn't say anything to me."

"I wanted to but when they told me Amelia was involved and …" Cam inhaled. "Well, Townsend is your middle name."

He lifted his head and his eyes flashed blue sparks. "It doesn't matter what my bloody name is. You should know I would never commit arson."

Cam raised the volume of her voice to match his. "Put yourself in my shoes. It was just too coincidental. My house burns down. You accept a position at a company you said you'd never work for. I finally agree to sell Castle the land they'd been trying to get for months. Then I find out Amelia and a relative, named Jack, hired the arsonist. What was I supposed to think?"

He jumped to his feet and paced to the other end of the kitchen. "You think it's a bloody big mistake because you know me and love me."

Like I knew and loved Oliver? It was as if the words rose from the top of her head in a dialogue bubble.

Jack wiped his hand across his mouth. "I am *not* the whacker who stole from you and left you at the altar."

"I know that. Please, come back and sit down. We need to talk about this. Please."

Jack returned to his chair and sat with his elbows on his knees. She waited for him to speak.

Cam leaned forward to catch his eye. "What happened after they took you to police headquarters?"

His jaw clenched. "I called Mum and her lawyer came. He told me to say nothing to the police." He sat up straight, his eyes drilling into hers. "They put me in a photo lineup but didn't show it to the bloke until this morning. I guess they didn't want to disturb his beauty sleep. Instead I spent the night in a cell. I was told about an hour ago that I was free to go. Their drug dealer couldn't identify me. The dickhead who paid him for the arson was an older man with gray hair."

Older? Gray hair? "Oh, shit."

Jack barked an ugly laugh. "Yes. My dear Uncle *Carl* Townsend used my name instead of his. All charges against me have been dropped."

"Did they arrest Amelia and her father?"

"Dunno. All I care is that I'm cleared."

Cam heaved a heavy sigh. "I knew it couldn't be you."

Jack's voice was low and frosty. "Did you now? You still gave them my name but."

Cam gave a slight shake of her head. "So they could rule you out. They wanted to know who Jack Townsend was."

"You thought I told the arsonist only my first and middle names?"

"I didn't know what to think. I gave them your real name because I hoped you were being falsely accused."

"You hoped?"

"Yeah, I hoped it wasn't you."

Jack gave her a long look then rose to his feet. His hand disappeared into the pocket of his overcoat, emerged, and slapped the tabletop like rifle shot. Cam jumped.

His key to the house lay there.

He was halfway to the back door when Cam leapt from the chair and ran after him. She grabbed his arm and, for a step or two, he dragged her along the kitchen floor behind him. The struggle ceased when he turned the knob.

"Jack, please, wait. I didn't know you would be arrested. I was sure you'd be cleared immediately."

He turned around, looking sad and defeated. "It's over, Cam. I can't be with someone who doesn't believe in me, no matter what others say. Maybe you'll always have trust issues. I refuse to prove my integrity to you."

He pulled his sleeve free of her grasp and walked out the door.

#

Over the next week, Cam sent Jack several emails to explain her actions, in various repetitions from lighthearted and casual, to stern and solemn, then groveling and desperate.

She asked him to reconsider and expressed her love. After the sixth one went unanswered, she stopped. Daily texts begged his forgiveness. He didn't respond to those either. She left messages on his phone and even tried contacting him at work. After ten days, she went from contrite and humble to unrepentant and angry.

Her final text read, *I'm done. I will never contact you again for any reason. FYI, I don't have trust issues. I'm just cautious of being fucked over.*

When her parents, Anthony, and Jeanine noticed Jack's absence, Cam told them they broke up. She didn't say why. Her standard reply was that it just didn't work out.

Detective Holmes called the week following Jack's release to inform her they arrested Carl Townsend for solicitation of arson. He was lawyered up and only spent a few hours in custody. His attorney advised him to not speak to them.

Detective Holmes asked, "Do you have any questions, Ms. Coleman?"

"Just one. Did you arrest Carl at Castle Construction and parade *him* past everyone in handcuffs?"

A beat of silence followed. "No. His lawyer called and brought him in. I'm sorry if Mr. Reynolds was inconvenienced, but we were just doing our job."

"Just so you know, I plan to inconvenience the hell out of Carl Townsend. Unlike your drug pedaling arsonist, I will *not* agree to any deal. I demand Jack's uncle be prosecuted to the fullest extent of the law. I want him to pay."

For the first time in his lying, cheating, assaulting life.

#

Cam prepared The Harte Estate to be put on the market. The flurry of work helped sublimate the pain from her broken heart. She cleaned, polished, or did physical labor until late at night then fell into bed exhausted. With Anthony's help, she moved furniture from her storage unit days before the listing was scheduled to go active. Some rooms would have to remain bare. She couldn't afford professional stagers for the eight-thousand-square-foot house or even the smaller gatehouse.

Anthony folded up mover blankets. "How does someone with no home collect as much furniture as you?"

Cam wiped her brow with the back of her hand. "I inherited a lot of it from my grandparents. Sometimes there were pieces left behind in old houses I bought. If my dad came across nice antiques, we would barter a trade. One day I'll have a house of my own for all this."

They headed to A to Z Salvage where she had unsold items on consignment. Cam's mother sat behind the front counter.

Anthony removed his cap. "Hello, Mrs. Coleman."

"Hi, Mom. Are Dad and Adam here?"

Abigail pointed in the general direction of the warehouse. "They're getting some columns down from the second-floor mezzanine."

Her mother referred to a pyramid of fiberglass-reinforced polymer columns, each weighing about five hundred pounds. Cam had manned the forklift when her father and brother stored them on the upper level decking.

"Do you mean those sixteen footers?"

"Yes. Someone ordered four of them. Do you need help with something?"

"No. Anthony and I are going to load up some of my consignment pieces to stage the house."

"Let me know what I can delete from inventory."

The hum of an electric motor came near when Cam opened the office door. Adam drove the forklift past them. Cam waved then motioned Anthony to follow her to where her things were stored. She selected a bed frame, bookcase, library table, and two dressers. They cleared a path and had just loaded one of the dressers onto a furniture dolly when her father's shout echoed through the warehouse.

"Watch out!"

A screech rent the air like a million ten penny nails scratched against a hard surface. Someone screamed in pain. There was the clatter of an aluminum ladder hitting concrete.

Cam ran and yelled to Anthony. "Call 911."

When she turned the corner, she stopped dead. Her father lay on his side, motionless on the warehouse floor. Blood seeped around his head. An extension ladder lay across him like a macabre teeter-totter. His chest rose and fell with shallow breaths. A fluted column, two feet in diameter, was strapped to the raised forklift mast. One end jutted out precariously. Adam was out of sight, but groans came from the mezzanine's upper deck.

Anthony skidded around the corner. He looked in horror at her father's body.

Cam grabbed one end of the ladder. "Don't move him. Help me put this up there." She pointed to the open double-wide gate in the safety railing.

Abigail appeared. "Oh, my God, Zane."

Cam set down her end of the ladder and blocked her mother. "Mom, go bring the EMT's here."

"But—"

"Go."

Her mother ran.

Anthony leaned the ladder against the second floor. "I'll go up."

"No. I will. You back up the forklift. Lower the column." She glanced at the broken body of her father. "Be careful."

When Cam's head cleared the steel deck, it was as she suspected. One of the decorative pillars had rolled off onto her brother. Adam lay on his back. His hips were pinned to the floor.

He turned his head as Cam stepped off the ladder. "Don't."

Another column perched near the edge, half off the stack. A slight bobble could send it crashing onto her brother's legs and ankles.

Adam's breathing was shallow. "Wait … help."

She moved closer. The ratchet straps which had bound the pile together now lay like dead snakes on the floor.

Anthony's head appeared. "What next?"

"Come up here."

Once he was on the mezzanine, Anthony moved without instruction to the rear of the stack and picked up a strap from the floor. Cam leaned forward, careful to not bump the protruding column. Anthony interlocked his hooked end with hers. She raised and lowered the ratchet handle. The webbing tightened. They moved to the next strap. When the column was secured, sirens wailed outside.

Abigail's panicked voice sounded from below. "They're over here."

Soon the area filled with emergency personnel. Cam and Anthony stepped aside. Her father was rolled onto a back board. The right side of his face was a bloody mess. He was whisked away in the first ambulance. At the same time, firemen used airbags and a hydraulic pump to lift the column off

Adam. Two EMT's slid him from underneath. He screamed and passed out.

Cam covered her mouth. Tears rolled down her cheeks. When the second ambulance left, sirens blaring, she looked around like a survivor who had just emerged unscathed from a scene of devastation.

Her mother's voice snapped her out of the daze. "Cameron Quinn Coleman, get down here. We're needed at the hospital."

Chapter 26

AT SIX P.M., Cam sent Sasha and the baby home. She promised to call her as soon as Adam was out of recovery. In the waiting area, she paced the room and hallway. In contrast, her vibrant, bubbly mother sat in unnatural stillness like a living statue, frozen in time and place.

Jeanine entered, hugged Cam, and sat next to Abigail. "I came as soon as I heard. How are they?"

Cam looked at the clock for the hundredth time. "Adam had surgery. His pelvis broke where the acid … acetab … It's the place where the head of his femur goes into the joint. Luckily, his leg bone didn't break. He won't need a hip replacement."

Jeanine cast an uneasy glance at too-quiet Abigail. "And your dad?"

"We're waiting to talk to his doctors."

Jeanine patted Abigail's hands which were clenched in her lap. "Mrs. Coleman, we're going to get something to drink. Do you want anything?"

In slow motion, Cam's mother shook her head like her neck was rusted in place.

Jeanine stood. "I'll bring you hot tea."

She and Cam walked to the elevator. Jeanine punched the down button. "What are you not saying about your dad?"

"He has a head injury. That's all we know. The last we heard he still hadn't regained consciousness."

"But Adam is going to be okay, right?"

Cam rubbed her eyes. "The doctor who operated on him warned us he'll have a limp until his muscles heal. If there's permanent nerve damage, he might be in a wheelchair the rest of his life."

"Don't worry. He's young and strong. Doctors always want to prepare you for a worst-case scenario. I'm sure he'll recover without a problem."

They sat at a small table in the hospital café. Cam sipped the coffee she ordered. "Anthony and I almost had the house ready for sale. I don't know when I'll be able to get it done now."

"What can I do to help?"

"My dad and Adam won't be able to work for weeks, months." *If they recover.* "I'll need to run A to Z and make sure their bills get paid. Selling The Harte Estate would be the best thing that could happen."

"Don't worry about the house. I'll take care of everything."

"Thank you."

When they returned upstairs, Jeanine handed a Styrofoam cup to Abigail. "Drink up, Mrs. Coleman. You'll feel better." She gave Cam tight hug before she left. "Keep in touch."

#

Thirty minutes later, Cam and her mother met with the neurologist who had done a CT scan on Zane.

The doctor spoke in clipped tones like he was delivering a message he had already repeated several times that day. "Mr. Coleman has sustained a contracoup injury."

Cam blinked. "A contra what?"

"His brain bounced off his skull on the left and rebounded on the right. This caused bruising on both hemispheres."

Abigail's voice quivered. "Will he wake up?"

"In time."

Next, they met with the orthopedic surgeon who had worked on Adam and evaluated Zane. Dr. Whipple's large hand enveloped Cam's completely.

She spoke aloud without thinking. "You have the paws of a bricklayer."

The doctor laughed. "It helps when I have to wrestle bones into place."

"Thank you for operating on my brother."

"You're welcome. I've just looked at your dad's X-rays. He fractured the head of his left humerus and clavicle."

Abigail's eyes widened with the new vocabulary words. "What are those?"

"He broke his upper arm and collarbone. We'll need to put them in a sling and swath to restrict movement for several weeks. He'll be prescribed physical therapy."

Their final consultation was with the maxillofacial surgeon who was a petite Pakistani woman. Her English was accented with a sing-song cadence. "Mr. Coleman suffered a closed fracture of his lower jaw. In my opinion, the injury will require surgery once he regains consciousness. He has a veddy long laceration near his jaw line. I will use that to do my repair and suture it nicely."

An hour after the last consultation, an ICU nurse informed them Zane was conscious again. "His doctor approved pain medication which has him sleeping now. You can see him for five minutes."

When they approached his bed, Abigail put her hand over her mouth. Cam had her arm wrapped firmly around her mother's shoulders. Her own knees wobbled. They stared for several minutes at the man who was once the strongest, most vibrant male in the family.

Zane now looked like a corpse. His skin was the same ashy-gray color of his short haircut. The gash on his face was swollen. He had tubes going into various parts of his body. Several machines around his bed flashed digital displays and beeped.

Cam laid her hand on his arm. It was warm. Abigail kissed her husband's forehead. She murmured with her lips against his skin. Then she stepped aside and headed for the door, dabbing at her eyes with a tissue.

Cam put her mouth close to her father's ear. "I love you, Dad. Don't worry. I'll take care of everything and everyone. Just get better."

#

The day after the accident, Zane was moved to a regular hospital room. His jaw had been strapped to restrict movement until surgery. He was only able to nod or shake his head in response. His coloring had improved. The prognosis for a full recovery was good.

Abigail laid her hand on his arm. "Darling, do you remember what happened?"

Head shake. He looked at Cam.

"Either a column on the stack bumped into the one on the forklift or vice versa." She sighed. "Whatever happened first, the one on the forklift swung out and knocked you off the ladder."

Her mother ran a hand over her husband's hair. "Your humor is broken."

Zane frowned.

Cam smiled. "Your humerus is the bone in your upper arm."

Abigail nodded. "Your collarbone is broken, too. It's why your arm is in a slingshot."

Zane glanced down at the double bandage then looked at Cam with raised eyebrows.

"It's called a sling and swath. The swath is the Velcro band around your chest. You also have a concussion and were unconscious for about six hours yesterday."

Abigail nodded. "They did a CAT scan. The doctor said you have contraband bouncing around in your head."

Zane's eyes moved from his wife to his daughter.

Cam rubbed her nose and smiled. "He called it a contracoup injury. It means you bruised both sides of your brain."

An older nurse in pink scrubs breezed into the room. "I need to check your eyes, Mr. Coleman."

Cam's father rolled them to the ceiling. His lips tightened into a thin line.

"Now, now. You know, we need to do this every hour for two days." She leaned closer and stared at his pupils. "Looks good." She turned to Abigail. "Is he oriented?"

"Uh, I don't think so. He's mostly English and German."

Cam jumped in. "He understands and answers questions just fine."

The nurse left and Abigail stared after her, shaking her head. "Why would she ask that? The swelling makes only his one eye look Chinese."

Before Cam could explain, Zane pointed to the bandage which wrapped his head.

Cam said, "You also fractured your jaw when you fell. The doctor said once you're cleared by the neurologist for surgery, you'll get it repaired. You'll be able to eat and talk after that."

Zane raised the index finger of his good hand in the air. He drew a letter A, then D, another A, and an M followed by a question mark.

Cam laid her hand on her father's sheet-covered knee. "When the column on the stack was jarred loose, it knocked down Adam and fell on him."

Zane grimaced.

"He has a fractured pelvis. They did surgery last night, and he's doing fine. Sasha is with him. A neighbor is watching AJ."

Zane made a walking gesture with the two fingers of his right hand.

"The doctor said Adam should walk again. He'll need physical therapy just like you're going to need for your arm and shoulder."

Zane blew out a gust of air from the side of his mouth and waved his free hand in a dismissive gesture.

Abigail came to life and pointed her finger at her husband's face. "You listen to me, Zane Coleman. You will do any exercises the doctor and therapists order, just like Adam will have to. At least, you'll be able to walk out of here on your own two feet and go home. *My son will be in a wheelchair and have to spend time at a rehab center. He won't be walking again without help for weeks.* So, I don't want to hear any crap about physical therapy being a waste of time. Is that clear?"

Zane nodded at his wife who continued to glare at him. After a few moments, he raised his finger and drew an A, then a line from left to right, followed by a Z. His wife said nothing. Her brow wrinkled. Both parents looked to Cam.

She gave them a weak smile. "Don't worry about A to Z. The warehouse has been closed since yesterday, but Anthony is going to open it the rest of the week. I'll do the paperwork and billing. My house is ready to sell, so I'll run the business until you and Adam are back at work." *I'll do my best to keep us from losing what we've all worked hard for.*

#

On the drive home, Cam received a call from Aunt Marjorie. She updated her on Zane and Adam's condition. "Things are looking a lot better than they did yesterday."

"I'm driving to Akron tomorrow morning to take care of the baby. I should be there around nine. Let Sasha know. I'll stay in her guestroom as long as needed."

"Thank you. I know both she and Adam will appreciate it. The neighbor isn't able to watch AJ every day. I thought I'd have to bring him to the warehouse with me."

"You can't do that. Besides, Sasha needs to concentrate on her husband right now. And Lord knows Abigail will have her hands full with Zane. I'll take care of the little guy."

#

On Friday, almost two weeks after the accident, Cam met Anthony at A to Z Salvage after visiting her father at home and her brother at the rehab facility.

She gave her assistant a hug. "I really appreciate all you've done."

A flush crept across his cheeks. "Ah geez, Boss, it's nothing. You and your folks have done more for me and my family than we can ever repay."

At closing time, Cam bade him goodbye, set the alarm, and locked the building. When she pulled into the driveway of The Harte Estate, she braked hard. Three box trucks with the names of two interior design firms and a staging company were coming toward her. She pulled to the side and the drivers waved as they passed. An unknown minivan and Jeanine's Lexus were in front of the carriage house. When Cam entered the main house, she stumbled to a stop inside the vestibule.

Islands of large Oriental carpets covered the foyer's hardwood floors. An octagonal oak table sat in the middle with an ornate floral arrangement. Farther back, a plush sofa and two leather armchairs faced each other with the soft glow of lamps on end tables. A showroom of furniture was placed in the living room. Satiny drapes hung from the iron curtain rods which came with the house. She gasped when she opened the leaded glass doors to the dining room. A mahogany table with twelve chairs was laid with china and crystal.

Footsteps sounded on the main staircase. Cam returned to the foyer. Jeanine and her mother descended the steps.

When they reached the bottom, Tina spotted her. "Oh, look. Cam's here."

Jeanine spread her arms wide. "Do you like what we've done with the place?"

Tears blurred Cam's vision. "Where? How? It's fantastic, but I can't afford all this."

Jeanine curled her hand and rubbed her fingernails in a polishing motion against her shoulder. "*I* called in favors. Rubber City Staging is giving you three months free furniture. So are Chez Delmonico and House of LaRose. I promised to tell everyone that, except for your antiques, all the furnishings are for sale. Now I just have to get the place under contract. By the way, the first open house is Sunday."

Tina looped Cam's arm through hers. "Come and see the library, then we'll take you upstairs. I had so much fun telling those men where to put everything."

Jeanine followed them down the hall. "I'm going to get every qualified buyer through this place if I have to kidnap them or have a showing at five in the morning."

Cam envisioned being awakened in the middle of the night as Jeanine flipped on the light, pointed out the natural woodwork, and told prospective home buyers to ignore the woman in bed. "I'll pack up my things and move to the loft tomorrow. If I'm going to be running my dad's business, I might as well stay there and be out of your hair."

#

On Saturday morning, Cam was in the kitchen cleaning out cupboards. Each dish, pot, or pan she packed was a painful reminder of when Jack used them. She stared at a browned plate. It was one of the dishes burned in the oven. Jack had worked for fifteen minutes to scour off all the crusted bits.

"Just throw it away," she had told him.

"Am I not hearing right? This from the woman who believes every old thing is worth saving."

"First of all, it's not old. And second, it's just a plate."

"Its value is in its function. It's not broken and needs to be made useful again. Like this old house."

In that moment, early in their relationship, Cam had fallen a little bit in love with Jack.

Her reverie was interrupted by the ring of the doorbell. She laid the plate on the countertop and went into the foyer. Her breath whooshed from her throat when she opened the heavy front door.

Jack's mother stood there.

Chapter 27

CAM MADE NO move to unlock the screen door. She and Brooke stared at each other like enemy soldiers across a demilitarized zone.

Finally, the older woman cocked her head and raised her brows. "Can we talk? Please."

After another moment of hesitation, Cam unlocked the handle and pushed the door open. Brooke walked into the front hall then stutter-stepped to a halt.

Her head swiveled around the decorated room. "Oh. My. Goodness." She turned in a complete circle until she faced Cam. "This looks fantastic. I had no idea it could be this beautiful. You must be so proud of what you've accomplished."

Cam's voice was flat. "This is the staging for the open house tomorrow."

Brooke's face fell. "How can you sell this place?"

"That's the whole reason for the renovation. I don't allow myself to develop feelings for the properties I work on." *Except I did for this one.*

"Well, you have done an amazing job. I can see why Jack was so impressed with you."

A stab of pain pierced Cam's heart. "What do you want to talk about, Mrs. Keller?"

The use of her proper name wiped the smile from Brooke's face. She indicated the nearby furniture with her open palm. "May we sit?"

Cam nodded and took a seat in one of the leather armchairs. Jack's mother sat across from her on the sofa.

Brooke leaned back against the plush upholstery. "My purpose for coming today was to discuss my brother, Carl."

Here comes the pity pitch. Cam crossed her arms.

"I don't know how much Jack has told you about his uncle but this latest blunder—"

"Blunder?" Cam turned her ear toward Brooke as if she hadn't heard her. "He *paid* to have my house burned down. He was *arrested* for solicitation of arson."

"You're right. He committed—"

"A felony."

"Yes." Brooke took a deep breath. "As a result, the board of Castle Construction has terminated Carl's employment."

Good. He deserves it. An errant memory of something Jack had said skittered across Cam's thoughts. "If I recall, the plan was to force mandatory retirement on him when he turned fifty-five."

"Jack told you?"

"He said it was one of the reasons he was willing to work for the company."

Brooke nodded. "Yes. Carl has been forced to retire."

"So, he wasn't actually *terminated*, was he?"

"No. But he has had to sell his shares of Castle Construction and have no further say in the company."

"And who bought his shares?"

Brooke studied Cam as if she had a new respect for her. "I did."

"I see. Now Carl can play golf at Portage Country Club whenever he likes, collect his pension, and has a shitload of money in his pocket. Well, that'll teach him a lesson."

Brooke frowned. "I didn't come here to argue. I want the same thing as you. Carl needs to pay for his actions."

Cam snorted. *Like that was going to happen.*

"A good portion of the money he's received from the sale of stock will go to pay his lawyer. His only earnings from now until the end of his life will be his pension unless he gets another job, which he won't. My guess is he will find himself a wealthy wife to support him after his legal battles are over. His lawyer will try to cut a deal with the prosecutor in exchange for a guilty plea. I urge you to reject any offer which does not include jail time."

Cam uncrossed her arms. "You *want* your brother locked up?"

"I want him held accountable. It's likely too late for him to learn from the consequence, but he needs to suffer a real punishment for once in his goddamned life."

Carl has hurt her also. "If it makes you feel any better, I already told the police I would accept no deal on the charges. I want him to pay for what he did, and not with cash. Whether he will be convicted and serve time is up to the justice system, not me."

Brooke sighed and flipped the ends of her silvery hair over her shoulders. "Actually, a punishment for him right now is the loss of power. He was always Castle Construction's golden boy. But after several of his underhanded shenanigans left the company financially responsible, the board voted to limit his control. I took over at that time. It was a huge blow to Carl's ego. Now his termination, I mean, forced retirement is another hit. He will claim, as you said, that now he can improve his golf game. But, in reality, he wants power, not free time." Brooke paused. "Do you plan to sue Castle for the arson?"

I hadn't thought of it, but I'm not going to let Brooke know that. "I haven't decided."

Jack's mother leaned forward in her seat. "Before you hire a lawyer, let me try to work out a financial agreement with you first. I would rather pay you the money which would go to attorneys and avoid more bad publicity for the company. I promise to be more than fair."

Cam said nothing. She had been compensated for the house fire by her insurance company and from the sale of the land to Castle. All she wanted right now was for the Silver Fox to be punished for what he did.

"Can we talk about you and Jack now?"

The question snapped Cam to attention. She jumped to her feet. "I have lots of work to do before the open house tomorrow. I think we're done here."

Brooke stared at her for a moment before she stood. Cam walked over to the front door and waited. When Jack's mother drew near, she opened it.

Brooke exited, stopped, and turned around. "My son doesn't want to discuss you either. But I'll tell you what I told him. It's okay to let go of your pride for someone or something you love. But it's not okay to lose someone you love because of your pride. Keep that in mind, Cam, and thank you for talking with me."

#

On the Saturday before Memorial Day, Cam stopped at her parents' house. She brought flats of impatiens. "I got flowers for your beds out front. I'll try to get them in this afternoon. If not, I'll finish tomorrow."

Abigail took her daughter by the arm and led her to a chair at the kitchen table. "Sit. Have you had anything to eat today?"

"Yes, Mom. I need to get this done then check on Adam and Sasha. Do you think she would want me to plant flowers at their place? With helping Adam and running after AJ, landscaping is the last thing on her mind." Cam tried to rise.

Abigail pushed down on her daughter's shoulders. "They're fine. You need to take a break."

"But the flowers—"

"Will wait. Besides, I want to plant them myself. Your father can sit out there with me. He could use a little sun. You, on the other hand," she grasped Cam's chin and moved her head from side to side, "are worn to the bone. If you don't slow down, you're going to have a metal breakdown."

Mental, Mom, not metal.

Living on fewer hours of sleep each night gave Cam a somewhat sedated feeling. It allowed her to detach herself from the sadness of losing Jack and her pitiable life in the warehouse loft. She had no time to feel, to analyze her situation, to attach importance or significance to anything except caring for her family.

Abigail pulled out a chair and sat down. "I want to talk to you about A to Z's finances."

"I've got everything handled."

"I know you do. But how much of your own money have you put into it since the accident?"

"Not much. I've just been covering the utilities and things."

"Cam, there's money in the bank."

"But sales are down without Dad and Adam there. I want you to have a cushion when you come back."

"You have expenses too. Are you even paying yourself a salary, from either C.C. Restorations or A to Z?"

"I'm okay for now. And you're right. I am a little tired. I'll go back to the loft and take a nap." She kissed her mother's cheek. "You don't have to worry about me, but I love that you do."

She left before her mother realized how jittery she was with fatigue and nerves. *Please, Jeanine. Sell The Harte Estate soon. Very soon.*

#

Her father and mother returned to work a week later. The doctor gave approval for Zane to spend four hours a day in the warehouse office with limited physical activities until his next appointment. He no longer had a headache or double vision. He sat in his office, answered the phone, and checked out potential salvage sites online. Adam and Sasha returned to A to Z three weeks later. As predicted, her brother still walked with a limp but had been cleared for everything except heavy lifting.

Cam and Anthony were outside the warehouse two days later. They had just loaded a pedestal sink and cast-iron bathtub into the truck for delivery the next day.

Anthony pulled down the rollup door and inserted the padlock. "You've been quiet today, Boss. Are you trying to find a way to tell me I'm out of a job?"

Cam shuffled back a step. "How did you know?"

"I've been expecting it."

"I'm so sorry."

She had agonized over this conversation for the past week. No matter how she juggled her finances, there was no way to keep Anthony on the payroll. If The Harte Estate didn't sell, she only had enough in cash reserves to cover the next six months.

"Hey, don't worry. Every new skill you've taught me I've put on my resume. It's a lot more impressive than a year ago."

Cam raised her eyes to meet his. "I can keep you on until the end of next week. My dad and I will give you great references."

"Actually, I have an interview on Friday morning at nine o'clock."

"That's wonderful. Just come in to work when you're done."

#

Cam was by herself at A to Z on Friday and expected Anthony to return from his interview at any time. Her mother and father were at a doctor's appointment. Adam and Sasha had just left to check out a century-old barn in Holmes County. When the bell at the front entrance sounded, Cam glanced at the CCTV video feed. It was Anthony. From his glum expression, it didn't appear the interview went well. When he entered the office, he removed his baseball cap and slapped it against his thigh.

Cam tried to catch his eye. "How did it go?"

In a flat monotone, he said, "I got the job."

Cam grinned, but Anthony still appeared unhappy. "What's wrong?"

Her assistant stared down at the countertop. "It's with Castle Construction."

Cam said nothing for several moments. *If anyone knows what a hardworking and trustworthy guy Anthony is, it's Jack.*

Her assistant rubbed the back of his neck. "I'm sorry."

"What for? Like in any other business, it's not necessarily *what* you know as much as *who* you know. If I had been in your shoes and needed a job, the first person I'd call would be Jack."

"You don't mind?"

Cam ignored his question. "What are you going to be doing?"

At last, Anthony sported a smile. "To start with, pretty much what I'm doing with you. But, get this, after a three-month probationary period, I'll get full benefits. For a little extra each month, I can have a family health plan and add my mom and sister."

"That's great news." *It's way more than I could ever offer him.*

"They want me to get my general contractor's license. The company will pay for the training."

"The pay is good?"

Anthony's smile wavered. "Uh, yeah."

"More than I'm paying you?"

He scratched his cheek. "Uh-huh."

"Glad to hear it."

"Um, Boss?" He shifted his weight from one foot to the other. "I talked with Jack when I got there." Anthony swallowed hard. "He, uh, asked why I wasn't going to be working with you anymore. I told him you had shut down C.C. Restorations to help out here. He got pretty upset after he found out about the accident."

The chime sounded. Cam glanced at the security monitor. Zane and Abigail came inside. She turned back to Anthony. "When do you start the new job?"

"I have to fill out paperwork, have a physical, and take a drug test next week. They want me the Monday after that."

She hopped off the stool and came around the counter. "I plan to work your ass off until then. Let's tell my parents your good news."

Chapter 28

THAT NIGHT AFTER A to Z closed, Cam heated up a Stouffer's frozen entrée in the microwave. The doorbell to the warehouse sounded. She checked the CCTV. *Let it be Jeanine with a sales contract.*

It was Jack.

He looked around and rang the bell again.

I might as well get this over with. She crossed the warehouse, disarmed the alarm, and unlocked the deadbolt.

Jack stepped back as the door swung out. Cam had never seen him in a business suit before. His charcoal gray jacket and pants were professionally tailored, worn with a white long-sleeved dress shirt, and a maroon striped tie. His unruly hair had been tamed, but an errant curl flopped toward his forehead.

With one hand on the door and the other on the jamb, she schooled her face into nonchalance and raised her eyebrows. "What do you want, Jack?"

He studied her. "May I come in and talk?"

"There's nothing to talk about."

He eyed the barrier she created with her body. "Why didn't you call me?"

With deliberate obtuseness, Cam replied, "I did and left messages. I also sent texts for more than a week."

"I never ... You're talking 'bout after we ... I meant after the accident. Why did you not tell me what happened?"

"My last text promised I wouldn't contact you again for any reason. Since you never answered me, I figured that's what you wanted."

He ran his fingers through his hair. "I understand. But I like your father and brother. I could have found some way to help. You talked with my mum. Why did you not tell her?"

"She doesn't know my family. Besides, she said you didn't want to talk about me."

"I didn't want to discuss our relationship with her, but she could have told me 'bout the accident." Once again, Jack scanned her from head to toe. "There are dark circles under your eyes and you're thinner."

"Listen, I appreciate you hiring Anthony. I hated to let him go but with Dad and Adam returning to work …" She shrugged. "Well, you know how it is."

"Your loss is our gain. He'll be a great asset to the Castle team." Jack cleared his throat. "Are you going to get C.C. Restorations running again?"

"That's my plan."

"Cam, I—"

"My dinner is getting cold, and I have a bunch of paperwork to do. I've got to go."

Before she could shut the door, he grabbed it. "Wait. I want you to know I'm sorry."

He stepped closer. His nearness made her uncomfortable. It was like triggers in her body ignited as the distance between them closed. Unlike with Oliver, Cam didn't hate Jack for breaking her heart. She was just sad.

He bent his head to look into her eyes. "I shouldn't have taken my anger out on you. When the detectives interviewed Amelia, she said it was her cousin, not her father, who hired the arsonist. That's why I was arrested. It was not because you gave them my name. They've charged her with obstruction and lying to the police."

A feeling of satisfaction warmed Cam. *Good. The bitch deserves to be punished as well.*

He tilted his head to the side. "Mum told me how great The Harte Estate looks. How's the sale going?"

Cam looked down at the ground. "It's ... um ... slow. Jeanine is working to drum up buyers, but it's a unique property. The number of people who would be interested in a place that size is small."

"Are you going to be all right financially until it sells?"

Cam flashed him a weak smile. "Sure. No problem. I can wait until the right offer comes along."

Her bogus bravado didn't seem to fool him, but he didn't question her further. His eyes softened. "Cam, I was wondering if we could—"

"No, Jack."

"You didn't let me finish."

She lowered her head and stared at her feet. "It doesn't matter."

He didn't speak for several seconds. "Is there nothing I can do?"

When Cam looked up at him, his expression made her heart beat faster, but past experience taught her that the misery of a failed romance didn't just hit and run. It stayed with you for months, sometimes years. She couldn't risk another broken heart this soon. "I don't think so."

He released the edge of the door. She stepped inside and shut it behind her.

#

A week later, she and Jeanine were having lunch when a male voice with an Australian accent said, "I have an order for pickup. The name's Reynolds."

Cam stiffened in her seat. She glanced up from her menu. Apparently, her friend didn't hear anything over the din in the restaurant. Cam's gaze shifted to the bar area.

Jack stood there in a navy-blue business suit and looked like he had just finished a GQ photo shoot. The young female bartender handed him a bag with a big smile. He thanked her and turned to leave. At that moment, he looked left and made eye contact with Cam.

Shit.

She stopped herself from ducking behind the menu. As Jack approached the table, she said, "Jeanine, look who's here."

Her friend glanced up as Jack stopped next to them.

"'Allo, Cam."

She nodded. "Jack."

He turned to Jeanine. "'Allo. Nice to see you again."

"You too. Would you like to join us?"

He held up his take-out bag. "Just picked up some tucker. I'll be eating it as I drive to Cleveland."

Cam sat in silence. With Jack near her, heat steamed beneath her clothes. Her jeans and sleeveless tee-shirt had become like an electric blanket. If it wasn't so cliché, she would have picked up her menu to fan herself.

Jeanine flashed a rueful smile. "Another time then."

Their waitress slowed her drive-by refilling of water glasses. She pointed her chin at Jack. "Are you joining them?"

He shook his head. "Can't today."

The waitress turned to Cam and Jeanine. "I'll be right back to take your orders."

Jack gave them an innocuous farewell smile. "I'm off. Enjoy your lunch."

As soon as he was out the door, the counter girl and another waitress, who had tracked Jack on his table detour, clasped hands to their chests, and rolled their eyes, whispering and giggling.

Cam smiled at their reaction. Then the realization that he was no longer in her life, although he was still planted deep in her heart, made her head drop. She stared blindly at the menu.

"Cam?" Jeanine reached across the table and laid her hand on Cam's arm. "Are you okay?"

"Jack was at A to Z last week after he found out about the accident. We talked, but I wasn't expecting to see him again so soon. I'm not used to being friendly with an ex-boyfriend."

"Sometimes, I think, that part is harder than the breakup. At least, that's what the divorced women with kids in my office say. You have to figure out a new way to be around him again."

"So what do you do? Act casual, like it's no big thing? Or do you let your feelings show?"

Jeanine clapped a hand to her chest. "You're asking me? Considering how nonexistent my love life is, I'm more clueless than you."

#

When Cam walked into her father's office the following week, she found him with the phone to his ear, his back to the door.

"I think that's a great idea, Jack, " he said.

Cam froze. Although she didn't make a noise, it seemed like some deep-seated instinct caused her father to spin around.

"I'll check and let you know. Bye." Her father looked at the phone. "That was your Jack."

He's not my mine anymore.

"Castle Construction is restoring an old print shop in Cuyahoga Falls. They can't use some of the original double-hung windows. I'm going to take a look at them. You want to go with me to see if they're worth salvaging? I'm meeting him there on Monday."

Her instinct was to make up an excuse, but she said, "Sure. I'll go with you."

It seemed as if her heart began to beat in double time. She left the office before she could change her mind.

#

Cam and her father arrived at the red-brick building undergoing renovation. From one empty square of a second-story window, cracked and stained ceiling panels were being tossed into a large dumpster below. Anthony's pickup, as well as Jack's, were two of the half dozen vehicles in the lot. Zane parked the box truck near an open overhead door. He grabbed two A to Z hard hats and handed one to Cam. When they entered, Jack and a workman were bent over a makeshift table spread with large sheets of paper.

He looked up. A wide smile lit up his face. "Be right with you."

Cam turned her back and tilted her head to study the walls and ceiling, checking out the structure as if it was the most fascinating building in the world. Her false interest masked her body's traitorous response to seeing Jack again. She meandered around the room as she tried to get a grip. Her temples pounded, the tips of her breasts tingled, the area between her thighs grew hot and swollen.

"What do you think?"

She whirled around.

Jack stood behind her, his hands on his hips.

"It's a solid building. What are your plans for it?" She was pleased she didn't sound breathless.

Jack gestured with an open palm. "Let me show you 'round."

Cam's gaze swept the room. "Where's my dad?"

"He's upstairs, checking out the windows."

"I should go and help him."

"Anthony is working up there. He'll help him if he needs it. I have other plans for you right now."

Oh God.

"You have a ripper eye for old buildings, so I'd appreciate your ideers. D'ya mind?"

Cam shook her head, pleased with his compliment. "Lead the way."

Jack walked over to where the sheaf of plans lay. "The building is being redesigned for an advertising and media communications firm." He pointed to the drawing then to the doorway where she and her father had entered. "That will be the reception area. We'll be replacing the overhead with double glass doors. By those windows will be one of two large conference rooms. Over here," he gestured behind him, "will be several smaller one-on-one rooms."

"What about upstairs?"

"That's for offices and creative work spaces."

Cam turned to face a staircase in the middle of the large open floor. "I see the stairs go down. Is there a lower level?"

"Come. I'll show you. We'll be moving the stairs to the side wall and installing a glass elevator here for all three floors."

Jack grasped her elbow, sure and firm. The warmth of his hand penetrated through the long sleeve of her A to Z tee-shirt. Her arm tingled with his touch.

"Watch your step." Jack released her when she started down the stairs.

As she neared the bottom, she gasped with delight. Straight ahead, a wall of dirty windows opened to a fantastic vista of the rippling falls of the Little Cuyahoga River.

"Wow. I wasn't expecting this."

"Isn't it great?" Jack walked over to the windows and spread his arms wide. "Believe it or not, this used to be the storage area. They had racks of paper and boxes covering this view."

Cam joined him and scanned the water as it danced over the rocks and cascaded downstream. "What are you going to do down here?"

Jack didn't answer. His shoulder brushed hers. Then, as though by accident, his finger entwined her pinkie. An arcing response ran up her palm and targeted her heart like a guided missile. She forced herself not to make a noise when her breath caught. Just as quickly as it happened, Jack's finger moved away.

He stared out the window. "My initial plan was to put in a kitchen area for a lunch room. But the client wants it upstairs closer to the conference rooms. What do you think?"

Cam walked from one end of the space to the other. "Why not have two kitchens? The one upstairs could be smaller, more like a bar, where beverages and snacks can be stored and prepared. Down here, you could put in a bigger kitchen for the employees to use. If they host any parties, this could be where the caterers work. What about restrooms? Can't have too many of those."

They returned to the first floor to review the plans again, and Jack made notes in pencil on them.

She leaned her hip against the table. "I love what you're doing here to repurpose the space."

"My apprenticeship with you really helped me see that historic buildings can be transformed into modern, fluid environments and still preserve much of the original architecture."

They climbed to the second floor where workmen were tearing down the grids of a dropped ceiling. Her father and Anthony worked on removing an old window similar to those in the basement.

Zane turned to face Cam and Jack. "There you are. I wondered where you two went. You're sure you don't want any of the windows on this wall, Jack?"

He shook his head. "This is where the client wants the rooms dark. We'll be bricking up the outside openings."

"Hi, Cam." Anthony tipped the brim of his cap at her.

It was the first time he'd called her by name instead of Boss.

She smiled. "How's your mom and sister?"

He gave her a quick update on his family. Cam didn't ask him how his job was going since his new boss stood next to her.

She pulled safety glasses and work gloves from the pockets of her cargo pants. "Well, I'll let you guys get back to your work, and I'll help my dad with these windows."

When she and her father left two hours later with ten windows secured in the truck, Jack was gone. On the drive back to A to Z, Cam stared out the passenger window without seeing the passing scenery.

What am I going to do about Jack?

Chapter 29

ON THE FIRST day of August, Cam was at The Harte Estate as the staging company and the interior designers removed the houseful of furniture. Several pieces were marked as sold. Cam made sure none of her antiques were taken by mistake, and the movers didn't damage the walls or floors. Her footsteps echoed through the near empty rooms.

It's going to be even harder to sell this place now.

Jeanine called from the foyer. "Is anybody home?"

Cam left the dining room and walked toward her friend. "Look around. Your work will really be cut out for you now. The furniture made a huge difference. I wish I had the money to keep it here a while longer."

"That's what I came to tell you. We have a contract."

The breath rushed from Cam's body. She felt light-headed and giddy. At the same time, a stabbing pain radiated through her chest. "Is it a good offer?"

Jeanine pulled a legal-sized paper from her leather portfolio. "The best. Full price."

"What's the hitch? Do they want me to hold the mortgage?"

Jeanine studied the paper in her hand. "No. It's for cash."

Cam's legs felt weak. "Is it from a developer?"

Jeanine nodded. "Sort of."

Cam's shoulders drooped, and she rubbed her cheeks. "He wants the land and plans to get rid of the buildings, doesn't he? Is it someone Susan Gardiner turned down before?"

Jeanine held out the purchase contract. "No. The houses stay, and the offer's never been made before."

Cam snatched the paper and bent her head to read it. The buyer was listed as Castle Construction. On shaky legs, she walked over to the main staircase and half-sat, half-collapsed onto the second step. Jeanine took a seat beside her.

Cam stared at the contract in her lap. "When was this written?"

"Mrs. Keller called me yesterday and said Castle wanted to put in an offer."

At the bottom was the signature of *Jackson T. Reynolds*.

Cam pointed to his name. "Only Jack signed this."

"I met him at my office today to draft it. Mrs. Keller verified he has Castle's authorization."

The sales agreement was for cash at the full asking price, with no contingencies or inspection. It was the kind of offer a seller could only dream about. Castle required a closing date of next Monday, six days away. In a week, all Cam's money woes would be over. She could look for another property, maybe several, and get C.C. Restorations going again.

Cam twisted to look at her friend. "You said the *buyer* told you the houses would stay. How do we know Castle means it?"

"We don't," Jeanine replied with brutal honesty. "Like with any sale, once the property changes hands, the new owners can do whatever they want. But Jack and his mother talked about an *enclave* they wanted to create. He showed me some preliminary drawings he made. One new house would be wheelchair accessible. He said he's pitched the concept to several people with aging parents, and they've expressed interest."

It took Jeanine another fifteen minutes to convince Cam to sign the contract. Afterward, she placed the paperwork in her portfolio and stood. "I'll notify Jack and get started on the closing. Are you going to be okay? Is there anything I can do?"

Cam remained seated on the step. "Yeah. Make sure I don't have to sit across the table from him or his mother at the title office. I want to sign all the paperwork before they get there."

Jeanine squeezed her shoulder. "If that's what you want, I'll take care of it."

#

The following week, Cam was notified by Jeanine's secretary that the closing was scheduled for Friday at one p.m. She sent her friend a text to contact her ASAP.

Jeanine called five minutes later. "What's wrong? Did something happen?"

"You're sure I'll be done at the closing before Jack gets there?"

Jeanine sighed. "Yes, Cam."

"I know you think I'm being silly. It's just that selling The Harte Estate is not like any other place I've ever restored. I fell in love with it. It's the worst mistake a rehabber like me can make."

"I understand." Jeanine's voice softened. "Jack knows you have more invested in the property than just your money and hard work. He's aware of how difficult this is for you."

"Maybe he is, but I still don't want to see him when I sign it over."

#

Cam struggled with an almost overwhelming depression the morning of the closing. *Get over it. You're the one who made the mistake of falling in love with a house.*

After she changed into a sleeveless blouse and summery skirt, she went into her dad's office. The outgoing mail sat on the corner of his desk.

She picked up the envelopes and put them in her purse. "I'll drop these off at the post office while I'm out."

Zane spun his chair around. "I know this isn't easy for you, Cameron. You wouldn't be in this position if Adam and I hadn't gotten hurt."

"That's not true. I'd still have to sell The Harte Estate. Selling to Jack and Castle Construction is the hard part."

"It'll be in good hands."

"And I'll be able to get out of your hair and start C. C. Restorations again."

Her father rose and wrapped his arms around her. He wasn't much of a hugger. "I'm so proud of you." Zane stepped back but continued to hold his daughter by her shoulders. "I love you. You deserve to one day have a good man show you how much *he* loves you too."

Cam sniffed back tears. "Thanks, Dad."

#

When she arrived at the title agent's office, Jeanine was there. Halfway through the process of signing the documents, the realtor's phone vibrated.

She checked the screen and headed to the door. "I need to talk to this client."

When all the paperwork was finished, a dull wrenching sensation gripped Cam's chest. *I just lost the first house I loved to the man I love.* She pushed back her chair and shook hands with the title agent. "I appreciate you letting me come in early."

"No problem. We do it all the time." She picked up the folder and left the room.

Jeanine returned. "All done? How are you feeling?"

"Resigned. Sad."

Jeanine put her arm around Cam's shoulder. "Do you want to meet for a drink later?"

"I'm better off by myself tonight." She put her purse strap on her shoulder. "Call me when you have my copies and the check. Thank you for all you've done."

The two friends hugged, and Cam left the office. She walked across the parking lot to her truck. She opened the driver's door and halted when a familiar voice spoke. One she didn't want to hear today, of all days.

"Cam."

She took a deep breath before she turned to face Jack. He stood next to her truck's rear bumper in a white dress shirt and Docker pants. His expression was either concern or pity, both of which were unwelcome.

She frowned. "Why are you here, Jack? Your appointment isn't for another half hour."

"I wanted to make sure you were okay."

"Why wouldn't I be? I just closed on a sweetheart of a sale."

He moved closer. "But you love The Harte Estate." Another step brought him within three feet.

"How would you know?"

"It was the way you lit up when a room was finished." Jack smiled. "You spewed loud enough for the neighbors to hear when the garage door bloke went inside to use the loo and didn't take off his boots. Sometimes you just looked at the house like a mum does at her baby. I know you wanted it to be where you could put down roots. It's a grand place for a family."

"You're right. But not for *my* family. It needs someone with deeper pockets than the Colemans will ever have. Jeanine says you plan to build your enclave."

Jack put his arm on the edge of the truck bed and leaned against the side. "I do. It's an ideer well-suited to The Harte Estate. Like creating a village. When older folks want to downsize and younger ones need space they just switch houses but stay together."

Cam tossed her purse inside the cab. "Well, good luck."

Jack grasped her elbow. His touch seared her skin. It took every ounce of willpower not to step into his arms.

"Forgive me, Cam."

"I already have."

He seemed taken aback by her reply, then a smile dimpled his cheek. "Does that mean we can—"

"No." She gave a small shake of her head.

"There has to be something I can do."

She grasped the steering wheel and hauled herself onto the driver's seat. "Let me know when you can turn back time."

She closed the door and started the engine. Jack stepped away, and Cam backed out of the parking space. She glanced at him before changing gears. He had his hands on his hips. She expected him to appear upset or angry with her refusal, but he didn't.

He looks as determined as when he vowed to finish stripping the bedroom wallpaper by the end of the day.

Chapter 30

WITHIN DAYS OF The Harte Estate closing, Cam purchased a house in Bath Township, a community fifteen miles west of Akron, and home to the sort of people who own horses or large breed dogs. Cam's latest preservation project was built in the early 1900s and in good condition, but a sign could be hung on the front door that read, *Welcome Back to the Seventies.*

She met with contractors to get estimates and schedule the installation of a new heating and air conditioning system. The house also needed to be rewired and all new plumbing installed. After the last meeting, she drove past The Harte Estate. Workmen, trucks, and earth-moving equipment were there.

Wow. Jack fast-tracked permits to begin his enclave construction.

She parked on the street and strolled up the drive. If someone stopped her, she'd claim to be a nosy neighbor. As an excavator tore into the ground, an unexpected pain made her gasp. Seeing the hole dug was the physical manifestation of her dream being dead and buried. She would never live in The Harte Estate as a homeowner.

She hurried back to her truck. Once inside, tears spilled from her eyes. She pulled up the neckline of her tee-shirt to wipe them away and rested her forehead on the steering wheel.

That's when the realization hit her like a trash can lid to the face.

She wouldn't be happy living anywhere, even in The Harte Estate, unless Jack was with her. After he had returned from taking care of his dad, she told him she could never leave Akron. At the time, living away from her family and running her business in a new country like Australia was unthinkable. But when she daydreamed about living in The Harte Estate, he was always there with her. His presence in the house was as deeply ingrained as the hundred-year-old hardwood floors.

Every memory she had of the house involved him. In the kitchen, her thoughts were of Jack cooking dinner rather than the original floor to ceiling cabinetry. She smiled remembering how they would clean the kitchen and dance on the black and white checkered linoleum while his phone's iTunes played.

In the library, she pictured Jack stripping the hideous wallpaper rather than the walls of built-in bookshelves. The dining room was where he rescued her from Gus rather than the place with a magnificent oak coffered ceiling. Her remembrances were filled with the hours they spent refinishing the floors, stripping woodwork, sanding plaster, and painting walls.

But what she missed most was Jack's To Do List. He numerated every room and horizontal surface on which they had made love as well as those they hadn't. The task involved the two of them debating positions which suited the location. It took weeks to complete Jack's list because, of course, some arguments were best settled with trial runs, and there were still a lifetime of places to love him in that house.

Cam started the truck and drove, her thoughts on Jack, her aching heart, and her unending love for him. It had been less than a month since they last talked in the title agent's parking lot. He had begged forgiveness then was about to ask something else. She had cut him off before he could finish.

Did he want to get back together?

Cam hit the steering wheel with the heel of her hand. She had to get in touch with him. She was ready to let him back into her life. Where would be the best place for them to speak in private? Definitely not at A to Z. A public place, like a restaurant, was too impersonal. Maybe she would suggest his condo. It was quiet. There would be just the two of them. Who knows how things would turn out? Everyone talked about how great makeup sex was. It would be nice to experience it for the first time.

Yes, the condo is perfect.

When Cam arrived at A to Z, she was surprised to see the parking lot filled with vehicles. Buyers were coming back. Inside the warehouse, her father waved at her. He was with a couple who examined rows of salvaged church pews. Adam's voice was off to her left where doors leaned against each other in wooden supports like drunken dominoes.

As she neared the office, Sasha exited with a young couple. "Come. I vill show you vere dose vindows are. Cam, someone in der want to talk wid you." Her sister-in-law winked.

Inside the sales office, Cam's heart stopped when she spotted the next customer. *Speak of the devil.*

Jack leaned against the counter, debonair in a well-fitted pinstripe suit and tie. He chatted with her mother. Next to him, a beautiful woman with long, dark hair stepped forward. She wore a fitted short skirt, topped by a silk blouse with a deep V, and impossibly high heels. She was his height in her shoes.

Abigail pointed. "There's Cam."

Jack turned toward her. "I was afraid we'd miss you. There's someone I want you to meet." He put his hand on the back of the Miss America look-alike and his white teeth flashed in a seductive smile.

Cam walked on leaden feet toward them, her face frozen. If she tried to smile back, it might look like a grimace. She held out her hand. "I'm Cam Coleman."

"Missy Maguire." The woman's brown eyes sparkled down at her with genuine warmth. "Jack's told me so much about you."

Has he?

Jack exchanged a knowing look with the woman. "Missy is Castle's new interior designer. We're all thrilled to have her on board. Me especially."

Cam nodded stiffly. "Congratulations."

Missy flashed a dentist's dream smile. "Thank you. I was so excited when Jack said A to Z has wonderful salvaged pieces I can use in my designs. We came right over to look around."

Why did they have to wait for me to do that?

Missy pulled her iPhone from a large designer bag. "You don't mind if I take photographs, do you?"

"Take all you want."

"If I see something that might work, is there a way I can reserve it?"

Cam looked at her mother. Abigail was glued to their conversation, her elbows on the countertop. "My mom can get you some *On Hold* tags to put on items. Just write your name and the date on them. The pieces will be held for sixty days. If someone wants them, we'll call you for first refusal."

Her mother held out a handful of tags, and Jack took them.

"Great." Missy grabbed Jack's arm and squeezed. Her generous bosom pressed against him. "Let's go. I can't wait to see what's here."

She took his hand and headed to the door. He opened it and placed his palm in the small of Missy's back to usher her through.

A part of Cam died inside as she exhaled a gusty breath. *So much for getting back together and makeup sex.*

Abigail busied herself at the computer, avoiding eye contact. The door swung open again, and Adam breezed in followed by Sasha. They headed to their respective stools along the long front counter. Cam retrieved copper polish and several tarnished exterior lanterns and took a seat off to the side. She needed the distraction of physical labor. Thirty minutes later she had buffed so hard a sheen of sweat dotted her brow.

"Is Cam not here, Mrs. Coleman?"

Her head lifted from her task. She hadn't heard anyone enter the office. Cam stripped off her gloves and stood. She focused on Missy and was again struck by the beauty of Jack's new girlfriend in a sexy *do me* outfit. The contrast with her own cutoffs, A to Z tee-shirt, and work boots was laughable.

Cam cleared her clogged throat. "Did you find anything?"

"Loads," Missy gushed. "This place is fabulous."

At last, Cam slid a glance at Jack. He studied her as if she were an unfamiliar bug under glass. A feeling of being as helpless as a trapped insect washed over her.

Is he making comparisons and wondering what he ever saw in me?

It took a monumental effort to hold back the thickness in her voice and the tears that pricked her eyes while she talked with Missy and Jack. By the time they left, Cam felt bruised and battered.

#

Despite beginning work on her new property, Cam had told Jeanine to be on the lookout for another. Her friend called soon after Missy and Jack had been at A to Z.

"You're not going to believe it, Cam. It's fate or your lucky day. Another century home in Bath Township just came on the market. It's not too far from the one you have. Are you free to look at it today? We need to act quickly. I think it would be perfect to renovate, and it's priced to sell."

After touring the property, Cam told Jeanine to contact the listing agent and put in an offer. "You're right. This place is perfect for a renovation. For the next one, how about looking a little farther away? Maybe in Canton or Massillon?"

Jeanine frowned. "Are you running away?"

"No, of course not. It's just that I've never bought property in another county. I think it's time I did."

"Remember who you're talking to, Cam. I'm the one who helped you pick up the pieces after Oliver left. You have that same look on your face. What happened? I thought you were doing so well after the breakup with Jack."

"I was. I mean, I am. I think it's time C.C. Restorations focused on somewhere other than the Akron area."

"That's not what it sounds like to me." Jeanine placed her hand on Cam's arm to halt her walk to the car. "You are a tough broad. You shouldn't run away from your family, your place of business, and your hometown because of a failed romance. You didn't do it after Oliver left."

Cam gave her a wry smile. "I didn't have to. He did all the running."

"You're right. Thank God he did, or I would have had to shoot the bastard."

Cam didn't laugh. "Please understand that I need to put a little distance between me and Akron for a while. But don't worry, it's not permanent."

Jeanine sighed. "Well, whenever you're ready to add another project, I'll help you check in other counties."

"Thank you. Driving past The Harte Estate is really hard and meeting Jack's new girlfriend affected me more than I thought it would. I would hate to run into them again."

Jeanine jumped like she had been hit with a cattle prod. "What? He didn't say— What new girlfriend?"

"Missy Maguire. He brought her to the warehouse. She's just been hired as the interior designer for Castle Construction."

"Did he introduce her as his girlfriend?"

Cam shook her head. "He didn't have to. It was obvious. They waited for me to arrive, so I could meet her. I guess he wanted me to know he's moved on. The way they touched and made eyes at each other, I could tell they're a couple. It was kind of a triple whammy. Boyfriend gone, check. The Harte Estate gone, check. New girlfriend, check."

"Oh, Cam. Men can be so stupid."

#

On Saturday, Cam manned the front desk at A to Z. Her parents had gone to Columbus for the weekend, and Adam was in the warehouse with a customer.

The office door opened and Missy breezed in. "Hi, Cam. I'm back." She was in white shorts and a tank top. A guy who looked like an ex-football player followed behind. At the counter, she beamed up at him. "This is my fiancé, Eric."

Without thinking, Cam blurted, "*Really*? I mean, that's great."

Missy opened her palm. "And this is Cam Coleman."

Eric's voice was deep and gravelly. "Nice to meet you."

"Yeah, I'm really glad to meet you too."

Missy squeezed his thick arm and pressed her breast against his massive chest, just like she had done with Jack. "We're remodeling our house in Fairlawn. I was telling Eric about all the wonderful salvaged pieces here. Jack insisted I bring him as soon as possible to see for himself."

Cam's mouth stretched into a smile so broad her lips ached. "Well, if you find anything of interest, let me know."

"Come on, honey." Missy slipped her hand in Eric's and tugged on his arm. "I want you to check out some pocket doors. They would be perfect for your office."

Seconds after Missy and Eric left, Adam entered. He looked through the window. "Isn't that the woman who came in with Jack?"

"Yeah."

"Nice-looking couple."

"They sure are."

For the first time in months, Cam could not stop smiling.

Chapter 31

AFTER ADAM WENT home and Cam closed up A to Z, she stared at her phone. Earlier in the week, she had been so ready to take the plunge, to revive her relationship with Jack. Now she didn't know what to do. Her misinterpretation of Jack and Missy's relationship was a prime example. What if she had misread other signs? Maybe he wanted to be friends again, not lovers. She was paralyzed, afraid to act. After Oliver humiliated her at the altar, she had jumped from love to hate in seconds. Now it was fear, not hate, that crippled her.

Do it. What have you got to lose?

She dialed Jack's number. It rang twice.

"Cam? Is that you?"

"Hi, Jack. Um … Listen, I was wondering … Are you busy tomorrow? I'd like to meet with you and talk. If Sunday's not good—"

"What time and where?"

It took a moment for Cam to catch her breath. "How about your condo? In the morning?"

"Come at ten. I'll make brunch."

Cam smiled. "You don't have to go to the trouble."

"It's no trouble. I like to feed you."

"And I like to eat."

They both laughed. It seemed to break the tension that made their conversation sound stilted and awkward.

"Okay, Jack. I'll see you at ten."

"Looking forward to it, luv."

Luv?

Cam hit the end button on her phone with a joyous whoop.

#

The hot, humid days of summer were still in full swing on this last day of August. Cam dressed with care to look attractive but not too sexy. She put on a casual white sundress. The spaghetti straps left her shoulders bare. The V bodice gave the illusion she was bustier than she really was. Her legs appeared less muscular with the slight flare of the skirt. She paired the dress with tan high-heeled sandals and a medallion necklace.

Not wanting to show up empty-handed, she stopped at the Acme grocery store and bought a bag of Akron's own Pearl Company coffee. In front of the condo entrance, she took a deep, cleansing breath before she knocked. Seconds later, Jack opened the door.

He bowed with a slight flourish, his arm stretched out. "Come in."

Once over the threshold, Cam handed him the plastic bag. "This is for you."

He looked inside. "Seattle Roast?"

"Your favorite."

"I made a pot this morning, and I'm almost out. Thank you." He leaned sideways and kissed her cheek. "Want a cup?"

Taken aback by the casual and unexpected show of affection, Cam nodded. She followed Jack into the kitchen. He poured and added the two sugars she liked.

Cam glanced at the pot, pan, and bowls littering the kitchen. "What are you making?"

"Eggs Benedict."

Jack had prepared her numerous homemade breakfasts from omelets to steel cut oats to a variety of pancakes. Never had he done Eggs Benedict.

She set her purse on a stool. "Can I help?"

He handed her a package of English muffins. "Split these open, toast them, then spread on butter. I've already cooked the eggs, but I need to reheat them."

She loved to watch him cook. It was like a well-choreographed dance. He stirred the Hollandaise sauce as it simmered. He flipped rounds of Canadian bacon. Using a round mesh strainer, he slipped perfect ovals of cooked poached eggs into gently boiling water. He flitted from one task to the next with grace, precision, and timing. She was always amazed when all the components of a meal were placed on the plates, cooked to perfection. The warm was warm, the hot was hot, and the cold was cold.

They sat at the dining table with coffee, orange juice, Eggs Benedict, and a fruit salad.

The butterflies in Cam's stomach flapped wildly. She picked up her knife and fork. "Do you want to go first, or should I?"

"Don't wait. I'm digging in." Jack cut through his egg, bacon, and muffin. He swirled the three layers in a puddle of Hollandaise sauce and popped it into his mouth.

"I meant, who should talk first, you or me?"

Jack chewed and swallowed. "Let's eat, then we'll talk. You're calmer when you aren't hungry."

Cam opened her mouth to argue, then shut it again. *Dammit, he's right.*

Jack caught her eye. "Have you started C.C. Restorations again?"

She told him about her purchase of two homes in Bath Township. She was about to ask the status of the construction at The Harte Estate. *Do I want to know?*

Jack said, "Your father looked good when the two of you came to remove those windows. I could see the scar on his jaw. That was the only thing that still showed from his accident."

"My mom and I told him he should have plastic surgery. You know my dad." Cam rolled her eyes. "He thought we were nuts to even suggest it."

"He could grow a beard. That's an advantage men have."

"My mom wasn't too keen on that."

"What 'bout Adam? Anthony said he was still walking with a limp."

"He was when he came back to work in June." Cam looked off into the middle distance. "Now that you mention it, I can't remember the last time I saw him limping."

There was a lull in the conversation. Cam was curious about the disposition of his uncle and cousin's legal cases but was afraid a discussion of his relatives might taint their so far pleasant meeting.

Like he had ESP, Jack said, "Speaking of families, Carl and Amelia pled guilty to the charges against them."

"Really? I'm surprised your uncle didn't fight it."

"A deal was worked out with the prosecutor."

Of course. Money talks.

"Amelia was fined and has to perform community service hours."

Without thinking, Cam blurted out, "Can we go watch her pick up trash along the highway? Maybe take pictures?"

Jack laughed. "I'd love to see that girl do anything that resembles actual work. I wonder if she'll follow through with whatever service hours she's been assigned. Mum says if she doesn't, she'll face jail time."

"Can we watch her wearing a prison jumpsuit? Maybe take pictures?" When they both stopped laughing, Cam asked, "What about Carl?"

"Dunno. I haven't heard what his punishment will be. He hasn't told anyone."

"I'll call and find out. As the owner of the house that burned down, I have a right to know."

"When you do, tell me and Mum."

Cam picked at her food. Although it was delicious, swallowing was hard. She was so nervous. "Uh, Jack, I need to ask you an important question."

He paused with a forkful of food halfway to his mouth. "Right now?"

She nodded. "I won't be able to eat without knowing the answer."

He laid down his utensils. "It must be serious."

"It is."

Cam shifted in her chair to face him. "When we talked at A to Z and in the parking lot at the title agency, you were about to ask me something. It was about us, but both times I cut you off. I wasn't prepared to give you an answer to the question I thought you were going to ask. Then I got to thinking." She shrugged with a humorless laugh. "Maybe you weren't wondering if we could get back together again. Maybe you just wanted to be friends. That's why I asked to meet with you today, so there's no misunderstanding. What were you going to ask me?"

Jack laid his knife and fork down. "Actually, one of the times I was asking if we could be friends. The other time, I wanted to resume our relationship."

Oh shit. Which was the second one?

'Which one would you prefer, Cam? Because right now there's only one I'm prepared to accept."

Now she was confused. He called her luv on the phone and Cam now. She took a deep breath. "There's only one I prefer too. I don't want to just be your friend, Jack. I love you. I want you back in my life and my bed, because you're still in my heart. If that's not what you want, then tell me now so I can finish my Eggs Benedict and leave."

Her heart thudded behind her breastbone. Jack didn't move, but the slightest trace of a smile lifted the corner of his mouth.

He said, "I love you too and always will. I never stopped even when I was angry and didn't think we could ever be together."

He reached across and clasped one of her clenched hands on the tabletop. Cam opened her fist and flipped her hand so it was palm-to-palm with his. He intertwined his fingers with hers, bent low, and kissed her knuckles. They sat in silence for several seconds, not looking at each other, but at their joined hands.

"Jack?"

"Yes, luv?"

"Can I have my hand back to finish my eggs?"

He laughed and released her. "All of a sudden, you're really hungry, aren't you?"

Cam had already cut a chunk off and had it in her mouth. She chewed and swallowed. "How did you know?"

'"When it comes to your appetites, no one knows better than me."

They finished eating, and Cam helped Jack clean up the dishes. She looped the damp dishtowel over the oven handle. When she turned around, Jack stood close, very close. He leaned forward, and his mouth covered hers. As the kiss deepened, the passion Cam had redirected for months ignited. When Jack pulled back, an inadvertent moan of protest slipped from her. She opened her eyes.

A muscle pulsed in his rock-hard jaw. "I promise I won't ever hurt you again, luv."

At least, not deliberately. "I know." She stared into his azure eyes. "I promise to never doubt you again."

Jack wrapped his arms around her and drew her against him. He feasted on her lips. She held his head in place, tasting him like she was starved. Both gulped for air when they separated, eyes blurry, mouths tender.

As if unable to resist her magnetic pull, he nibbled a line of kisses down her neck. "God, it's been hell without you."

They held each other tight. Cam gloried in having Jack in her arms again.

After a time, he lifted his head and stared at her. "Are you not happy, luv?"

Cam reached up and stroked his cheeks. "Of course, I'm happy."

"Then why are you crying?"

"Because you're my second chance."

He brushed a tear off her cheek. "Second chance at what?"

"Love. Being happy. Finding someone who accepts who I am and what I do. I feel like you're a gift I didn't deserve but received anyway."

#

Cam and Jack resumed their relationship with caution. They didn't move back in together, although she spent every weekend at the condo. When she told her parents she and Jack were together again, her mother cried.

Cam rushed to Abigail and held her. "Mom, what's wrong?"

Her mother smiled, but the tears kept falling. "I was terribly worried that Jack's ship had failed."

"Don't you mean sailed?"

"You were so heartbroken after Oliver left. Then when you and Jack broke up, I was afraid you would suffer from that awful post-dramatic stress again."

Post-traumatic, Mom.

"Five years ago, there was nothing I could do except be there for you when you needed me. But this time after the breakup, the accident happened, and it was *you* there for *us*. I love you and want you to be happy."

Cam enveloped her mother in her arms. "I am happy, Mom. Jack and I are taking it slow, but we are definitely back together."

Her father raised his coffee cup as if in salute. "That's good news. I like Jack. He loves you and can cook."

Chapter 32

CAM SAT UP and looked out the windshield. She and Jack had eaten at their favorite restaurant and instead of turning left for Northside Lofts, he kept the truck headed west. "I thought we were going back to the condo."

"I have something I want to show you at The Harte Estate."

Cam's breath caught in her throat. "What is it?"

He gave her a quick glance and smiled. "You'll see when we get there."

The last time she had set foot on the property was a shortly before their reconciliation. Since then, work was being done but no large-scale construction. By now, she expected the framing of one or more new houses to be visible from the road, but there was none. Soon winter weather would set in and delay whatever new construction plans Jack had.

"Close your eyes, luv."

They were a block away.

Cam frowned. "Why?"

"I want you to see the place with fresh eyes."

Cam heaved a sigh and closed her eyes. Soon the truck turned left. She waited for the crunch of tires on the gravel drive. There was none. She frowned. The truck finally rocked to a stop.

Jack's hand touched her shoulder. "Are your eyes still closed?"

"Yes." Cam drew out the word with a hint of annoyance.

"Don't make me blindfold you. Although, I know how much you love it." He chuckled.

Her lips twitched. The driver's door opened and closed. Cam unfastened her seatbelt. With the sound of the passenger door being released, she swung her legs to the side.

"Hang on. I'll help you." Jack's hands assisted her sightless clamber out of the vehicle.

"Now can I open my eyes?"

"Not yet."

She tapped her foot on the ground. "I feel asphalt. Did you redo the gravel drive?" She bent to touch it.

"Bloody hell. Can you just wait a minute?" He moved her a few feet forward then slammed the door shut. "Take my hand."

She stumbled after him. They crossed from a hard surface onto the softness of the lawn. The metallic clanking of a gate being opened sounded.

Jack led Cam onto another hardscape and moved her into position. "Okay, open your eyes."

On the ground before her lay a shimmering rectangular pool of clear blue water surrounded by inlaid bluestone. Several red-gold leaves floated on the surface.

She turned to Jack, eyebrows raised. "You put in a swimming pool?"

"It seems to be what people want even though the season in Akron is short. I had a natural gas heater installed. Next week, a company is coming to install a winter safety cover. What do you think?"

"A long time ago, we talked about how an estate this size should have a pool. I was expecting the enclave houses to be built first though." She twisted to look behind her.

Jack grabbed her shoulders. "Don't look at anything else. There's more to see. You know what to do."

Cam sighed and closed her eyes. Jack walked her back through the open gate and across the lawn. Once situated where he wanted her, he allowed her to open her eyes. A ten-foot-high chain link fence enclosed a green clay tennis court. It was situated where the old one had been.

Cam clapped her hands. "I love that you rebuilt this. It looks perfect, although I wonder if the original one was fenced in." She pointed to where orange-tipped construction stakes were laid out in an open area between the new court and pool. "What's going to be there?"

"That's where I wanted to get your input. I was thinking a pool house that could double as a covered pavilion for the tennis courts. Or a separate building that could be used as an office or studio with a bathroom. Or maybe a nice storage shed for all the equipment. Do you have any ideers?"

Cam pursed her lips. "I guess it depends on what the homeowner wants."

"You're right. I just wanted some options to propose. That's why I've only surveyed the site. I'm waiting on a definite answer from the new owner."

Cam's heart dropped. "The Harte Estate has a new owner?" Jack hadn't mentioned the property was sold.

"The deal hasn't been finalized, but I'm hoping it will be soon. Think on what could be built here." Jack took her hand and led her to his pickup. "There's one more thing for you to see."

Cam hauled to a stop. "Don't I have to close my eyes?"

"Not anymore."

He parked in back of the gatehouse. When they rounded the front, she halted again. On either side of the drive where a chain link fence and scrubby bushes had once separated the property from the street, there was a barrier of mortared stone. It was similar to other houses along Portage Path.

Eyes wide, she turned to Jack. "You built a wall?"

"Since I had the stone masons here doing the pool deck and the walkways," he pointed to a new sidewalk that led from the gatehouse's detached garage to the front porch, "I decided to add the wall."

"I love it."

Thick columns topped by coppery post lights sat on each side of the driveway opening. Embedded into the face of one pillar was a bronze plaque the size of a placemat. Cam expected to read The Harte Estate, but her brain couldn't process the letters. They made no sense. It was as if they were written in a foreign language.

Etched into the metal were the words, *Coleman-Reynolds Manor*.

Jack stepped in front of her blocking her view of the plaque and handed her an envelope.

She stared at it. "What's this?"

"The deed. In your name."

Everything seemed to move in slow motion, like a film running at half speed. Cam blinked at Jack.

"... so they felt it was only fair."

Cam was light-headed. "W-what? I'm sorry. C-could you say that again?"

"I said, because you didn't sue Castle Construction, which you had every right to do, the board voted to deed the property back to you. They felt it was only fair." Jack moved closer. "But there's a catch, luv. I built the pool and tennis court and own two of the six acres for new enclave houses."

Cam rubbed her forehead. "We each own part of the estate?"

"That's right, but there's a way to fix that."

Jack took her hand in his and knelt on one knee. "Will you marry me?"

"W-what?"

"Marry me so we can both own Coleman-Reynolds Manor and live happily ever after in the main house. When or if we need a smaller house or an ADA place for our parents, I'll build it. For now, we can use the gatehouse for guests. What do you say?"

"Jack, you don't have to do this. I love you, and I'll live with you wherever you want." Her eyes filled with tears. "*My* heart estate is with you."

"I know, luv. I feel the same. But I want you to have this place. It's where we fell in love and where we can love each other for the rest of our lives. I told you once before it's a grand place for a family. Let's make it our family." With his lopsided grin, Jack repeated the question. "Cam, will you marry me?"

Cam threw her arms around his neck. "You're damn right I will."

www.ingramcontent.com/pod-product-compliance
Ingram Content Group UK Ltd.
Pitfield, Milton Keynes, MK11 3LW, UK
UKHW041430180426
11947UKWH00007B/372